FACES ON FRENCHMEN STREET

HALEY WARRINGTON

First published in the United States of America 2025 by Lake Country Press & Reviews.

Cataloging-in-Publication Data is on file with the Library of Congress.

ISBN: 979-8-9922275-8-1 (Paperback edition)

ISBN: 979-8-9922275-9-8 (Ebook edition)

Author website:

Editor: Rebecca Puhl

Cover Art: @jessamyart

Cover Design: Rae Valtera

Formatting: Juliet Bridges

Lake Country Press

Publishing & Reviews

To Isabelle, my best friend and the person who never let me give up, no matter what.
May we all find someone who reignites our passions for what we love.

CONTENT WARNING

Please note that FACES ON FRENCHMEN STREET deals with sensitive topics such as depression, loss of close family members, parental emotional abuse, and side character pregnancy

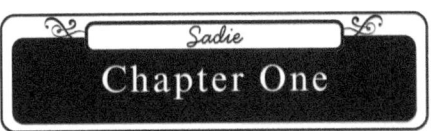

Sadie

Chapter One

Here's the thing about funerals in the middle of a New Orleans summer: They're hot. Sticky. Uncomfortable to the highest extreme. Yet, the sun shines. I lose the most important person in my life, and that damn glob of light a billion miles away has the audacity to continue shining.

If there's one thing I knew about my dad, it was how much he loved the sun. When my grandparents died, he commented on the heat and vibrance of the day. Now it's him lying in the casket in front of me, and I'm not sure I'll ever get over this.

Twenty-five years did little to prepare me for a moment like this. Walking onto the church podium, trying my best to keep my composure by staring at the little fleur-de-lis patterns littering the walls. The hardwood is silent. Not a damn thing about the day around me is sad except for me. No creaky flooring, no rain, nothing to symbolize something bad happened.

But it did. The worst thing, and my family will never be the same.

I squeeze my speech flashcards in my hand so tight, I'm certain they'll break skin any second. Once I make it to the top, I clear my throat and set the cards down. Dad had amazing community outreach. He was a member of a well-off band on Frenchmen Street. Clearly, I'm not the only one hurting from his loss, no matter how much it feels that way.

My mom, Andrea, sits in the front row, blonde hair tied up in an unforgiving bun. She'll have a headache later. The redness in her otherwise gray eyes probably won't go away for the foreseeable future.

Katherine, my sister, is next to Mom. Kat, or as our dad used to lovingly call her, KitKat, could be my twin if we weren't separated by a two-year time span. Her brown hair is much longer than mine and pin-straight. The green eyes we inherited from Dad are a lighter shade in her.

And then Mason, my best friend. His usually messy sandy hair is brushed neatly. I meet his gaze, hoping the deep chestnut color can calm me. He chews the inside of his cheek, the sullen look on his face proving this is as dire as I thought.

After him are an empty spot for me, then my cousin Gabe, and my Aunt Naomi. Naomi, the complete opposite of my father, has blonde hair and an overwhelming blue stare. Gabe looks a lot like her, minus the sometimes horrid attitude, and instead of blonde, he has brown hair like Kat and me.

Being with them should make me stronger. Make me believe in myself, believe that I can get through this.

In all honesty, I don't have high hopes.

I don't recognize most of the other people in here. They've played music with him or seen him play or something along those lines.

I glance up at the ceiling. He's up in the sky somewhere, and if the sun has to continue shining, at least I know he's looking out for me. If you're born and raised in New Orleans like me, you believe in the supernatural. Ghosts. Vampires. Witches. All of it. Maybe he'll come back to haunt our house. At least we'll know he's around.

Tugging my fingers through my hair, I pick up my flashcards.

"Hi, everyone," I start, voice catching in my throat. "My name is Sadie Dupont, I'm William's daughter. I wanted to start by thanking everyone for coming. He, uh...he really would've appreciated the turn out, honestly. He is—*was*—such a people person, as I'm sure everyone here knows."

Breathe, Sadie, I think to myself. *Just fucking breathe.*

"I think I'm luckier than most. My dad was taken much too early, but the twenty-five years I was able to spend with him meant more to me than he ever could've known." My breath hitches, so I cough to try and hide it. "Not everyone gets to spend that much time with their fathers, and certainly not ones as amazing as William Dupont. Many of you know him as Willy, the trumpet player, on Frenchmen Street. He inspired the love of music in me, too."

Movement catches my eye. The door opens, parting to

show the last person I ever expected to see here. Black hair. Towering height. Icy blue eyes that meet mine from across the room. They freeze me to my spot, making my lips part in shock.

Cole.

What the hell is Cole doing here?

I fumble with my flashcards, gaze flicking between them and Cole. Struggling to find my spot, I pick a random one and start again.

"Um, he taught me so many things," I continue, my heartrate tripling in speed. "From my love of music to everyday living. He taught me to live each day to the fullest, and I don't think he regretted a single moment of his life."

My speech isn't anywhere near over, but I can't stand being under the scrutiny of the man across the room. His stare weighs me down. Suddenly, my mind isn't on the flashcards. It's on the night I met him. The night that would undoubtedly change my life, for better or worse.

"Why are you looking at me like that?" I'd asked.

"I figured you'd be used to having eyes on you."

"None like yours."

The exchange rings true to this day. Being a bartender in the French Quarter has its perks, but I wouldn't say having eyes on me was one. Only Cole's. It's only ever been Cole's.

Panicking, I realize I've been standing there in silence, staring at the man across the room. "Thank you all for coming. God rest his soul."

I let out a shuddering breath as I rush off the stage, sitting back in my seat between Mason and Gabe. I lean into Mason for comfort. He shifts and wraps his arm around me, squeezing me.

"It's okay," he whispers, rubbing his thumb against my skin. "It'll be over soon."

But it won't be, and I'm sure Mason, of all people, knows that. I look up at him. "Did you know he would be here?"

"Who?" Mason furrows his eyebrows, turning to see the back rows. As he shifts back, he curses under his breath. "I swear, I didn't."

Gabe inhales, his shoulder nudging mine. His jaw tightens when he realizes what we're talking about. The pastor drones on in front of us, but I can't pay attention. Not when I know *he's* here.

"Say the word, Sadie," Gabe mumbles. "I can get him out of here."

"Don't bother." I shake my head. "He won't talk to me. He's smarter than that."

I say it, but I don't mean it. My pulse races at the thought of Cole across the room. Is he here for me? To support me? I don't know why else he would be, considering he didn't leave a great impression on the rest of my family.

No. I don't need his support, nor do I want it. We both burned that bridge a long time ago, and we have no reason to try and build it back up. I've been fine without him. In fact, I hadn't thought about him in a while until today.

Mason and Gabe, being overprotective as per usual, flank my sides. Both of them were friends of Cole's at one point, but for Gabe, family loyalty won out. He reminds me of the older brother I never wanted in the first place.

Cole stares forward as the three of us walk past, but I catch him in my peripheral. He rubs his jaw. Before I know it, he's gone from my sight, but not my mind.

It comes back in waves. The sudden intrigue I felt for him. The tug toward him couldn't have been anything but cosmic. I'd laugh in the face of Fate for the shit she pulled on me if I didn't have to watch my father's casket get loaded into the horse-drawn carriage.

Mason is tall, but Gabe's height should be illegal. He has to be at least a head and a half taller. A twinge of annoyance bubbles when they refuse to leave me alone, like I'm a child who'll get lost in a grocery store.

"Thanks, dads, but I can handle myself. You can be more than a couple inches away from me." I pause, sighing as the two of them stand there, blinking at me. "Whatever this is you guys are doing... It's appreciated, but not needed. Please go support whomever needs it the most."

Mason's brows furrow. "Um, Sadie."

"Okay, fine." I roll my eyes. "Gabe, be with your mom or something. Macho Mason will protect me."

The coachman waits for my signal to start, but I wait for Gabe to give in. He nods, sharing a glance with Mason before walking toward Naomi, who's standing with my mom and Kat.

"He's trying to help," Mason murmurs, crossing his arms over his chest.

I nod once at the man, and the jazz music begins. Taking a deep breath, I try to feel the melody the way I used to—

deep in my soul, intertwined with everything making me who I am. It's not the same. Not without Dad.

The outside of the church is intimidating, even as it disappears along the horizon as we start our march. He always said he wanted a funeral like this. One that starts in the church he adored, continues on with a parade in his honor, and ends when he's laid to rest in our family tomb. How unfitting. He doesn't deserve to be shoved in a stone prison, reduced to a slab with a name, yet that's how we'll all end up. Dead, alone, and encased in pounds and pounds of concrete.

"Look," I tell Mason. "The last thing I need is for Cole to come up to us and start trouble. What happens if he brings up The Incident in front of Gabe?"

"You think Gabe doesn't know?" Mason asks.

"I assume not, considering he doesn't hate your guts." I shake my head. "I need to not be worried about any of that today, okay? For now, it doesn't exist."

The thought of it makes my stomach twist. Guilt encompasses my heart, and as I glance behind me, I catch the gaze of the person it hurt the most. I quickly look away, tightening my jaw and facing forward.

This is the worst day of my life—my father's funeral—and I'm thinking of The Incident. It's been five years, yet the heartache comes back full swing. Leave it to me to uproot not only my relationship, but my family as well. Maybe things really do come full circle. Karma's a bitch.

Any other time, music would be able to quell this unsinkable anxiety. My mom walks with Kat a few feet ahead. If it weren't for Mason, I wouldn't be keeping a steady pace. I'm sure I'd be turning in the opposite direction, running away and never coming back, not until I could redo everything. I'd never let Dad in that damn car.

It'll take a good hour for us to walk to the cemetery, so we have plenty of time to talk, but Mason is silent for the duration. I run my fingers through my hair.

"Sadie."

Hearing Cole again startles me. Mason tightens his grip on me. When I don't say anything back, Cole picks up his pace until he's walking next to me. I've cried too much today already, so as soon as the tears well up, I fight them off.

"I only want five minutes, Sadie." Cole's voice is deeper than Mason's, yet somehow so much softer. Everything about Cole is softer than Mason.

"I'll be okay, Mase." I let go of his arm and meet his gaze. "Catch up with Kat, will you?"

Mason's jaw tightens as he looks between Cole and me. Right when I think he's going to put up an argument to stop me from being alone with Cole, he gives a brisk, firm nod and picks up his pace until he's leaning down to talk to Kat. Following a few muttered comments, Kat whips her head around to glare at Cole.

"You stopped dying your hair," Cole whispers, arm brushing mine. My skin jolts as if he's lightning, steady bolts of electricity escaping from his touch. "And you cut it."

Yeah, I did. Up until my breakup with him, my hair almost reached my tailbone. And I spent ungodly amounts of money to dye it silver.

"What are you doing here?" The question escapes me before I can stop it.

"Mason told me what happened. I'm sorry, Sadie. I know how close you two were, and I wanted to tell you that."

It's been years. Five years, to be exact, and somehow his voice still sinks into my chest and reverberates around my entire body. It's warmth in the never-ending blizzard I'm in.

"It's not your responsibility to tell me that, Cole."

"You seem different," he says, as if he's not the one who made me different in the first place.

As soon as my heart rate spikes, I hear my dad's voice.

Daddy used to struggle with this too, Peanut. The best way to deal with it is breathing. Here, do it with me.

Inhale.

One, two, three, four.

Hold it.

One, two, three, four, five, six, seven.

Exhale.

One, two, three, four, five, six, seven, eight.

My pulse slows, and I follow that up with another deep breath.

"Look." I sigh, still unable to bring myself to look at him. "Thank you for coming. But I've obviously got a lot going on here, and I don't have the capacity to talk to you."

"You can't even look at me."

"It's not that I can't. I don't want to." My heart thunders from being in close proximity to both my father's casket and Cole.

"Right," Cole murmurs. "Guess I deserve that."

"If you don't mind, I'd like to get back to my family."

"Since when is Mason part of your family?"

If there weren't a hundred people behind me, I'd stop walking. I'd stop this whole thing right now, because apparently, Cole Anderson thinks he has any right to ask me questions about Mason. I scoff, finally looking into his bright blue irises.

"My dad loved Mason." It's not meant to be a jab, but that's how Cole takes it. He recoils ever so slightly, but quickly recovers.

"Brought him around a lot, did you?" Cole shoves his hands into the pockets of his pants.

For everyone else's sake, I try my best to remain calm. "Actually, yeah. He's been a really good friend to me the past five years. My dad kept telling me to date him."

"You didn't? You're not?"

"None of your business. You choose today of all days to talk to me? For the first time in five years?"

"I've wanted to for a while. It never turned out to be the right time. Not that I'm saying it is, but I really did want to tell you I'm sorry for your loss." Cole touches my arm. If it weren't covered by the black fabric, I'd feel those stupid fucking sparks I always felt from him. I know that because I feel them anyway, no matter how dull they are through the dress.

I allow those sparks to soothe me instead of tear me up from the inside out.

"Whatever happened between us is bad history, Sadie. I still care about you, and I'm worried. When Mason told me about this, it broke my heart. You guys are the last people in the world who deserve this." Five years has done him well. Defined cheekbones lead to his knife-sharp jawline, and unlike Mason, he's embraced the stubble on his face. Cole Anderson has changed. At least...on the outside.

I'm not willing to find out about the inside.

"Thank you, Cole," I concede, fidgeting with my hands. "For saying that, and for coming."

"I don't mean to intrude," he says.

I can't help the short laugh escaping my lips. "There are dozens of people here I don't even recognize. You're not intruding."

"That look your sister gave me says otherwise." He shrugs, biting back his smile.

"You know how Kat is." I frown after I say it. Cole doesn't really know Kat. Not anymore. Kat was eighteen when he met me, and she was an entirely different person back then.

"How are they holding up?"

I shake my head and inhale sharply. "Not well at all. I mean, I expected it from Kat, but I never thought I'd have to force my mom out of bed."

"You know," Cole starts. "You've grown a lot, Sadie. Will must've been proud of you."

"He was." I press my lips together. We talk in hushed tones even though the jazz music drowns us out.

"He still is." Cole's chest rises. "I'll let you get back to your family. But...if you ever need anything, and I mean anything at all, my number's the same."

"Thanks," I say, unsure of how to respond to the last part.

While I'd love to say I deleted Cole's number after The Incident, I didn't. I stared at it almost every night afterward for months wondering if I should text him, call him, reach out, or leave him alone for good. Obviously, I chose the latter.

Like Mason was listening, he hangs back so he can walk by my side. Cole disappears into the crowd of people behind us with a single nod at Mason. Sighing, I lean my head on Mason's shoulder.

"You okay?" Mason asks, letting his hand rest on my hip.

"Of course." I give him a small smile. He knows when it's fake or real, so he seems satisfied to see I didn't have to force that one.

I didn't think it'd be possible for me to appreciate Cole's presence again, but it feels like it did the first night I met him. It scares me. It makes my phone suddenly so much heavier in my purse. Cole Anderson isn't what my dad wanted for me. That alone is enough.

That alone makes me want to finally delete that number forever.

Chapter Two

FIVE YEARS AGO...

My aunt's bar, and coincidentally my place of work, isn't as packed as normal for a Friday night. Until things pick up, Gabe's working in the back on some sort of paperwork he claims is important.

I turn around to start making a customer her drink, and I catch myself in the mirror behind me. After I flick my hair over my shoulder, I admire it. It took many, many sessions to get it from my natural brown to this silver color. Even in my ponytail, it reaches the middle of my back.

A flash of bronze from the trumpet on the wood-paneled back wall catches my attention. Flimsy tables (that nobody ever sits at) line it. Within each panel, old jazz instruments hang, along with various signed posters and vinyl records, even if they don't get used all that often. The bar stretches along the length of the room, with a small section at the end cut off so I can walk out.

I give the girl her drink and see someone else has approached. In a place like this, people don't usually sit down. Not for long, at least. Nowhere near as long as he has. He's scrolling through his phone, the light from it making it easier to see his features.

His hair is dark. Brown or black, but I can't tell even with his screen on. Striking blue eyes reflect whatever he's looking through. Defined cheekbones lead down to a strong, sharp jawline, even when he's resting his head against his palm. He's handsome—ruggedly so, but this seems like the last place he wants to be. If I didn't know any better, I'd say he's bored.

The corner of my mouth ticks up in amusement. I don't see that here very often, so I don't want to bother him. He's definitely here for someone else. While the music is loud, I swear my ears have morphed with superhuman ability, allowing me to hear over it. Bored Man doesn't notice when I walk up to him. Bracing my palms on the bar, I decide I'm going to bug him and see what he wants.

"Well, you're definitely not a tourist."

He almost drops his phone in shock. Strange, considering he came and sat here. Someone was bound to talk to him eventually.

He clears his throat. "Definitely not."

His voice, reminiscent of the deep bass around us, vibrates past the music, through where I'm leaning, and caresses my arms even though we don't touch. It lights up my skin, setting the back of my neck on fire. Am I blushing? It's not often someone's voice makes me blush, and certainly not here of all places. He looks me up and down, but it feels as if he's staring right through me.

"Dare I say you look...bored?" There's a flirty drawl to my voice, it's been ingrained in me since I started working here. Flirting makes money.

"Incredibly." With a deep inhale, he nods and sets his phone on the bar.

"Not much of a talker?" I stand up straight, gesturing behind me. "Do you want a drink?"

"I'm okay." He narrows his eyes at me. "I'm the DD. Hence the boredom."

After a moment of being locked in place together, I figure he's not keen on conversation. Looking behind him, I snort in exasperation when I see one of my favorite regulars out on the floor. His name is Mason, and he makes it his goal to go home with another girl every time he's here—including multiple (more like hundreds of) attempts at me.

"Do you know Mason?" the man asks, tilting his head in curiosity. When it clicks in my mind, I nod.

"You're DD'ing for Mason?" I scrunch my face up. "You may as well drink. He's not gonna need a ride."

"What makes you say that?"

"For starters," I say, leaning forward. "He never leaves alone. If you're friends with him, I'd think you'd know that."

His gaze trawls over my body, or what he can see of it behind the counter. He lingers at my chest for a beat before snapping back to himself and redirecting his attention to the counter. Did he think I wouldn't notice the way his eyes snagged? He's not the first man here to appreciate my breasts.

"And you?" He grabs his phone and slides it into one of his pockets.

"I'm sorry, what?" I frown, straightening myself out as I look at him.

He worries his bottom lip as he considers—as though he's hedging his bets with his next question. "Do *you* usually leave alone?"

Men say things like that to me all the time, and I don't know why it sounds any different coming out of his perfectly shaped mouth, but fuck. My heart beats as fast as my head spins, and I squint to take him in. Now that he's not looking at his phone, his shoulders have uncurled, and they're broad and strong. The way his gaze takes me in makes me feel like he sees me as more than just some bartender in a bar in the French Quarter—and damn if it doesn't feel good to be seen.

While I'm processing what he asked, the doors to the backroom swing open and Gabe appears through them. He wears a black T-shirt tucked into jeans, and of course, there's a permanent frown plastered on his face.

After taking one look at the man in front of me, his eyebrows furrow. He's next to me in the blink of an eye, folding his arms over his chest.

"Off-limits," Gabe says. "Especially for you."

Rolling my eyes, I nudge Gabe away before turning my attention back to Bored Man. "To answer your question, yes. I do."

"No answering his questions." Gabe scrunches up his nose. "Cole's an old friend of mine."

The name Cole fits him perfectly. A smirk forms on his lips, but he doesn't say anything else in front of Gabe. He glances between us, meeting my gaze as if he's daring me to say anything else.

"I'm his cousin," I explain to Cole, ignoring Gabe's presence. "He's not the boss of me."

Before Cole can open his mouth to respond, Mason approaches. He's definitely a lady killer—complete with round cheeks, messy blond hair, and brown eyes. Once a week he graces me with his presence, and every time, without fail, he goes home with a different girl.

"Sadie, baby, I need another drink." Mason leans on Cole and throws his arm over his shoulders. "He could use one, too."

"I tried, Mase," I say. Mason never fails to bring a smile to my face, no matter how much I deny he does. "Your usual?"

"You know me too well." He grins. "You can still know me better. That offer is always on the table. Just say the word."

"Does anyone in this place listen to me?" Gabe groans, massaging his forehead.

"What was that?" Mason puts his hand over his ear as if he's trying to hear Gabe better. "I'm sorry, did you say something?"

"You're awful." A laugh escapes me as I turn around to make his drink.

Mason's usual is a whiskey sour, and I swear, if he was the only person to ever order it, I'd still have it committed to memory. The man never branches out with anything other than his women.

As if we've done this a thousand times before (we have), I slide the glass across the bar into his outstretched hand. He winks at me and pats his friend's shoulder. "Sadie, Cole will get your finest shot of tequila."

A couple walks up to the other side, leaving Gabe to begrudgingly walk over to them to see what they want.

"No, I won't." Cole glares daggers at Mason. "I don't want to drink."

"I'll take a shot with you," I offer.

Mason fakes a gasp. "What the hell, babe? You don't drink with me."

Normally, I don't get along with guys like Mason. He's overly flirty, and I'm not sure he really knows when to stop. And while he's probably not serious, he's respectful of me. Sometimes, he's pretty vulgar, though.

"He seems like more fun than you." I purse my lips to stop my laugh when I see his face contort in faux shock.

"This is betrayal," Mason replies before turning to Cole. "If you get to take her home first, I'm gonna be so pissed."

"You know what?" When Cole looks at me, it feels like those blue eyes stare right into my soul. "Let's take a shot."

Mason winks at me as he walks back toward his lady friend, like he did me a big favor or something. Grabbing the tequila from the shelf and a couple shot glasses, I debate on if I should do this. I'm definitely not supposed to drink—not legally or on the clock—but I guess I'm okay with it today. One shot won't hurt, and I'm only three months shy of legal anyway. I smile as we clink the glasses together. While I fight the urge to gag at the feeling of it burning down my throat, Cole seems unbothered. The only sign he doesn't like it is the scrunch of his nose and a quick shake of his head.

Gabe glares at me while he mixes a drink. I wave him off, knowing he won't do anything about it. The best part of having a cousin who's practically an older brother is that he'll tell me when I'm wrong, but he won't tell anyone else.

"Sorry about Mason," Cole says, setting the glass down on my side of the bar and garnering my attention. "He's not exactly shy."

I give him a wide smile. "Don't worry. I'm not either."

He shrugs like he believes me, like he's conceding to what I say, but keeps staring at me. Usually, I'm able to tell what people are thinking when they look at me, but not him. His face is blank. Whether that's a good thing or a bad thing, I'll probably never know.

"Why are you looking at me like that?" I cross my arms over my chest, the flirtatious tenor falling back into my tone.

"I figured you'd be used to having eyes on you." Cole smirks.

Hook. Line. Sinker. He's making it easy.

"None like yours," I tell him, watching him shift in his seat. The smirk falls from his face.

"And is tonight one of the nights you'll be going home alone?" Words like that should be spoken confidently, but he says them in a quiet, controlled voice.

"Oh, so you're a rulebreaker." I tease, putting my hand on

my hip. "But since I can't leave until four, I think it's safe to say yes."

"Sadie..." He says my name like he's tasting it on his tongue, and he pauses before he continues like it's a good taste. "I'm a patient man."

God, there's something about him that has me hanging on to every word he says. I can feel his voice all over my body. It takes a lot for a man to render me speechless, but he seems to do it easily. I *do* always go home alone. I certainly don't take men from here home. They usually only hit on me after they're drunk.

Cole's not drunk.

And Gabe be damned, I'm trying to remember if my apartment is clean enough for someone to come over.

I look over in Gabe's direction once, and he's so enthralled with the couple he's talking to, I don't feel bad for considering what Cole's saying. What Gabe doesn't know wouldn't hurt him. Not my fault his friends like me.

"We'll see."

Cole sits for another half an hour or so, but as soon as Mason leaves, he does too. I don't know if my sigh is relief or disappointment. Maybe he's not as patient as he thought. Or maybe, he decided this was a bad idea...which it is. For the rest of the night, I struggle to get him out of my damn head. It's like those blue eyes of his will forever be in my memory. If he comes back with Mason any time soon, he might actually get the chance to come home with me.

. . .

WE CLOSE AT THREE, and I'm walking to my apartment by four. Hints of music float in the air, but it's nothing like it would be if I was walking this street six hours ago. New Orleans is a large city, meaning things don't close or turn off the music until late (or early, depending on who's answering that question). The streets are filled with melodies and bass almost all the time. It's a comfort for me.

The area of Frenchmen I'm walking in is next to pitch-black. A few streetlights are thrown in every now and then, but not enough to make a difference. Behind me, where the bars and restaurants flash neon, a street performer freestyle raps. When I walk past, he says something about my shoes—how they're too tall to walk on the cobblestone, I think. Galleries line the homes and businesses. Every once in a while, a couple people will be sitting on one, laughing through the dead of night and sometimes, even spilling alcohol over the edge.

After growing up here, the stories you hear about the supernatural make you laugh. Sure, I believe in ghosts. Maybe vampires. But at the end of the day, I haven't seen anything to prove any claims. When it comes to witches though, especially New Orleans witches, I always believe.

Smoosh all of them together, and you have the French Quarter—the pinnacle of tourism in the city. It's beautiful, straight down to the architectural history of the buildings. Fascinating enough, though it's called the *French* Quarter, most of the buildings are of Spanish origin.

When someone grabs my arm, my instincts kick in, and I

don't even have a second to process before my fist connects with a jaw.

"Fucking Christ, Sadie!" Mason groans, holding his face. "It's me. Who the hell taught you to hit like that?"

"Shit." I wave my hand through the air as if that'll stop the pain exploding in it. "Who told you it was smart to come grab a girl walking by herself at 4 a.m.?" After the pure agony of hitting Mason starts to subside, I notice his companion. Cole's eyes gleam even in the dark.

"I told you, Mase." Cole's voice sinks into my belly, and I wish it would stop doing that. Damn it.

I cross my arms over my chest, waiting for Mason to say something else. He's too busy rubbing his jaw, a pout gracing his face.

"Remind me to never piss you off," Mason says, eyebrows furrowing. "That was pretty badass, though."

Cole stifles a laugh.

"What are you doing out here?" I scold them both. "I need to get home. And what happened to the girl of the night?"

"She bored me." Mason shrugs, finally dropping his hand back to his side. "Nobody can ever compare to you."

I snort. "Yeah, I'm going home."

"I'll walk you," Cole offers before Mason can say anything else.

"I'm okay." I shake my head and start walking away from them.

Cole waits a moment, like he wants to follow me, but he doesn't want it to be weird.

The feeling of his eyes on me melts every ounce of willpower I have, so I turn around and look at him. "Fine. You can walk me to my building. No further."

Cole smiles and pats Mason's shoulder before he meets me where I'm standing. While he's walking next to me, he slides his hands into his pockets.

"Why are you walking by yourself?" he asks, gazing forward.

"Because I live around the block," I answer, giving him a slight shrug. "And, as you can tell by Mason's face, I don't really need anyone to protect me. I've got it."

"Yeah, that's true." Cole smiles. "I told him not to grab you like that."

"He's pretty drunk. I know Mason well enough." I reach up and remove the tie from my hair. It falls to the middle of my back. As I run my fingers through it, heat rises to the tips of my ears when I notice how Cole's eyes cling to my every movement.

"You have pretty hair." He lifts his hand to play with a couple strands. "It's long."

"It gets in the way." I finally glance at him. "What's your goal here? Tonight, I mean."

"Getting you home safely." He raises his eyebrows at me. "And unlike Mase, I'm not drunk at all. So, I'm not nearly as fun."

"You seem like the type that doesn't need alcohol to have fun." I grin, more to myself than at him.

"I...am as boring as they come." He nods, but a laugh

escapes his lips. "Mason can be really convincing sometimes. I prefer to consider myself something of a classy drinker. Anything strong on the rocks, and only on occasion."

Instead of responding right away, I admire how much taller he is than me. At this proximity, I have to tilt my head upward to see him. His gaze flicks to mine. Fumbling to come up with a response now that I'm caught, I blank.

"What about you?" he asks.

"Well, I have three months before I can buy my own, so I take whatever I can get." I laugh to myself.

"Are you gonna get fired for taking a shot with me?" He nudges my arm, sending a firework of sparks down my body.

"Oh, Gabe's not gonna say anything." I wave him off. "He's the one who buys me alcohol in the first place."

The smirk falls off his face when Gabe's name leaves my mouth. We come to a stop outside my building, and I turn to face him in silence.

"So, if bro code didn't exist, would you be coming upstairs with me right now?" I brush my hair off my shoulder before clasping my hands together.

His chest rises as he contemplates what he's going to say. Running his tongue over his teeth, he looks away from me. "You just had to be related to him."

My confidence soars. Taking a step toward him, I get close enough to hear him stop breathing. "You know, there's this creepy guy who lives on my floor. Um, you should come with me, in case he's outside."

"Sadie," he warns. His voice sinks into my chest and ping-pongs around until all of my coherent thoughts have left my brain. "You wouldn't lie to get me to go upstairs, would you?"

Gulping, I shake my head. "Who? *Me?* How ever could you think of me like that?"

"I don't know," Cole trails off.

"What's the worst that'll happen?" I ask. "Worst case, you'll have to fend off some creepy old man."

He wets his lips, biting back the smile on his face while his eyes drag over me. The chill follows immediately after them. "And the best case?"

"Well, best case is there's no creepy man outside. And you drop me off and leave." I watch him finally smile like he's a movie. God, if he *was* one, he'd be my favorite. I'd replay that damn thing over and over again.

"You don't even know me," he says. "Not even one thing."

"Fine," I reply in defiance, holding my hand out to him. "Hi. I'm Sadie Dupont. I work at that bar down the street, and I live in this apartment building. I'm a Capricorn."

He shakes it and blanks for a moment, face void of emotion, before he regains his composure and a small smile returns. "Cole Anderson. I work at a boring ass company, and I live in Gretna. I think I'm an aquarium."

"Right, an aquarium." I nod, chuckling. "Not a city boy?" Our hands are still connected in the middle since neither of us wants to let go. The shock of his touch comes back tenfold, and I find I enjoy it more than I should.

"Well, I'm not a *boy* and I don't live in New Orleans...so no, not a city boy." His eyes don't leave mine the entire time he speaks. Others could find this intimidating, but I find it welcoming. Like he's letting me see a little piece of his soul through the blueness.

After that, a brief moment of semi-silence encases us. Faint music plays, bounding from the French Quarter in waves. It shouldn't be this hard to figure out what to say to him, especially not when it looks like he's hanging on every word. He leans forward slightly, his height towering over me.

"If you want to help defend my honor against a weird dude that lives on my floor, then let's go." I turn away from him and head toward the front door of the building.

This is most likely the only time he'll be here—or even in that bar—and if the creepy man is a figment of my imagination, he'll never know. Hesitating for a moment, Cole decides to follow me. His arm brushes mine as we make our way up to the second floor.

The darkness hides his hair color from me, even though I've tried hard to figure out if it's black or brown. He's quiet until we make it to my door, his hands in the pockets of his jeans as I stick my key in the lock.

"Well." His voice barely reaches my ears. "No creepy man waiting for you. I should go."

I unlock it, cracking it open before I turn back to him. With less than a foot of distance between us, my stomach flips. I think of kissing him, and what could happen if I bring him inside my apartment.

"Sadie," Cole warns me again, but his gaze flits down to my lips. He's already leaning forward, whether intentional or not.

"Cole." I grab his shirt, pulling him into me. He gasps, but before I know it, my back is pressed into the doorframe. I'm half in my apartment, but he's completely out of it.

The heat of his body rolls into mine, and suddenly, it's hard to breathe. Warmth cascades through me, and his scent floods my nose with bourbon and vanilla. He's absolutely divine.

We stare at each other for a brief second, one that feels like an eternity, before his head dips down to connect our mouths. It's tentative at first, slow and hesitant as he gets comfortable with the idea. I throw my arms around his shoulders, pulling him flush to my chest.

He only had one tequila shot, but I still taste it on him. The fireworks shooting from our mouths feel sinful, yet I relish in it. His hands travel along the bare skin of my back. I arch into him, desperate for the feeling of him. His tongue parts my lips, a graceful dance turned into a battle for control. He doesn't know what he's in for with me.

As much as I wish he'd just push me into my apartment and keep whatever this is going, he pulls away from me, breathing raggedly. He reaches up to cup my cheek, thumb rubbing my flushed skin.

"You're not making this easy for me," Cole comments.

"Never said I would." I grin. "In fact, I pride myself on making it harder."

"Something tells me you don't have much of a problem with that. I should go." He bites back a smile.

"Or," I say, placing my hand on his chest. "You could come in. I wouldn't tell."

He rests his forehead on mine. "You...are so much trouble."

"Come in," I repeat, softer.

He contemplates it for a second, but the wall burns down behind his eyes. "Fine."

Chapter Three

My dad instilled his love of music in me. Or maybe it's genetic.

We used to play together as a family, a four-member jazz band. My dad, since he played on Frenchmen all the time, was an expert trumpet player. I don't say that lightly. Even when sight reading, his performances were virtually flawless. Music was his life. Despite bringing us along, he could've been a one-man show. He knew how to play other instruments, too. Piano, trombone, clarinet, saxophone, and many others.

I learned how to play most of those by the time I was eleven. Play, yes...Perfect? Absolutely not. The creation of music is easy and hard at the same time, considering pitch, placement, and pretty much any slight slip can turn a brilliant song into something entirely different.

Of all the instruments my dad taught me to play, the piano is the only one I'm even remotely good at. I play like second nature, like I'm one with the keys, even as life without him turns as black and white as they are.

"You'll feel the rhythm in your bones, Peanut," he'd said to me the first time he was teaching me. "You can look at sheet music every day, every time you play, but it's like reading. You can be a perfect replication, or you can take your own creative license. Always be yourself, even in music."

He sat next to me at the piano bench and even taped labels on the keys, so I'd know which notes were which. The first song I learned was *Fly Me to the Moon*. Every time I'd play it, mistakes and all, without fail, William Dupont would sing along.

Maybe that's why I haven't played since he died. When I do, I'll expect his angelic voice to accompany me. He can't do that from Heaven, though, no matter how hard he tries or how much he wants to. I'm alone. Sure, my mom and my sister are still here, but it feels like they're fading as fast as Dad did.

It's been three weeks. I figured it'd get easier, that I'd want to get up in the morning.

It doesn't. And I don't.

Dad was our family glue, and without him, I'm the only one willing to pick up the slack.

If I close my eyes and try hard enough, I can see his face. Picture the prominent smile lines and crooked grin. Even hear him. And sure, the last thing I told him was that I loved him, but it was over the phone. I don't go home as much as I should. The last time I saw him in person was a week before his death. He'd told me, "I'm glad life's treating you well, Peanut. You deserve it."

Life is no longer treating me well. Hell, life seems to go on for everyone except for me. It's funny how things our loved ones say are unremarkable at the time, taken for granted, and are only deemed important after a loss. And I hate reducing him to that. A loss. He's so much more than that. A gaping fissure in the universe, a black hole swallowing everything around it, infinitely bigger than a loss.

Mason tiptoes around me like he's waiting for me to explode. I haven't stopped thinking of Cole since he showed up at my dad's funeral. Cole from five years ago wouldn't have done that. But the last thing I need to think about is him, and everything we went through. I'm different. He's...hopefully different.

I don't care to find out.

Mason acts like he's my therapist. He asks me every day how things make me feel; how I'm holding up, blah, blah, blah. While I think about my dad every second, the more Mason talks about him, the worse it gets.

"Sades, you're zoning again."

I do that a lot. Whenever I get in a car. "Sorry. What did you say?"

"I asked you if you've talked to Cole since the funeral," Mason says.

Gabe looks over his shoulder at me in the back, expectant of the answer himself.

I shake my head. "Nope."

"Really?" Mason's eyebrows furrow, but he knows better than to take his eyes off the road.

"He told me to text him if I ever needed someone." I stare at my hands in my lap, picking at my cuticles.

Gabe snorts, leaning back in his seat. "Did he happen to mention his fiancée?"

For some reason, my heart sinks in my chest. I fidget with my seatbelt and stare out the window to avoid both him and Mason. Cole hadn't mentioned anything like that, but it's not like he's obligated to. I've had people come in and out of my life since him, and that's none of his business, either.

After a pause, Mason asks, "Were you thinking about it?"

"Absolutely not." I scoff. "Doesn't matter if he became a saint in the last five years."

"Good." Gabe nods once. "Keep it that way, Sadie. Seriously."

"I appreciate the concern, but I promise I can look after myself," I grumble, running my fingers through my hair.

"Trust me, I know that," Gabe replies. "But your brain gets all fucked up around him. It did back then, and it probably would now, too."

Instead of responding, I bite my tongue. Last thing I need at the moment is to get into it with Gabe as we're pulling up to my house. Regardless, he's right. I'd never admit that to his face, but he knows better than anyone how I acted in the wake of what Cole and I left behind.

As Mason puts the car in park, I notice someone else is here. A black SUV takes up Mason's usual spot, glittering in the unforgiving summer sun.

"Who is that?" Mason asks.

"No idea." I unbuckle my seatbelt, sliding over to the right side to get out on the grass.

"I can come in."

I give him a pointed look. "I'm sure it's fine. You don't have to be my protector, Mase. I've got it. Plus, Gabe's staying. Thanks for the ride."

I get out of the car, shooting him a quick "goodbye" and a "drive safe" before he pulls away. Like most Garden District homes, ours stands proudly at two stories and is painted in a faded pink. Railings surround the porch and the gallery on the second floor. The sun shines through them, leaving lace-like patterns on the grass as I walk up to the door. That's where they get the name iron lace. Since it's shrouded in old live oak trees, it's almost impossible to see inside the house from out here. Resurrection ferns cling to the branches. They're a lush green from the summer rains.

The house is complete with seven rooms, four bathrooms, and fourteen-foot ceilings. It's worth rings up at about 6.5 million. It sounds like a lot, but we never paid for it. The Dupont family home was built in 1945, and we've kept it in the family since, passing it down to the first-born child of every generation.

Which means, yes, it's technically mine.

It's always been mine, and both my dad and I take—*took* —great pride in it.

Every time I walk into the house, I expect to hear some sort of jazz record playing and a loud "Peanut!" coming from dad.

Instead, the foyer is a long and silent hallway, two rooms off to the side before it opens up into the kitchen beyond that. A staircase takes up a little less than half the hall, covered in Victorian-style carpet. The majority of the floors are dark oak wood, which creaks in places under my feet. It's beautiful. No matter how creaky it is, it's home.

"Mom? Who's here?" I call, but she doesn't respond.

Gabe trails behind me. Sighing, I walk past the music room without so much as a glance. The dining room is what stops me. And no, it's not the beauty of it. In fact, I can't even process the intricate details when I see who's in my fucking house.

My mom sits at the head of the table, in Dad's seat, with Kat behind her. Every other chair is taken. By the Andersons. Cole's family. The largest real estate moguls of the Garden District. Anger bubbles deep in my stomach, and I grip the door frame instead of moving forward.

I laugh. There's no other possible reaction to that. "Oh, hell no."

"Sadie, I wasn't expecting you home yet." My mom clasps her hands together.

The Andersons are definitely an attractive family. Cole and his brothers get their black hair from their dad, even though his is flecked with gray. I blink vacantly for a moment, shaking my head. When I meet Cole's gaze, it's clouded with guilt.

Cole's the only sibling with those icy blue eyes. Clark, his older brother, and Carter, his younger brother, both have brown eyes like their dad's. Cole gets his from his mother.

"Yeah, obviously." I scoff. "What the hell do you think you're doing?"

"Sadie." Cole's voice makes me flinch.

"No, my mom can tell me." I hold up my hand to stop him. "Because I know she's not trying to sell this fucking house."

"You don't understand," Mom says, tears welling in her eyes. "I can't live here."

My ears ring, pulse thrumming as my hands fidget at my sides. If I don't step away, I'm going to say some really terrible things that shouldn't be said, even if I mean them. Everything hurts. *I* hurt. For me, for Mom, and especially for Dad.

Dad's voice plays in my mind, faded and warbly almost as if it's coming through a walkie-talkie.

Daddy...struggle with this too...best way...breathing. Here...

It's no use. My heart races, and my entire body feels weak, like I'll fall down with the next gust of wind.

"It hasn't even been a month." My voice breaks, and I clench my fists at my sides.

All of the Andersons are staring at the table except for Cole. He's looking at me. It's suddenly too much, all of it is just way too much.

"Hear them out," Kat says, although guilt pulls her lips down into a frown.

"You know damn well he'd be disappointed by this." I look up to the ceiling, begging for the strength not to ruin her heart all over again. "He's probably turning over in his fucking grave. You know, the one that we left him in twenty-four days ago."

"Sadie Nicole, that's enough–"

"No, it's not! I've busted my ass to get you out of fucking bed every day, and this is what you do? With them?" I rip my fingers through my hair. Gabe grabs my wrist, and Cole stands from his seat.

"Cole, sit down," his father commands.

The old Cole would've listened, but the new Cole doesn't even acknowledge he's said anything. If I wasn't so upset about this, my heart would've skipped. Maybe he is different.

"I've taken care of you and Kat. I moved back in to make sure you were okay. You were gonna sell it out from under my feet?" I try so hard to ignore Cole, to forget that his family is here, but a dam's been broken.

I've held my anger back so well until this. Honestly, I get that my mom and sister are devastated. That they may need some extra help. There's nothing wrong with needing it, but good fucking Lord, where's my support?

I take a step back, glaring at her. "You should be ashamed of yourself."

Dad loved this house. It was his father's before him. And while Andrea is a Dupont, she doesn't carry the same love for all things New Orleans that Dad did. Sniffling and nails digging into my palms, I storm out of the room, wishing that I could fucking scream my lungs out.

I lost my dad, and now I have to lose the house, too?

When I make it to the kitchen, I brace myself on the island, fighting the tears. I have to be the strong one. I can't break down like this. Gabe follows after me, furrowing his brows and gently touching my back.

"I'm sorry, Sadie."

Right when I open my mouth to speak, I hear Cole's voice instead.

The walls are thin. It's one of the only things I dislike about this place. Cole doesn't know that, so I catch every word coming out of his mouth.

"All due respect, Mrs. Dupont, but Sadie's right. You should give this more thought before you decide to sell. And...we both know it's her house. It belongs in the family."

Cole.

Fucking hell, my heart feels like it's going to jump out of my chest and land straight in the garbage disposal. I slap my hand over my mouth as the tears fall. And then I look up through blurred vision, managing to recognize Cole standing in the archway.

"Can we talk?" he asks, hands in his pockets.

Cole dresses impeccably. He always did, even at twenty-three. His button-down is blue, making his eyes brighter and warmer. There's not a wrinkle in sight. Typical Cole.

"Bad idea," Gabe interjects, shaking his head. "You should go back to your fiancée and leave Sadie alone."

"Gabe," I scold him before turning my attention back to Cole. Under any other circumstances, I'd say no, but I think he earned it for what he said to my mom. "Outside."

Cole crosses his arms over his chest, delivering Gabe a cold look. "Not that it's any of your business, but she's not in my life anymore."

Ignoring the way my stomach twists, I take a step toward the back door, and Cole moves to accompany me. Gabe's jaw tightens, as if I've committed a felony for disobeying his command.

We step onto the back patio, gray stone stretching from the door for about twenty feet. I wipe my eyes before I look at him. His eyebrows are furrowed as he rocks on the balls of his feet.

"Are you okay?" he finally asks, gaze trailing over me.

I give off a sad chuckle. "I wish people would stop asking me that."

"Right." He presses his lips together. "I thought she told you."

"It would appear that she did not." I sigh, itching the top of my head.

"I'm sorry. I should've let you know."

"I'm not your responsibility, Cole." *Not anymore.*

With a deep inhale, his chest rises. I wait and wait for the exhale, but it doesn't happen. One, two, three seconds of silence sweeps over us, eyes locked together. He finally lets his breath go.

"I didn't say you were. You were never a responsibility, mine or otherwise."

Ah, memory lane. A long, bumpy road I can't seem to get away from whenever I see Cole. I know I need to change the subject, but most of the memories I have with him are good ones, and I desperately need something positive to cling to.

"It's been a while since I've seen your family." I clear my throat since it's scratchy from yelling. "I guess the second impression wasn't any better than the first."

"Oh, come on." The corner of his lips ticks upward. "It was better than your mom's first impression of me."

It's the first time I let out a real laugh in three weeks. "Yeah, I guess you're right."

He was probably about ten feet away from me, so I'm not sure how he's right in front of me. It makes me remember how tall he is. How good it felt to be in his arms, to have his head rest on top of mine.

"I'm sorry, Sadie."

Wow, that's loaded. Sorry for my dad. Sorry for me. Sorry for the past.

"People die all the time," I say, shrugging. "Everything happens for a reason."

"Do you really think that?" Cole puts his hand on my arm.

I tense, but it's not bad. "Not at all. I want to tell my mom she's insane, and make Kat get her shit together, and burn the fucking world down, but who am I to do any of those things?"

"Doesn't matter who you are." Cole shrugs. "Only that you're grieving. Do what you need to do to feel better. You're the only one in your family that hasn't done that. You deserve to grieve, too."

I let his words sink in. They float around in my chest and sink into the deepest part of my heart, wrapping around it and squeezing. Besides The Incident, everything was good. We were good. And now, that's apparently all I can think of.

"Seriously," he continues, squeezing my arm. "If you let that sit, it's going to kill you. You have to get it out in whatever way works for you."

"I could really use a fucking punching bag."

He smiles. "Some things never change, do they?"

"Oh, no way. Violence is a fundamental part of who I am." I furrow my eyebrows, voice dripping with sarcasm.

"I miss talking to you," he says, tilting his head. His hand drops back to his side.

And then, he hugs me. Sometime during our conversation, he got close enough for physical contact, and I don't hate it. My breath catches. The dam I worked so hard to reconstruct after the kitchen completely shatters, tears welling and blurring my vision.

It's so easy to fall into this rhythm with him. He rests his head on top of mine and rubs my back, heart thrumming in his chest. I breathe him in. His scent is different, but still innately him. A gentle mixture of vanilla and mahogany floods my senses, and I let it and his embrace relax me.

"Everything will be alright," he whispers. "I promise."

Hundreds of people have said that to me, yet Cole is the only one I believe.

"Thank you," I murmur.

He takes a deep breath, and I realize I'm not the only one reminiscing. This is dangerous. Absolutely everything about this is dangerous. Reminiscing leads to feelings, and feelings lead to mistakes, and mistakes lead to more heartbreak. That's the last thing I need at the moment.

"Sadie, I–"

The back door opens, and he sighs, pulling away from me. Carter stands in there, lips pursed, as he realizes what he interrupted. He's a lot like Cole in many ways, and really, the only one of Cole's family I got along with. Cole clears his throat.

"We're leaving," Carter says.

Cole steps away. "Okay."

He looks back at me once, giving me a slight nod before he slides his hands back in his pockets. After he takes a few steps, the urge to call out to him resurfaces.

"Cole."

"Yeah?" He turns to me, eyebrows raised.

"I missed talking to you, too."

His face softens for the briefest moment, before he responds with a small smile. Time slows as he walks toward his brother. Carter's dark eyes meet mine as Cole passes him. He doesn't carry Cole's confidence or his perfectionist personality. I don't have time to react when he, too, gives me a nod before closing the door behind him.

I'm not expecting the shaky breath that leaves my lips, but I quickly put my hand on my forehead. Whatever the hell that was definitely cannot happen again. Cole is bad news. Good memories aside, my dad would be disappointed if he saw that.

Apparently, my mom isn't the only one doing things that'll make him turn over in his grave.

Sadie

Chapter Four

FIVE YEARS AGO...

Cole follows me in hesitantly, contemplating leaving my door open, but deciding to close it in the end. He glances around nervously, scratching the top of his head as he takes a deep breath.

When I turn the light on, we both flinch from the sudden change in brightness. His eyes flutter shut as he adjusts to it. My heart stops. His hair is definitely black, his jawline seems sharper, and I swear his eyebrows are perfect. Maybe he's thinking the same thing about me. How silver my hair is, how green my eyes are, and how revealing this outfit is. God, it's one thing to see all of him in the dark, but it doesn't do him any justice. Something happens in my chest, and I'm suddenly not thinking about what he'd look like with fewer clothes on.

I like him like this, and it's weird.

"I can't do this with you." Cole shakes his head but doesn't move to exit. "I shouldn't have come up here."

"Ask me what the worst-case scenario is." I take a step closer to him, desperately itching to reach out and touch him. His jaw tightens the longer he looks at me.

"What's the worst-case scenario?" Cole asks. He doesn't give me the impression that he restrains himself often, but he's fighting every urge he possibly can. His eyes give him away.

"Worst case is you walking away from me." I step away from him, contradicting what every cell in my body wants me to do. "Do you want a drink?"

"Sure." With one word, Cole cements his stay here, even if nothing else happens. He follows me into the kitchen. A bunch of useless crap sits all over the faux-granite counter—mail, a pack of bottled water, and a box of cereal. He glances around, almost fondly, and takes in everything my apartment has to offer.

"I have whiskey," I tell him. "It's cheap shit, but it's the only alcohol I have."

"That's fine," he replies with a smile, leaning against the counter. It's weird how well he fits in here. Maybe he's just as messy as I am, and it makes him feel better about his choices tonight.

I grab two glasses and my whiskey from the freezer.

He watches.

I pour the bronze liquid.

He keeps watching.

I hand him his glass.

He's *still* watching.

"Um," I start, sipping on my drink. "You said you live in Gretna. What brings you to the French Quarter?"

"Mason," he replies with ease, cringing at the taste of the whiskey. "It's his birthday."

"Shit, I punched him on his birthday?" A laugh of disbelief escapes me. I'm positive I'll have bruised knuckles tomorrow, but I'll be okay. His jaw? Definitely worse.

Cole laughs, too. "He deserved it. Most likely the best birthday present he's ever gotten."

Cole takes care of himself. His hair is brushed to perfection, eyebrows groomed, and fingernails manicured.

He taps his nail on his cup, small sounds following it as he does. The *pings* from the glass match my heartbeat perfectly as if he can hear it. *Ping, ping, ping.* I sigh, setting mine down on the counter.

"Do you do this often?" He raises his eyebrow at me.

"What? Lure men into my apartment?" I ask, watching a pink tint rise on his cheeks.

"I guess that's what I'm asking, yeah." He scoffs at himself and shakes his head slowly.

"Not often, no," I tell him. "I almost never bring men from the bar here."

"Almost never?"

"You'd be the first." I sip my drink before I walk out of the kitchen. Cole follows. His gaze is still on me as I take a seat on the couch. He sits on the opposite side as if he's scared to be too close to me. Maybe he thinks I'll bite.

"Oh, so I'm special?" He leans back on the cushion, hiding his grin by running his tongue over his teeth.

I send a glare his way. "It's unprofessional."

"I guess you're right." He shrugs, bringing his glass to his lips. I take in the shape of them and recall how they felt pressed on mine in the hallway. That hits me like a ton of bricks, and it dawns on me there's a chance he might want me in the way I want him.

When I scoot closer to him, he watches me closely. A dark intensity fills his stare. Prying his cup from his hand, I lean across him to put it on the side table. I throw my leg over his lap to straddle him. He gulps and furrows his perfect eyebrows as I sink into his lap. His hands clenched against the couch cushion as he tries his best not to touch me. We both fear that spark. The way it makes everything else disappear except for each other. The way it makes me want him with every ounce of my being.

"Sadie..." Cole trails off, his eyes leaving chills as he drags them over every part of me. "I can't."

"Can't, or won't?" I whisper, dragging my lips on his neck. He lets out a sigh and drops his head on the cushion behind him.

"Both. We can't have sex." It's the least flirtatious way to say it, yet I can't help but like the words when his neck rumbles beneath me.

"Who said anything about sex?" I lean back, making sure to watch for his reaction as I tease him.

"Oh," he says. "You invited me into your apartment at four in the morning, and you're on my lap, kissing my neck. What am I supposed to think?"

I smirk. "You make very convincing points. Maybe I invited you in here at four to sit on your lap and kiss your neck."

Cole lets out a short laugh, his eyes rolling. "So, if I do this, you wouldn't think I wanted to have sex?" He grabs my hips and helps me lie back on the couch. Shifting, he climbs over me and rests comfortably between my legs. I gulp and hope he doesn't see.

"Not at all," I reply, breathless. "This tells me you cuddle a body pillow at night."

This time, *he* kisses *my* neck. Arm flexed, he keeps a minuscule distance between us. He nips my collarbone, and the pit of my stomach flips. My breath hitches as the smallest noise of surprise leaves my mouth. His lips pull into a smile.

"And this?" he whispers. "I think this is pretty suggestive."

I'm glad he can't see the involuntary eye roll. "You made your point. I'll stay off your lap."

"Does it *feel* like that's my point?" Cole removes himself from between my legs. When he stands from the couch, he grabs his glass from the table and finishes it off.

"I wouldn't know. You're kind of cryptic, Cole." I lift myself up on my elbows.

"We probably won't see each other after tonight." Although he's being honest, my heart wrings in my chest before sinking into the furthest depths, never to be found again.

"And?"

"And I don't know if I could have sex with Gabe's cousin," he replies, avoiding my gaze. "It's weird."

"It's not really that weird," I say, scrunching my face up at him. "But it's fine. He'd probably be pissed."

I think the night will be awkward after that, or that he'll leave, but it's not, and he doesn't.

We end up outside on my gallery. He must have a much better tolerance than me. He's on his third glass of whiskey, and I'm still nursing my second. We're both leaning on the railing, looking up at the starless sky. Our eyes strain as we try to find one—Cole swears he'll be able to, and all I can do is laugh. After all, this is New Orleans. Light pollution makes it impossible to see stars.

"See?" He points off into the distance. "There's one right there."

"No." I giggle, sipping my drink. "That's definitely a helicopter." He tilts his head as he looks at it before he laughs, too.

"Shit, you're right." He drops his gaze down and taps his cup on the iron railing. "Maybe you should cut me off, bartender."

"I don't know, if I didn't live here, I might've thought it was a star, too." I nudge his arm, the event on the couch a faraway memory.

"Damn helicopters," he says, humor laced in his voice. "Why do they get to be stars? Doesn't *everyone* want that somehow?"

I take him in like this. The only light out here is from the window that separates my gallery from the inside of my apartment. His eyelids droop, somehow making the bags beneath them more prominent. Probably because it's 5 a.m., and he's awake with me. It's like he rips through my chest and tugs at my heartstrings, leaving me wondering if I'll really never see him again.

"Are you getting all psychological on me?" I tease him.

"Maybe."

"Well, I don't think I want to be a star." I crinkle my nose as I look back to the sky.

"Why not?" He frowns, eyebrows knitting together. "I think you'd be the prettiest star, Sadie."

My heart skips a beat. Nobody's ever said anything like that to me before, but that's probably because it's not a normal thing to say. Nothing about Cole is normal. I don't know if I love it or hate it.

Cole isn't normal because if he'd been anyone else, we would be sleeping together.

Cole isn't normal because if he was, he wouldn't say things like that to me.

"Maybe I *should* cut you off." I shake my head at him and try my best not to let him see the way that affected me. "Tell me more about you."

"There's really not all that much more to tell." He acts like he doesn't notice I'm moving closer to him. "I grew up in Gretna; still live there. I'm a boring man. Not very many hobbies, not much of a life, obviously. Mason's my only friend."

"How long have you known him?"

There's a gleam in his eyes as he smiles. "Feels like fucking forever. Probably six or seven years...Maybe it just feels like forever because he's such a pain in the ass."

"Oh, right. *Mason's* a pain in the ass." I chuckle, chewing gently on my thumbnail.

Cole's smile widens. "Okay, okay. I'll explain it then. First of all, he drags me out everywhere. I can't remember one time where I willingly left the house to go somewhere with him. And secondly, he keeps me out all night. I never get any sleep if he's involved."

I drink, acting as if I'm in thought for a moment. "Mm, maybe he's a lot more like me than I realized."

"I wouldn't go that far," he quips. "Luckily for you, you're much cuter than he is. I'll let it slide."

"Wow, thank you so much for doing me this amazing favor." I can't stop the abrupt laugh from leaving my throat.

Cole takes a step closer to me, closing the distance between us as the grin slowly falls from his face. He swallows hard. His gaze trails over my face and stops on my lips.

"I want to kiss you."

"Then do it." I shrug.

"I shouldn't."

"Shut up, Cole. Do it."

He does.

His lips are softer on mine this time, lacking the need he felt out in the hallway. I smile into his kiss. With a starless sky as our backdrop and the scarce lighting casting shadows, our night is romantic, even if that's not his goal. He delicately wraps his arm around my waist, just enough to make sure I'm pressed into him. His lips trail to my neck, and I tilt my head back to give him the most skin I can.

"I should be honest," I murmur, gulping. "I lied about the creepy man living on my floor. I wanted you to come upstairs."

Cole chuckles against my skin, only removing his lips from me to speak. "I know."

I'm not sure how long we're out on the gallery, but I lose track of time. Neither of us knows what to expect from the other. When we go into my room, I decide I need to change. He sits on the edge of my bed, taking in the off-white walls and dark flooring while his fingers run along the blue comforter on my bed.

Grabbing clothes from my drawers, I turn my back to him. His attention is on me as I pull my top over my head. It's basically a bralette, so I'm definitely not wearing a real bra under it. His gaze sends chills all over my body. I slide the T-shirt on. The black fabric covers me to the middle of my thighs as I take my shorts off and let them slide to the floor.

When I finally face him, he's smiling at me like he enjoyed the show, even if it wasn't much of one. For a moment, I wonder if he's changed his mind. If he wants to give into the urges written across his face as he shifts forward to rest his elbows on his thighs.

"You really are beautiful, Sadie," he says as I approach, wrapping his arms around my waist. As much as I ache to be on his lap again, I refrain.

I kiss him as a thank you. He accepts it, his tongue inviting itself into my mouth. All of this feels so natural. Like

I've known him for years. Like we were meant to meet and be alone in this room together. His hands grip the back of my thighs, pushing my shirt up until his hands are on my ass. The heat in his touch offsets the coolness of his eyes.

"What are you thinking about?" I ask him, unable to discern it from his face.

"How nice your lips feel on mine," he whispers, squeezing me and pulling me closer. "How nice it would be to give in to you."

"It would be nice," I confirm, smiling at him even though I know he won't. His hands are still on me, but he doesn't do anything else. They rest there.

"Why don't we?" Cole furrows his eyebrows. He trails his touch up further, my shirt dragging. As he reveals more and more of my skin, his gaze travels along my body.

"You don't want to feel bad about leaving after." I run my fingers down his arms, hoping he feels the same sparks I do. "You think my cousin would hate you forever." My heart pangs at the thought of him leaving.

"That's not...that's not why I would feel bad after, Sadie." He doesn't offer anything else, but his hands disappear from my body. Cold air replaces his warmth, and with a sharp inhale, I try to shake the feeling off. Climbing into my bed, I meet his stare from where he stands at the foot of it.

"Coming?" I ask, patting the opposite side. "You can take your jeans off if you don't want to sleep in them."

"I'm okay," Cole replies, settling in bed next to me. Sighing, he pulls me into his chest. "Tell me more about you."

I laugh. "Well, I'm Sadie. My favorite color's blue. I work

at your friend's favorite bar. He also hits on me a lot, but I'm pretty sure he's joking. The only reason I have that job is because my aunt owns the place."

"Tell me about your family." He kisses the top of my head.

"My family's pretty great." I shift to rest my leg across him. "Lived in the French Quarter until my grandpa died ten years ago. We moved to the Garden District since it's a little more peaceful over there. My parents are amazing. My sister's a dumbass. She's only two years younger than me, but she's six times the trouble."

His chest shakes as he laughs. "I don't know about the trouble part."

"You'll believe it when you see it. She's a shithead." I blush as soon as the words come out of my mouth. He deflates a bit, but he doesn't say anything about it.

Cole changes the subject, continuing to pry more information out of me. Before the night is over, we know more about each other than anyone else does. We don't sleep, either. The sun rises around seven, and we're still talking.

We discuss dreams, motivations, aspirations—things I've never told anyone. I'm dreading the moment he'll get up and walk out the door, but I know it'll happen. He'll leave, and I'll never see him again. I hate thinking like that, because talking with him all night is something I've never experienced before. I've never been *interested* in someone enough to sit and listen to their life story.

Cole Anderson is one of three kids, all boys. He's the middle child, meaning he got picked on a lot by his brothers. Apparently, his parents are boring. He refers to himself and his family as that a lot—boring. I don't think I agree. If any of them are like him, even in the slightest, they'd most likely be the most interesting people I've ever met.

As soon as the jazz music starts to flow through the windows from the cobblestone New Orleans streets, he tells me he should go. I consider asking him to stay, but I know better. He kisses me sweetly as he leans over me, and then I walk him to the door, the hard flooring cold under my feet. He stands there for a moment.

"I'm sorry," Cole says, his hand reaching up to brush my hair behind my ear. "I really wish we could have more than this."

I don't ask him why we can't. It's only because he doesn't think it's right. All I can do is smile at him in response.

"We can." I move his hand from my face and place it back at his side. "You'll realize how addicting I am, and you'll be back."

He knows I don't really mean it, but he gives me a sad look anyway, almost like he wants it to be true. Turning away from me, he opens the door.

"You should get some sleep, Sadie." He walks away after that, closing it behind him.

The jazz music from outside dances with the sunlight, intertwined as it comes through the window. If I wasn't so upset about Cole leaving, I would've enjoyed it.

Cole

Chapter Five

As soon as I'm back inside Sadie's house, I regret not saying anything to her when I walked away. Carter pats my shoulder. His lips press into a thin line as he gives me a knowing look, but I wave him off.

My parents and Clark are waiting by the front door with Sadie's mom. I catch my dad's gaze and quickly avoid it. He's got a way with words. As in, without speaking at all, he tells me how severely disappointed he is in me—from the frown on his face to the way he stands straight as a pin. Both for what I said to Andrea, and for going outside with Sadie. He never liked Sadie, but it wasn't his job to like her. It was mine.

I walk right past him through the open door without acknowledging any of them. They can be mad at me all they want, but that's not going to make me change my mind about this damn house. After years, I was hoping they'd give up.

Once we're all in the car, it's time for the lecture.

I'm twenty-nine years old, and my dad still lectures me. Our seating arrangement is kind of funny. Middle seat. Middle child. Even though I'm the tallest, I'm in the middle. Fucking birth order.

"What the hell were you thinking?" Dad's voice is stern, like I'm still a ten-year-old boy. "We've been trying to get this house for years."

"Kind of shitty of you to use someone's death as a way in." I clasp my hands together in my lap. Clark shifts, grimacing. Carter sighs.

They don't argue with Dad. Nobody argues with Dad.

Except for me, as of five years ago.

I think Sadie's confrontational personality wore off on me, and I genuinely would not want it any other way. It irritates me to no end how many traits I got from my father. The black hair. Sharp jawline. Resting bitch face. Does that apply to men? Because if it does, we've got it.

"Right." Dad scoffs. "*That's* why you don't want us to move forward with this."

"You know what? You're right. Sadie deserves better than this."

His face darkens. "You dated the girl five years ago, so don't you think it's time to get over her? What would Miranda think?"

My mood sours at the thought of *Miranda*.

"You're more upset about me breaking up with Miranda than she is." I massage my forehead, sighing. "I don't have to have feelings for Sadie to want good things for her."

Carter snorts, dropping his head into his hand. There's a line even I can't cross with Dad, and I'm treading pretty damn close to it. His word is law. Always has been, always will be.

He doesn't respond to me, so I allow myself to fall back on the seat. My mind trails back to Sadie the second it gets quiet in the car. God, the second I saw the look on her face when she walked into the dining room...I wanted to sweep her off her feet and take her away.

But that's the thing about Sadie. She doesn't want to be rescued. She doesn't want to be swept off her feet, and I think that was always my favorite thing about her.

And she's beautiful. Even more so now than five years ago. Her hair is shorter, falling right below her shoulders, and natural in color. I felt it today. Without the chemicals from the dye, it's so much softer.

I wish we didn't leave things the way we did. Throughout our entire hug, she was stiff as a damn board, until she started crying. I'm pretty sure she hates me and my family.

The only thing I regret about my relationship with Sadie is the end of it. She's the one who got away. And I'll probably hate myself for the rest of my life for letting that happen. Sadie deserves the best, and my family swooping in to buy that fucking house right after her dad's death is not it.

William was Sadie's best friend. From the brief time I was with her, she told me so many stories about how amazing he was. What an odd thing to think about—how some dads can be so great, and then... there's mine.

I doubt my dad even has a best friend. Maybe Mom, but it seems like she's more of a puppet than anything. She doesn't have her own personality, either. Not like Sadie. That's another reason I enjoy her. She has real thoughts and feelings she's not shy about sharing.

My mind slips from Sadie to Miranda. When Sadie and I were together, nothing was boring. Time flew. With Miranda, everything dragged. I wasn't happy with her, no matter how much my parents wanted me to be. The only person who's ever made me feel like I could do anything was Sadie, even if I was shit at showing her how I really felt.

Carter nudges my shoulder, breaking me out of my Sadie-induced trance.

"What?" I ask, frowning.

"Mom asked if you're staying for dinner."

"Oh." I pause, contemplating if I should. "Can't. I have plans."

Lying to them has gotten much easier. I try to separate myself from all of them except Carter as much as possible. They're not good people. And I've recently come to the realization that *blood* doesn't constitute *family*. Carter is good, and Clark isn't absolutely terrible. My parents are the worst.

"With whom?" my dad asks as he shifts the car into park. "You seemed quick to jump to Sadie's defense."

"Why do you suddenly want to know?" I narrow my eyes at him, refraining from rolling them.

My mom turns toward me. "Cole, don't talk to your father like that. He's allowed to be curious."

"Sure, if he's not doing it to be a dick." I shrug. "He wants to make sure I'm not going out with Sadie. And to answer your question, I think you did a pretty good job of getting her to hate me, so *no*, I'm not hanging out with Sadie tonight. Are we done?"

Clark sighs and pinches the bridge of his nose. "Can't you be civil for a few minutes? This arguing is really tiring."

"What's so bad about Cole going out with Sadie, anyway?" Carter asks.

"Sadie hating you has nothing to do with us." Dad scoffs. "It was your own stupid mistakes that did that."

"Go ahead," I say. "By all means, answer Carter."

"We want that house, Carter," Mom replies. "It's a conflict of interest if Cole has feelings for a Dupont."

"Right. Didn't work out with Sadie, so maybe I'll give Kat a try." I scoff.

"Yes, and we're the reason Sadie hates you," Clark retorts.

I shift in my seat, clasping my hands together. "Can we get the hell out of this car?"

Carter's door shoots open, and he all but tumbles out of it to escape the terrible tension filling the air. Sighing in relief, I follow him out. I don't say anything else to my parents or Clark. Carter has always been my favorite brother.

My parents live in Gretna. Up until three or four years ago, Carter and I lived in the guest house on the other side of the property. A miniature version of the original home, both towering white prisons. The windows are covered with shudders. Black accents the railings to the galleries and the porch that wraps around half the structure. The main house is three stories while the guest is only two. It comes with nine bedrooms, a completely oversized kitchen, and many more useless things. All it does is remind me how it's much too big for a family of five.

I don't like to spend too much time looking at it. Most of my childhood memories are in there, and seeing it brings them all back. Not a single one was decent. From a young age, we were groomed into business. Into perfection.

I had such an overwhelming need to make everything perfect that I lost myself along the way. By the time Isaac Anderson was done with me, there was absolutely nothing left. I was a shell of a human, much like my mother. Apparently, I was the only one with enough sense to get the hell away from here.

Carter walks with me to my car. "You've gotta be careful, man. The last thing you want is to get cut out of the will. Who knows when he'll finally hit the dust?"

"Fuck his will," I grumble, shoving my hands in my pockets. "I don't want his money. Especially not if it comes from the Duponts, or anyone like them for that matter."

"She did that much damage?" Carter raises his eyebrows.

"It's not damage, Carter," I deadpan. Carter means well. He always does, but that doesn't change how much I don't want to talk about this.

"Then what is it?"

"Her dad died. She was close with him, and it doesn't feel right to use his death as a way in. I care about her. That didn't end when we stopped dating." I fidget with my hands, biting the inside of my cheek to make me stop there.

"I've broken up with people before. Don't think I've ever

still cared about them five years afterward." Carter shifts on his feet.

"Then you've never been in love. It doesn't ever go away." I pause, inhaling. "I should get going."

"Are you...are you thinking about pursuing her?" Carter asks.

"Okay, for one, it's not the 1950s. And two, I just got out of a long-term relationship. So...no, Sadie isn't on my mind. I wasn't joking when I said she hates me. I'm the last person she wants to hear from." I open the door, ready to climb in the front seat.

"Cole...I don't think she hates you. And I'm sure you're far from the last person she wants to see. There's gotta be someone worse." Carter smiles, nudging my arm.

And for some reason, that makes me laugh. Maybe it's funny. Or maybe it's because I know he's wrong. "Thanks. But my time with Sadie's long passed. We've both moved on."

Here's the thing about being in love, about having someone who got away: you can try to move on. You can pretend it doesn't eat you alive every second of every day. But it does. No matter how hard you push yourself forward, nobody will be able to compare to *that one*.

Sadie brought out a side of me I didn't know existed. Until her, I never knew all the things my parents did were wrong, that a child shouldn't go through the things I went through. So... yes, she has a piece of me that no one else ever will. Miranda didn't come close.

By the time I get back to my house, it's dark out. The French Quarter is lit up this time of night, but it doesn't do much to aid me on the street I live on. I walk in, throw my keys on the granite counter, and fall onto my bed, directly face planting into my pillows. It's only seven. I shouldn't be this damn tired, but the day's events prove I need more rest than I thought.

With my head on my palm, I watch, mesmerized, as the ceiling fan turns. Being away from Sadie for so long helped me pretend to move on, and seeing her today set me back. I don't bother changing. Sleep won't be easy tonight, no matter what I'm wearing. When my phone starts buzzing in my pocket, the last person I expect the call to be from is *her*.

She's calling me.

I feared she'd deleted my number after all this time. Honestly, if I were her, I would've.

"Hey," I answer.

"Hi." Her voice is a sweet, sweet melody, a song sinking into my chest and forever playing there. Beautiful, even over the phone.

"Everything alright?"

"Not really." She pauses. Sounds follow from her end as she shuffles. "I wanted to say I'm sorry."

I frown, my eyes starting to dry from staring at the fan too long. "Sorry for what?"

"For Gabe being such a dick. And about your engagement. I'm sorry it didn't work out." Despite *her* calling *me*, she doesn't appear to want to talk for long. She speaks in short sentences, to the point where it sounds like she's holding herself back and cutting herself off.

"Sadie." I wet my lips, sitting up on my bed. "Sometimes

things just aren't meant to be. And as far as Gabe goes, I've known him forever. He doesn't faze me."

"Okay." She pauses. "Not that it matters. He shouldn't have intervened in something that doesn't have anything to do with him."

"Right. Well, I'm sorry, too."

We sit in silence for a moment, and if she's anything like me, she's basking in the thought of us talking like this. After not seeing her for years, it's like everything is hitting me like a semi-truck, all over again.

"It's..." She sighs, almost in defeat. "Nobody's stood up for me since he died. They don't mean it when they ask if I'm okay. Or when they tell me everything's gonna be alright. Not like you do."

I'm speechless. There's nothing I can say in response to that.

"Everyone's scared that we're all gonna fall apart. And, I mean, they're probably right about that, but still. It's nice. So...thanks." A slight pause. "Wow, I didn't even think to ask if you were busy. Sorry if I interrupted anything fun. Or...even anything not fun, I guess, because either way an interruption is an interruption–"

Yep, there's the Sadie I know. "Sadie." I try to stop the smile from spreading on my face. "I'm alone in bed at 7:30. It's safe to say you have not interrupted anything. Fun or otherwise."

"Okay, well, that's all I called for. Don't worry, this won't be a habit. I'll let you get back to your life, and I'll go back to mine, and hopefully, my mother won't try to sell my damn house. Mason'll be here soon, so I should go."

My heart sinks. It's not my place to worry about her being with Mason, but I do regardless. I have no doubts that Mason is a good friend to her and the rest of her family. But Sadie lost her dad. She's in a vulnerable place, and I'm not sure Mason is the person she should seek comfort in.

Like I'm a better choice. Or a choice at all.

"Alright. It...it was nice seeing you. Really."

Another pause. Another contemplation on what to say next. "You too, Cole."

Sadie

Chapter Six

FIVE YEARS AGO...

I want it. Never in my life have I ever wanted anything more.

At least, that's what I try to convince myself when I see the picture of the bookshelf on the box. I frown, trying to figure out what color it is. The store is bustling, even mid-afternoon on a Tuesday. The only bad thing about living in a tourist town—everything is so damn busy all the time.

I wiggle the box out of the shelf it's on, gasping as it *thuds* to the floor.

"Shit," I curse under my breath, looking around to see if anyone saw that. While I don't need help, I do want to make sure I'm not embarrassing myself. I brush my shorts off, even though nothing dirtied them.

I roll my shoulders like it'll make me stronger. Squatting down, I force my hands under the box. I lift, but I only get it up halfway before it tumbles out of my hands.

Now, I'm angry. I cannot believe I'm being defeated by a God damn *bookshelf*. Hoisting it upward, I finally get it high enough—until my stupid cart rolls away. The box smacks against the floor, way too close to my feet for comfort. I groan a little too loudly, tempted to leave this dumb thing where it's at.

"Wow, you have no trouble socking Mason in the face, but a *bookshelf* does you in?" *Cole*. There's humor in that stupid voice of his, but my pulse is already thrumming. I turn to look at him with a frown, which I have to *fight* to keep on my face when I see him.

The striking blue eyes. Raven black hair—not a single strand out of place—and that smirk on his pretty face.

Leaning on the store shelf, he crosses his feet at the ankles. He's wearing a maroon button-down today, sleeves rolled to his elbows and the bottom tucked into his black pants. Muscles on his biceps strain the fabric. His shoulders, much more visible in the store lighting, are broad, even with his arms folded over his chest. I almost forget to follow up my frown with words, but I do anyway.

"How long have you been standing there?" I growl at him, deciding against stomping my foot like a toddler. "Do you enjoy watching me struggle?"

Cole's smirk turns into a smile. "C'mon, Sadie, I'd never do that to you. I *am* a bit shocked to see you in this situation though. I don't think I saw any books in your apartment."

"I have books," I say, a short laugh escaping my throat. "There are tons of things in my apartment you haven't seen. You were too busy being a dick."

His smile falters, and his eyes take me in, trailing over my body as he chews on his bottom lip. I can't help but wonder why his gaze snags. My shorts go down to the middle of my thighs, and I'm in a plain T-shirt. Nothing special or remotely attractive.

"I was being chivalrous." He defends himself, shifting away from his spot and taking a couple steps toward me. "I'll do it again. Let me help."

"Don't you know chivalry is dead?" I glare at him, moving between him and the box and holding my hand up. "I don't want your help."

My palm lands flat on his chest, and I want to curse under my breath when I feel how firm he is. My fingers curl into the maroon fabric on instinct. As soon as I do it, I realize what the hell is happening. The corner of his lips twitches upward, and his eyes—in a move so quick I almost don't notice—flick down to my mouth.

"Okay, maybe you don't want it, but you clearly need it. You're going to hurt yourself." As much as I hate to admit it, he's right. I'm going to end up dropping it on my feet or pulling a muscle trying to get this into my car.

I sigh in defeat, retracting my hand from the warmth seeping through his shirt and stepping aside. "What are you doing here? I thought you lived in Gretna?"

"I do." He lifts the box and sets it into my cart. "It's not that far. I come here to see Mason all the time."

"You told me you didn't usually hang out with him."

"No, I said I don't go out to bars very often," he points out, raising one of his perfect eyebrows at me. "Why are you so angry today? Besides the bookshelf."

"Are you really asking me that?" I glare at him. His confusion makes me want to scream, but I keep it in. If he hasn't been thinking about me every second since he left, then I don't want him to know *I've* been thinking of him.

He's really close, and I'm realizing how tall he is. He towers over me. If he were to hug me, he could rest his head on top of mine. *Comfortably*.

"Is...is this about Friday?" He scrunches his nose up as he asks, like he feels awkward talking about it. "Sadie, I'm sorry if I hurt your feelings."

"My *feelings*?" I laugh, much louder than I should. "Worry about your own." I turn away from him and grab my cart, pushing it forward. He follows me, but I don't say anything to him.

"So, you understand why I did it?" His hands are in his pockets as he walks next to me.

"Nope," I reply, refusing to look at him. Peripheral vision does *not* count. Not if he can't tell. "But understanding it would mean I cared about your decision. You know what I wanted that night, and it didn't happen, so that's that, I guess."

He's taken aback by my forwardness, especially with so many people around, but he doesn't let it deter him. "I don't know, it seems like you care about my decision." He grabs my arm to stop me from walking.

"Did you not see what happened to Mason when he grabbed me?" I shoot at him, glaring.

"Yeah, except I'm not Mason, and it's not 4 a.m.," he points out, not letting go. I don't like that I still feel the sparks, but I *hate* that it looks like he can, too.

I jerk my arm away from him, pulling my cart out of the way of the public. He stands in front of me, looking like he wants to scold me, and it makes me want to walk away from him even more.

"You weren't acting like this on Friday."

"Cole." I think my voice startles him. "It's not Friday anymore. It's actually Tuesday, and you should really keep up on the calendar. I don't give a damn about it. You're the one bringing it up. Sounds like you regret your decision, not me."

He feels bad. I see it in those icy blue eyes of his, because it looks like they're melting.

I grip on to my cart. "Thanks for the help, and all the conversation Friday, but it's better for both of us if we just never see each other again."

"Okay." The word comes out hitched, so he clears his throat. "Yeah, I guess you're right."

Him giving up so easily irks me. The irritation sparks in me, but I take a deep breath.

"Sadie, wait." He makes my heart skip a beat.

I turn around once more to face him, seeing the conflict written all over his face. How is this so hard for him?

"How...how are you going to get that in your apartment?" He approaches me, gesturing to the box. "If you can't lift it into your cart, I doubt you'll be able to carry it up the stairs."

"No." I shake my head. "It's not your concern. I don't want your help."

"Look, if I'm never going to see you after today, I may as well make this a good encounter, right?" His eyebrows pinch, almost like he's begging.

"Don't you have your boring job to get back to or something?" I scowl.

"Nope," he says, shoving his hands back into his pockets. "I'm all yours today."

"Great," I mutter under my breath, but he smiles as I glare at him. "You can drop the box off right inside the door. Then you can leave." He's good at that, anyway.

I check out, and he helps me load the box into my trunk. He moves towards his car, letting me know he'll meet me at my apartment. I'm not sure if I regret letting him help me or not.

I tug the tie out of my hair in frustration. It's October, and the humidity here is absolutely dreadful. It makes silver strands stick to my skin, and I sweat as soon as I step outside. It rains on and off in New Orleans a lot, but hurricane season is the worst.

For a brief second, I hope he'll get lost on the way to my apartment. I don't want him remembering where I live, even though he stayed up all night with me and told me things about himself I'm not sure other people know, completely okay with never seeing me afterward.

It stings for sure.

But when I pull into my parking lot, he's there, standing outside of his car. I refrain from bashing my head against the steering wheel, because I know he can see me. He drives a black sedan. I swear, he's the embodiment of his dumb, *boring* job. The one I still have no idea about.

He grabs the box out of my car, and we make our way into the building.

"So," he starts, unbothered by the weight he's carrying. "Tell me more about you, Sadie."

I laugh. "Absolutely not. You got enough already."

"I could never know enough about you," he replies. Our steps are in sync as we go up to the second floor, but I try my best to ignore it. I could've sworn I hated the idea of him coming up here, but a tingling feeling in my belly tells me it was a good choice.

"Why do you act like you want to know me and then agree to disappear?" I finally ask. His face changes from relaxed to guarded almost immediately.

"It's what you want." He presses his lips into a thin line. "You were the one who said it in the first place. I respect you too much to challenge you."

"I guess." I've *never* wished for a man to respect me less, but I guess he's the exception—*again*.

We stop outside my door and he waits for me to open it. I do, holding it so he can walk in. He does—barely—and sets the box down. Then he's in front of me, and he has that stupid look on his face telling me he doesn't want to leave. He gave me the same look on Friday. Or actually, I suppose it was Saturday, because it was around seven in the morning.

He drops his arms to his sides as he exhales. "It was...it was really great to meet you, Sadie."

This is it. He's going to walk out, and I'll never see him again. His eyes will never leave those stupid chills all over my body. God, what's he going to do? Avoid the French Quarter for the rest of his life?

He still hasn't moved, though. The door hangs open, but neither of us moves to change any part of this. His eyebrows slant further the longer he looks at me. I bite my lip, wondering how the hell we ended up here.

"All you were supposed to do was drop that off," I say.

"That's what I did."

"Why would you want to?"

"You asked me to." He shrugs, pausing and shifting on his feet. "Did you ever consider that maybe I'm just being nice?"

I laugh. What the hell else am I supposed to do? "I didn't ask, you offered. And to be honest, you don't strike me as a nice person."

"That's coming from you? Wow." A small chuckle escapes him, and he bites the inside of his cheek to contain it.

"For one, I'm a fucking pleasure to be around. A complete and total sunshine. Nice people do tasks they're asked to and then they leave, or offer to help with something else." I walk toward the kitchen, and like the lost puppy he is, he follows me.

"What else do you need help with, your majesty? Shall I put together the bookshelf for you?" he says, leaning on my counter as I grab one of my water bottles.

The door's still open, but neither of us says a thing. Neither of us is going to close it, because that's too...permanent. If we close it while he's inside, he's probably not going to leave. And then we'll have another night like Friday. If he closes it on his way out, then it truly is the end of whatever the hell this is.

I send a glare his way. "No, thank you."

"Give me something else to do," he says, exasperated. "Because I wasn't lying when I said I didn't have anything to do today. Enlighten me."

"Oh, I've got it!" I feign enthusiasm before dropping back into having zero expression. "You could go home."

"Insufferable." Cole sighs and takes a step closer to me. "Fine, I'll go. If you need anything else from me, don't."

"I hate to break this to you, but I didn't exactly need your help in the first place." I shift impatiently.

When he's right in front of me, I think back to Friday, to how his lips felt on mine. The last time he was this close, the pull toward him was unlike anything I'd ever felt. Maybe the magic was only in that night, because it's not as strong today.

Maintaining his stance, he has to crane his head down to look at me. He crosses his arms over his chest.

He fakes pondering. "Actually, you couldn't even lift the box from the ground."

I scoff, recoiling. "The cart rolled away."

"Yeah. Sure. Keep telling yourself that." He leans forward, his face close enough to mine for him to notice how my breath hitches. "Maybe you are a complete and total sunshine, but those rays might be a bit too bright for me."

Oh, how rare it is for a man to leave me speechless. My jaw hangs open as I register what he says, and before I come up with a smart-ass retort, he smiles.

"When you fly too close to the sun, you get burned," Cole tells me. "I'd rather not."

"Yet, here you are."

"Here I am."

"Are you burning yet? Not only are you as close to *the sun* as you could possibly get, but I would so enjoy seeing that." I blink at him once, twice, three times before he scratches his forehead.

"Does that mean you don't want me to leave?" He quirks an eyebrow at me.

"You wish." I don't mean to get closer to him, but the step forward comes before my logical thoughts do.

"I think you're too stubborn to admit it," Cole replies. "You don't want me to go any more than I want to."

"For different reasons, of course." I nod. "You want to be around me, and I want to watch you burst into flames as you said you would."

"That's kinda sadistic, no?"

Glancing at the clock on the wall, I tap my wrist. "Time's ticking. Make up your mind."

"I'll see you around." Much to my distaste, he moves away from me.

"Doubtful."

"Always a pleasure, Sadie." Cole waves me off as he walks toward the still-open door. He glances back at me once before he pats the frame and leaves.

As intriguing as he is, this is for the best. Finding where he left the box on the floor, I drag it toward my room, out of breath by the time I get it over there. I'm suddenly much less interested in this bookshelf. Now it's going to remind me of him.

No matter how hard I try, thoughts of him continue to race through my mind.

A small hope buds like a blooming rose, one wishing he'll come back in, kiss me, and tell me I'm what he wants. But I know better, especially after ten minutes pass. I sit there with my deconstructed shelves, staring at the door for half an hour.

Tying my hair up, I push the box the rest of the way into my room. Cole may never be here again, but this stupid bookshelf will be. And like the couch, it'll be a constant reminder of him.

Great.

Sadie

Chapter Seven

Today has probably been the longest day ever. Getting off the phone with Cole feels weird, awkward even. I can't believe I called him. Obviously, he was surprised, but it didn't feel as if it affected our conversation. If anything, it was the same as it always used to be.

I lay in bed, staring up at the ceiling with my phone on my chest. Taking a deep breath, I consider telling Mason. About Cole. Or even about what he said to my mom earlier. From the start, Mason's had the same opinion when it comes to Cole and me. Bad idea. Always a bad idea.

But God damn it, he's so familiar. It feels good to talk to him, especially when I need someone to be there just for me, and not my entire family. Maybe that's selfish, but it's nice to think of myself for the first time since Dad died.

Mason will be here soon. I wasn't lying to Cole when I said that, but the disappointment hung heavy in his voice afterward. And like magic, as soon as I start thinking of Mason, the front door opens. I head downstairs.

It's not Mason that walks in, but Kat. Her eyes are wide as she practically slams her belongings down on the kitchen island before I come in, frowning at her.

"Hey, is everything okay?"

"No, Sadie, it's not." Kat rests her head in her palms. "Nothing is ever going to be okay again."

I hesitate. Kat hasn't exactly been doing well after Dad's death, but I never thought it would come to this. She's strong. The chronic worrier in me comes out, so I pull out one of the stools from under the counter and sit on it.

"Care to elaborate?" I ask.

Kat's eyelids flutter, a sharp inhale making her chest rise. "I'm pregnant."

"I'm sorry, what?" I choke on my saliva, clutching my throat while I cough. "You're what?"

"Pregnant."

"But, how? Who?"

"Do I really need to explain to you how I got pregnant?" Kat scoffs, rolling her eyes. "I've been on birth control for so long that I didn't think not getting my period was weird. But then I started craving the weirdest fucking things, so I went to the doctor today. I'm six weeks along."

Stunned, I sit there with my jaw dropped. Out of the millions of ways I could respond to her, I'm almost positive the way I do isn't right. "Where the hell are you gonna put it?"

Kat glares at me, tugging her fingers through her hair. "That's honestly the least of my concerns at the moment."

"Okay, sure. Who's the dad?"

"I don't know."

"You don't *know*?" I recoil, looking at her and trying to gauge how honest she's being.

She shifts on her feet. "Sadie, this is serious."

"No shit." I slide my head from side to side.

"You're insufferable sometimes, you know that?" She snorts, a small smile cracking on her face.

"Part of my charm." I shrug, grabbing the stack of mail from the counter. "Are you gonna find out who the dad is?"

"Short of calling the men I've slept with in the past few weeks, I don't really have a way to do that." She massages her forehead, a sigh wracking her chest.

"You've got two built-in babysitters." I sort the envelopes into three perspective piles for the three residents of the house.

"How kind of you," Kat says, stretching.

"Well, you know you have options, right? You don't have to go through with it if you don't want to."

Mason walks into the kitchen, hesitating when he sees both of us. "Late night kitch-intervention, huh? What'd you do this time?"

"Ha, ha." Kat gives him a dirty look. "None of your business."

"Oh, come on, KitKat." He puts a hand over his heart, narrowing his eyes at her. "You'd dare leave me out of the conversation?"

"Of this conversation? Absolutely." She fakes a smile.

"Sadie?" Mason turns to me.

"Oh, sibling privilege. Sorry." I scrunch my nose up.

"It must suck to be so badly outnumbered." Kat runs her fingers through her hair. "Well, I'll be upstairs if anyone needs me. Sadie, keep your mouth shut."

My jaw drops. No matter how much she knows I'm prone to spilling secrets, she didn't need to call me out on it.

"Night, KitKat. Better get plenty of beauty sleep," I tease her.

Glaring, she flips me off as she retreats toward the stairs. I sit in silence for a moment, wondering if I should press her any further. Mason goes right into the fridge.

"Oh, yes, help yourself," I say.

"You know I will." He sticks a straw into a juicebox.

Yes, a juicebox. Because Mason is basically a toddler. Although I guess I can't say much, considering they're mine.

Mason approaches the island, palms bracing on it as he narrows his eyes at me. "Oh, something's up. Spill."

"I can't." I shake my head. "She said I can't tell anyone, so shut up and drink *my* juicebox."

"This isn't funny." He leans closer. "Tell me."

"You can't say anything." I point a finger at him.

"Sadie, I'm your best friend. Why would I ever say anything to anyone?" His forehead wrinkles as he speaks. Tapping his foot on the hardwood flooring, his expectant look remains.

"Fine." I turn toward the stairs to make sure Kat's gone before I continue. "She's pregnant."

Mason immediately stiffens. His eyebrows go from raised to furrowed, his incessant tapping stopping.

"You said what?" he asks, voice small like the air rushed from his lungs.

"Kat's pregnant." I pause, chewing the inside of my cheek as I register his reaction. "Why are you freaking out?"

As soon as the words come out of my mouth, it clicks. I freeze, clenching my fists. Then, I back away from him, eyeing him up and down.

"Mason, why are you freaking out?" All the humor in my tone is gone.

His hands end up in his hair when he turns away from me. "For fuck's sake, Sadie, do I have to spell this out for you? I fucked your sister."

Oh my God, I don't think I've ever been so angry in my life. In an instant, my blood boils, and my heart rate quadruples in speed. Mason seems to know what's going through my head before I do, because when I turn around to go upstairs, he grabs my arm.

"Don't do this right now."

"*Me* don't do this?" I push him away from me. "You're a hypocrite! And she lied to me!"

His breath catches. "It's not what you think. But the last thing she needs to be is stressed out. Let's talk about it. You and me. And then we'll talk to Kat tomorrow. You need to do your breathing–"

No matter how right he is, I can't even hear my dad's voice this time. My mind is completely and utterly blank except for the burning feeling in my chest. I give a bitter laugh, planting both feet on the bottom stair. "Fuck you, Mason."

And then, I turn my back on him and stomp the rest of the way up. Mason is supposed to be my best friend. After all the things we've been through, I figured he'd have more respect for me than to sleep with my sister. My little sister.

"God damn it, Sadie!" Mason calls up the stairs, starting to follow as soon as I get to Kat's bedroom.

I slam the door open, making her jolt up in bed. Her green eyes are wide with shock as she looks at me, and then, she closes them in recognition when Mason shows up behind me.

"*Mason?*" My voice is unrecognizable when laced with so much spite.

I don't typically let my anger get the best of me. Not anymore. But between this, and my mother trying to sell the house, and the fact that my dad is dead, I can't let this go. Why is everyone in my family out to get me?

"You slept with *Mason?*"

Kat stands up from her bed. It takes me a moment to remember that she's pregnant, since it's far too early for her to show. When I glance back at Mason, he's not looking at me. He's staring straight at Kat, his eyes glistening with an emotion I've never seen from him before.

"Somebody tell me what the hell is going on!" I yell, looking between the both of them.

"I told you not to tell anyone," Kat grumbles, wrapping her blanket around her shoulders. "Mase, I was gonna tell you, but I just found out. And I'm scared out of my mind, so I needed a little bit to process."

Everything seems so foreign right now. No clues, no signs, absolutely nothing pointed to Mason and Kat. I narrow my eyes at Kat before I turn on Mason.

"*You.*" I point at him. "If you don't get out of here, I'm gonna scream." I turn back to Kat. "This is the most fucked up, selfish thing you have ever done. He's my best friend, and you–"

"God, **Sadie**, not everything's about you!" Kat yells, arms flailing through the air. "You're not the one that's–"

Oh, the way my heart's about to burst out of my chest and pummel the shit out of her face.

"Kat, stop!" Mason steps between the two of us. "Give her a damn minute. Sadie, you need to breathe–"

Great, I can leave the pregnant lady alone and turn on Mason, instead. "Tell me to breathe one more *fucking* time."

He faces me, eyebrows knit together. "You're going to say something you regret, and we both know it."

"If you knew me so well, you wouldn't have slept with my sister." I smile and scrunch my nose. "But I guess that explains why you've worried about her so much the past few weeks. God, I'm an idiot. Well, I hope you're both ready for a baby, considering the two of you wouldn't know how to raise one if it told you how."

At that, I slam the door on my way out. The slight possibility I'm overreacting weighs on me, but I hold every negative feeling back until I make it to my room. I don't know why

I'm crying as I sit on the floor next to my bed. Everything seems to be ganging up on me lately. This is when my dad would sit me down and explain to me the importance of family. Of friends. And how both Kat and Mason are adults, and they can do whatever the hell they want.

But Dad's not here. And there's no one else to talk me off this God damned ledge.

I should've seen the signs. Noticed the way he looks at her, maybe.

When the door opens, I don't look up. I already know it's Mason. He sits next to me, taking a deep breath as he prepares to speak. My knees are cradled to my chest, my chin resting on them.

"I'm sorry," Mason says. "For not telling you and lying to you about it. But..."

He pauses, wetting his lips as his head shakes once.

"But, Sadie, I have feelings for her. Real ones. And I know that that's probably the last thing you want to hear, but it's true. I'm not sorry about it. We both know I'm not good enough for her, and she definitely doesn't feel the same way about me, but I'm going to raise this baby with her. Whatever you want to know, I'll tell you."

I blink back tears, almost choking on the pride that makes me want to send him away and never look at his stupid face again. "How?"

"Um..." His chest deflates as he swallows hard. "It happened twice. And you know she means something to me if I do that. We... happened to be alone at the right time, I guess."

Alone at the right time.

Kat and Mason.

Mason and Kat.

Why do they get to have a *right time* when I never seem to get one?

"Please don't be mad at Kat. I was the one who came back after the first time. If you're gonna hate anyone, it should be me." Mason's eyes trail over me, looking for any sign of reluctance or discomfort.

"Is this why you've been talking about settling down?" I ask, voice weak.

"Yeah." His hands fidget in his lap. "And honestly, I really planned on telling you. I think Kat did, too."

"And then my dad died."

"And then your dad died," he confirms, nodding slowly.

My head thunks on the bed frame as I blink back tears. "I didn't mean what I said. I was pissed. I *am* pissed."

"You have every right to be mad at me." He takes a deep breath. "Sure, the whole baby thing probably isn't ideal, but I'm thankful it's her. Someone who I genuinely care about, for more reasons than one. I'm not going to hurt her. I promise."

"Wouldn't matter if you're perfect, Mase," I attempt to joke. "She's still too good for you."

"Don't I know it." Mason snorts, a sad grin spreading across his face.

Since I have no more questions, I fall silent, taking in his features. The round cheeks, wide brown eyes, how his ears might be a bit too big for his head. This is Mason. And Mason wants Kat. My God. Stranger things have happened,

I'm sure, but this is something I never expected to come to fruition.

"I... I talked to Cole earlier." Mason inhales, chest rising. "He said he saw you today."

"It's funny," I say, giving a short laugh. "He's the only part of today that hasn't completely fucking sucked."

Mason blinks a few times, face blank.

"You should go back to Kat. You've got more to figure out with her than you do with me."

"Maybe this is an overstep, but don't fall back into all of that, okay? Be careful." Mason pats my leg as he shifts to stand.

"Ah, yes. Careful. Like you were when you impregnated my sister six weeks ago." I raise my eyebrows at him, fighting to keep the anger down.

"Oh, I was. You know me. Always careful." He gives me a small, sad smile. "Seriously, Sadie, I don't know that Cole's good for you. Especially at a time like this. And...don't forget that he's got a fiancée."

"Actually, he doesn't. But maybe all of this would be easier to understand if it didn't feel like he's the only one that actually cares about me." My eyes don't stray away when I say it, and I see a pang of hurt cross over his.

Mason nods, hand on the doorknob. "I deserve that, I guess."

"Mason."

"Yeah?"

I pause, wondering if I should even say what's coming to

my mind. "My dad liked you. So, if it had to be anyone, at least it's you."

The words feel odd on my tongue, weighing me down and knocking the air out of me like a cinder block landing on my chest. I'm so tired of being angry. At Mom, Kat, Mason, all of them. I am beyond the point of being sorry for their feelings. Their emotions and heartache.

What about mine?

Why do I constantly care about everyone else, yet people seem to never care for me in the right ways?

My mother tried to sell the house, knowing how much it means to me.

Kat, my sister, slept with my best friend and got pregnant.

Mason ruined my relationship with Cole.

And for some stupid ass reason, Cole won't get the hell out of my head. I hate it. Mason hates it. But nothing I do to stop myself seems to be working. He's everywhere. Nowhere. Stuck in the walls of this house and in the stars outside.

I saw him twice in the past two months. That's it. Seeing him those two times did a number. I crave talking to him. He always made me feel normal. Listened to. Even when my parents or Kat didn't.

In eight months, I'll be an aunt. Kat will have her baby, and things might go back to normal. Mason will take care of her.

My phone buzzes on my bed. Standing, I crawl beneath the blue, cotton comforter before I look at the screen. Fate works in mysterious ways. I say that because there's no way this—Cole texting me right when I'm thinking about him—is anything other than fate.

> COLE
>
> It really was nice seeing you today. Hope everything is good.

My heart seems to think I'm twenty all over again. I remember the first time I met Cole, and how he was the first man who caught my attention in a way that made it impossible to forget him.

I loved him, whether I ever admitted it out loud or not.

And love like that doesn't go away. No matter how much time passes, the only reason I've been so good about keeping Cole out of my head was because I hadn't seen him in years. This is the last thing I want or need. Mason was right. Cole could not have worse timing, considering I'm fragile enough as it is. It won't take much for him to weasel his way back into my life.

He shouldn't want to. Not when the weight of everything we put each other through isn't lifted. Some things are better left alone. No matter what I'm feeling now, it doesn't make up for anything. We've grown apart.

My time has passed. *Our* time has passed. I have to respect that, even if he's the only one I want to talk to.

I toss my phone on the bedside table without responding.

If I stare at the ceiling fan long enough, counting each time I see the same blade whirl in a complete circle, maybe it will be enough to distract me from this.

Not just Cole, but everything that happened in the past

month. Clutching the treble clef charm on my necklace, I begin the count as I rub my fingernail over the grooves.

One.

Two.

Three...

Somehow, I end up on four-hundred-twenty-six, and I'm still not tired. I'm empty. Absolutely drained. Even as the whole world crumbles around me, as everyone else fades away, one person remains after a night like this.

Cole.

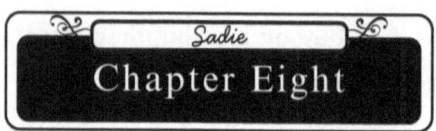

Sadie

Chapter Eight

FIVE YEARS AGO...

The bookshelf has been put together for four weeks. I built it the day I bought it to try and distract myself from Cole. It worked. For the hour it took to finish it, that is.

I have to work tonight, and no matter how much I try not to, I still have the tiniest hope that Cole will show up with Mason. He hasn't yet. I should probably get the hint at this point. Mason hasn't mentioned a single thing about him, either. Any other time, he'd be asking me for every detail of the night.

If I had to guess why Cole's been bothering me so much, I'd say it's because I haven't been that attracted to a guy in... a while. Of course, I'm not exactly sure why he's so attractive to me.

Damn it, Sadie. Stop thinking about him.

I check the mirror one more time before I leave. My roots are starting to show prominently, and I cave to the urge of leaving my hair down. I like my outfit today. The pink halter top tucks neatly into the black skirt.

I'm heading toward the door when my phone rings. Groaning, I set my purse down to dig through it.

"Yeah?" I answer.

"Sadie, it's Mom." Hearing my mother's voice is like being wrapped up in a warm hug. "I wanted to make sure you're still coming for dinner next week. We haven't seen you in almost two months."

"Hey, Mom. Yeah, I'll be there," I confirm, grabbing my shoes from near the front door. "I'm about to leave for work, but for sure dinner."

"You're not still walking there, are you?" She's only trying to look out for me, but it still bugs me a little.

Andrea Dupont is a kind woman. She turns forty-three this year, but she's aged gracefully. While she's always been an amazing mother, she can be overbearing toward my sister and me.

"I am. It's down the street," I grumble, grunting as I finally get my foot into the heel. "You can stop by tomorrow if you want. I'll be asleep til around noon. That okay?"

"Yes, but please be careful. The French Quarter is hardly a place for a young girl to walk around by herself," she says. "Love you, Sadie. I'll be over tomorrow."

"Love you, too, Mom."

We say our goodbyes, and I hang up the phone. I usually

talk with Mom for hours when she calls. She's the type of mom I can tell anything to. Especially since I'm twenty now, she doesn't get mad at me for the decisions I make. Not as much as she used to, at least.

I haven't told her about Cole, though. Oh, she'd kill me for that. Inviting a man into my apartment at 4 a.m.? She wouldn't be Andrea Dupont, lovely mother, but rather, Andrea Dupont, death bringer.

I welcome the distraction my mother brings. Instead of Cole, I'm thinking about dinner next week, and how long it's been since the last time I've actually seen my family. Kat will demand updates, and I'll have to tell her about him. She'll ask me so many questions, my ears will have fallen off by the time I go home.

Halfway through the night, I give up on trying to keep my hair down. I tie it up quickly before I continue making drinks. These nights are the ones that leave me a bit frazzled, but I've always liked a challenge. Leah, my favorite coworker, and I will make a bunch of money tonight, so neither of us is going to complain. She has midnight-colored hair, and her eyes are obsidian.

As I'm mixing a drink over my shoulder, a hand slides across the bar with a card. Mason taps it a few times, gaze stuck on me while I finish up the cocktail. Another night of the exact same thing. He'll wrack up a large tab, but at least he tips well. I give him a pointed look, but take his card anyway, swiping it and ringing up his first drink to open up his tab.

After I hand him his whiskey sour, he sits at his usual spot at the bar.

"Haven't found a girl worthy of you yet?" I chuckle at him, taking a second to stop and have a conversation with him.

"She's standing right in front of me," he jokes, tipping his glass to his lips. "I like that shirt, babe. It looks good on you. You should let me take it off you later."

"Ha, ha," I say with sarcastic drawl, rolling my eyes. "But thanks, I know it does. That's why I wore it."

"C'mon, it'd look even better on my floor." His face splits into a large grin. "And I've barely had any of my drink, so you know I'm serious."

"Classy, Mase." I snort. "I'm really busy tonight."

"Sadie," he replies, pouting. "Where's your spark? You haven't flirted back in weeks."

Despite his joking personality, his eyebrows furrow in concern. I'm taken aback by that—by him being worried about me—because I never thought Mason cared about... anything, really.

Well, Mase, the last time I flirted back with a guy at this bar, I took him home. And instead of no-strings attached sex, I got conversation. Yay, me.

Mason would give Cole so much shit for that. I'd love to hear it.

"Is this about Cole?"

I glare daggers at him before I turn to help the couple approaching the bar. Mason still frowns at me as I make the two drinks.

Okay, now I'm actually concerned. Mason hasn't left the bar yet, even though there are plenty of women on the dance floor. He could probably pick one of them up. I don't think I've ever seen someone say no to him.

He's waiting for my answer, but I go out of my way to ignore him. While I love flirting with Mason, all he does is remind me of Cole.

Mason eventually gives up and walks away. The bar bustles with people and loud music. After grabbing myself a water, I get back to what I do best.

Once it nears midnight, people start shuffling out—Mason included. He gives me a look that tells me our conversation is far from over. I roll my eyes in response. Leah and I try to clean as much as possible while people are still here. The faster we do, the faster we get the hell out of here when we close.

The line of people waiting for drinks would be overwhelming to me if Leah wasn't here. I'm not as frazzled as I was, and we have enough free time now that we can joke around with a few regular customers. Sometimes, we dance together when things slow down.

I step away from her to get some water and check on the rest of the bar. At the end of the day, I've always loved this job. As long as we're getting the drinks out, we can do pretty much anything we want.

I turn around, almost choking on my water when I see Cole's face.

He's sitting in the same spot, drinking in every inch of me. His blue eyes seem a bit darker this time—warmer, I'd say. His hands are clasped together, his broad shoulders accentuated by the flashing lights behind him. My heart thrums, skipping a beat every time one of the brighter hues flare.

Giving myself a mental pep talk, I walk over to him. "What are you doing here?"

"Is that how you guys talk to customers?" Cole raises his stupid, perfect eyebrow.

"Apologies, *customer*, thanks for coming," I shoot back. "If you're here for a drink, I'll grab Leah." I turn away and take a step in her direction.

"Sadie, don't do that."

For some reason, I listen to him. Maybe it's the exhaustion from my shift, but I exhale and shuffle back to him. "Seriously, why are you here?" I lean on the bar. "What happened to never seeing each other again?"

"I changed my mind," he says simply, shrugging. As much as I hate it, those words make my mind whirl, as if I'm ready to do whatever the hell he wants no matter how illogical it is.

"Cole, I'm working." I glare at him. Despite the gleam of humor in his stupid eyes, I really wish he wasn't here.

"Will you keep talking to me if I order a drink?"

"I guess I don't really have a choice, do I?" Another fire sparks in my gut. Why can he change his mind and expect me to swoon all over him?

"You always have a choice, Sadie." He furrows his eyebrows. "If you want me to leave, I will. If you haven't been thinking about that night for the past few weeks, then that's fine."

"You say that like you have." Gears begin turning in my head as I process his words.

"I have." He rolls his eyes as if it's the biggest inconvenience in the world. "Trust me, not my proudest moments."

"Look." I stop leaning on the bar and cross my arms over my chest. "If you're going to talk to me, stop acting like I'm not worth it because of Gabe. That's bullshit. I know better than that. Stop acting like a little boy and tell me what the hell you want, *bro code* or not."

His eyes widen but rake over me, slow and precise, snagging on my lips, my chest, and what he can see of the tightness of my skirt. I try to ignore the chills he leaves in his wake, but it's impossible. The corner of his lips twitch upward.

"Fine. I want your phone number. And I want to take you out on a date." The words surprise me, but not as much as his next ones do. "And I really want to fuck you."

My jaw drops, and I'm pretty sure that thigh clench was involuntary. The chills turn into undeniable fire, slick with heat. He said that to me in public. At my job.

"Oh," I choke out, trying to clear my throat. "That's... that's a turn of events."

"It should probably happen in that order, but I'll be fine with any one of those things happening first." His gaze finally returns to mine, and he smirks.

How is it that he leaves me speechless all the time? I mean, Cole doesn't strike me as a man who would say things like that, but here he is, saying them right to my face.

My heart spins in my chest. I finally scoop my damn jaw off the floor and hold my hand out to him.

"Give me your phone."

He smiles, pulling it out of his pocket and unlocking it before he hands it to me. I don't mean to look at his other messages when I go to type my number in, but I see Mason's name on there. The message came through around the time he left. I avert my eyes before I can read it.

After I send myself a text, I put his phone on the bar and slide it back to him.

"I'm serious, Sadie. I want to take you on a date."

"And the other thing?" I ask, fire spreading up my neck.

"You look...amazing tonight," he replies.

I close my eyes and take a deep breath, reaching up to tighten my ponytail. When I turn away from him, my first instinct is to latch onto the treble clef necklace resting on my collarbone.

"We'll see how you feel when I get off." I muster a flirty tone, but all I want to do is ditch this place and take him back to my apartment. With an hour and a half until we close, tonight is going to drag.

"I have no doubts I'll feel pretty damn good." He chuckles, tapping his fingers on the bartop.

"We'll be done by three," I tell him and take a step away. "You'd better be here."

"I wouldn't dream of missing out on you twice."

● ● ●

To say I spend the rest of my shift completely distracted is an understatement. I messed up at least three drinks. And while I'm going to regret the half-ass cleaning job tomorrow, all I want to do is get the hell out of here.

When Leah and I walk out, Cole's waiting for me. I smile to myself.

She frowns, crossing her arms over her chest. "Sadie, Gabe's gonna kill you."

"Don't worry. What he doesn't know won't hurt him." I grab Cole's wrist and pull him in the direction of my apartment. "No telling on me."

"He's my boss!" she calls out after me. "At least be safe!"

Cole laughs with me, allowing me to drag him along. "Are we really doing this?" he asks, fighting a smile.

I let go of his wrist and match his pace as we walk. "If you're gonna back out, at least do it before we go upstairs this time."

"I'm not backing out." His voice, firm and baritone, sends vibrations and shivers through my skin and into my bones.

Cole snakes his arm around my waist and stops me, pulling me into him. I stifle my gasp and stare up at him with wide eyes. Regardless of the intensity behind his bright blue gaze, his hands move gently down to my ass. I arch as he squeezes. My breath catches, and the urge to have him overtakes every other thought.

The air crackles around us with every passing second. I gulp, waiting for him to say something. Instead, he kisses me, his lips meeting mine in a flurry of want. I tangle my fingers in his perfect black hair, tugging on it.

"We have to keep walking." He taps his fingers on my spine before separating from me.

The rest of our journey is silent, yet far from awkward. We're charged with electricity, his skin sparking against mine. The last time we'd hit this crossroad, I had to make up some weird, old man living on my floor. Tonight, it appears neither of us needs any convincing.

As soon as we're inside my apartment, Cole has me pressed to the wall. His lips find my neck, a laugh rumbling from them as my head drops back with a solid thud.

Still connected at the lips, he leads me toward my room. Hand trailing up my back, he, with a slow, aching precision, pulls the tie out of my hair. His eyes snag as his fingers thread through silver strands. Sighing, he runs his tongue along the base of my neck and walks me toward my bed.

"Good God." I push him back.

He drinks me in with an eager, dark look as I pull the top over my head. The air crackles around us, as if one, tiny spark holds the power to ignite our ticking-time bomb. He swallows hard and clenches his fists, gaze flitting downward when I send my skirt to the floor.

That spark ignites. Tension explodes.

We shed the rest of our clothing, ending with me straddling him on the edge of the mattress.

"Is this how you want it?" he asks, fingers digging into my skin as he grips my hips. "On top?"

I drop my head on his shoulder and kiss his skin. "Yes."

Bodies merge, and I swear he knows exactly how and

where to touch me. Those perfect nails of his bite into my hips, the lines between pain and pleasure blur. His sounds meld with mine. He finds places no one else has with a tender gentleness I never knew could exist.

I'd be embarrassed by how fast it was over for me if he wasn't following shortly behind. Holding onto his shoulders tightly, I watch as his eyelids flutter closed. A low groan escapes his lips while his head tilts back.

We sit there for a few moments, basking in each other's embrace.

"I can't believe I passed on this last time." He chuckles, sliding his fingers through my hair.

"Yeah, that was pretty stupid." I scratch gently down his arms. Lifting myself from his lap, I swing my leg over so I can lay flat on my bed. He joins, turning his head to look at me. Eyes dark, he caresses my cheek. I smile at the contrast of his current gentle touch and the needy bite of his grip from mere moments ago.

"I like you like this," he whispers. His voice sounds like a song, and I've suddenly never heard one as beautiful as the words coming out of his mouth. "You've got the prettiest fucking smile."

My cheeks are already red, but my blush darkens them. I look up at the ceiling and take a deep breath. "You really want more than this?"

"Oh, yeah," he says. "I really do like you."

And then a slight, near nonexistent pause.

"Honestly, when you saw me, I thought tonight was going to go very differently."

I laugh. "Don't get cocky. I see a lot of faces on Frenchmen Street."

"I don't want to be just another face, Sadie." Cole swallows hard, reaching up to brush my hair behind my ear.

"I doubt you ever could be." My laughter fades into a soft smile, and I lean forward to kiss him.

We talk and laugh for the rest of the night, much like last time. I'm surprised we still have more to learn about each other. But thankfully, when the sunlight and music start dancing through my windows together, he stays right where he's at.

● ● ●

Sleep weighs heavily on me as I wake. Cole stirs next to me at the sound of the alarm blaring. His eyes are still closed when he pulls me closer to him, groaning. As much as I want to enjoy this, the stupid sound is making it hard. I shut it off, rolling onto my back.

"What time is it?" Cole asks, voice raspy.

I can't even take the moment to appreciate the sound when sleep tugs at my eyelids.

"Fucking 11:55," I reply. "I have no idea why I'd have an alarm." I wrack my brain for possibilities, but I blank. He pulls me back to him, his bare skin hot on mine.

"Then sleep more," he offers, kissing the top of my head.

Closing my eyes, I shuffle closer to him. The front door opens, and the approaching footsteps remind me of what—*who*—the alarm is for.

My mother.

"Shit," I curse under my breath, alerting Cole. "Whatever you do... don't freak out."

"Sadie, why is your front door unlocked?" My mother's voice gets closer to my room. "Are you awake?"

I sit up, clutching my comforter to my chest. "Mom, I'm awake, can you—"

She walks in. No knock. She walks right in.

I'm not sure who's more shocked—Cole or my mom. She's frozen for a moment, her jaw dropped. Her blonde hair is up in a ponytail, and her gray eyes are wide as she looks between Cole and me.

"You told me noon. Oh, God, I—"

"Mom, can you... wait outside please?" I cringe, hoping this doesn't look too bad. She scurries out of my room, shutting the door behind her.

"Your mom?" Cole is suddenly wide awake, face paling. "Holy shit, Sadie."

"I forgot she was coming," I hiss under my breath. "Stay here."

Climbing out of bed, I grab some clothes out of my drawers. I'm trying to be as fast as I can, but it doesn't help having Cole's stare on me. He seems to snap out of whatever it is by the time I'm done. Hopping out of bed, he grabs his clothes from the ground.

"What do I do?" he asks as he pulls his boxers on. "This is how I'm meeting your mom?"

"No! Well, I guess, but for the love of God, stay here."

"Sadie, wait," Cole says, beckoning me over to him. "Come here."

As soon as I approach him, he cups my cheeks. In a sweet, gentle melody, his lips work with mine. Harmony. Perfect harmony. Pulling away from him, I clear my throat and quickly regain my composure.

Time to face my mother.

She's pacing in the kitchen, her head in her hands.

"Jeez, Mom, you act like that was the end of the world." I lean on the doorway, hoping this won't be as awkward as I think it'll be.

"You didn't even tell me you have a boyfriend. I thought you told me everything." She seems more upset about that than the fact she walked in on me naked with a guy she doesn't know.

"He's... he's not my boyfriend, Mom." I shrug. "So, I still do tell you everything."

"Jesus, Sadie, you're sleeping with random men now?" She furrows her eyebrows at me and crosses her arms over her chest in her motherly fashion.

"No?" I say, almost like I'm questioning myself, too. "Things are... complicated."

"Complicated? What does that even mean?"

Since I'm not really sure how to answer her, I pretend like I'm thinking about it. The last thing I need is to piss her off. A door opens, and my head swivels toward my bedroom. I see Cole, fully dressed in his attire from last night. Sighing, I drop my head in my palm. I hope he knows what he's getting himself into.

Much to my surprise, he walks up to my mother with his hand extended. "It's great to meet you, Mrs. Dupont. I'm Cole Anderson."

Mom is as shocked as I am when she takes it. Her eyebrows furrow, and their hands are slow and hesitant. "Anderson... why does that sound so familiar?"

Well, that can't be good.

"My father works real estate in the Garden District, so the name's everywhere," he replies easily, retracting his hand after a few moments.

"Oh." Mom pauses. "No, wait. You're one of Gabe's friends."

Cole stops, running his tongue over his teeth and clearing his throat. At the lack of denial, she turns on me.

"Sadie Dupont, does he know about this?"

"It depends on what you mean by 'this.'" I scratch the top of my head. "Um, no. Not really, and if you really loved me, you wouldn't tell him."

"Did you just pull that card on me?" She frowns.

"There's nothing to tell him right now," I explain. "Give me some time to figure it out at least."

She purses her lips, studying me closely. "Fine. Why don't you bring him to dinner next week? A week is plenty of time to figure out how to tell your cousin."

My face gets hot, heat rising up my neck to the tips of my ears. "I don't think that's the best idea."

"Why not?"

"He's busy... and stuff. He works with his dad." I shrug, looking at Cole to support my claims.

My blush gets deeper when I see the quirk of Cole's eyebrow. His eyes are so much brighter in the sunlight— iridescent and shining like the near-still water in a bayou. He bites back a smile.

"I guess it would depend on the day, Mrs. Dupont." His gaze flicks between my mother's (still) shocked face, and my own.

"We said Wednesday, right, Sadie?" Mom tilts her head at me.

"You know, I don't think we picked a day. But I don't think Wednesday works for Cole." I slide my hands into the back pockets of my shorts. "He'll have to come next time."

"Actually, I'm completely free on Wednesday," Cole interjects, a grin forming regardless of his attempts to keep it back. "If that's alright."

I have absolutely no clue what's happening. Does he actually want to meet the rest of my family? Oh, God, I was hoping to have a bit more time with him before they scared him off. I stutter around my words, but Mom answers for me.

"That's perfect," she says, smiling as she looks between us. "And for both your sakes, I won't say anything to Gabe or Will. Yet."

That's probably smart. William Dupont, my father, hasn't quite come to terms with the fact that I'm an adult, and that I do adult things. I steal a glance at Cole. His face flashes with recognition. I open my mouth to ask him about it, but Mom continues before I can.

"Well, I will see you both next week then." She smiles at

us before grabbing her keys. "Sorry for the interruption earlier. I'll leave you two alone. Be safe!"

Cole's chest deflates with a sigh after she walks out the door. He puts his hands on his hips and looks at me with raised eyebrows. "I think she likes me."

I snort, shaking my head. "I'll report back after Gabe finds out. Don't be too sure of yourself just yet."

Chapter Nine

Bayou St. John sends me into a trance.

I haven't been back to this place in years. Mostly because it reminds me of Cole, even though the tree we used to sit under has since fallen and been removed by the city. The sun beats harshly on my skin. I needed this, regardless of how I feel about him. Staying away from him has to be my priority, but I said absolutely nothing about staying away from places that remind me of him.

The warmth he brought me is embedded in places like this. Here, I'm at ease.

Cradling my knees to my chest, I stare out at the water, to a single tree leaf swirling in the middle.

It brings me back to a memory far beyond Cole. Beyond Kat and Mason.

My dad was always good to Kat and me. Friday nights

were a novelty in our house. Dad would come home with three dozen roses, and we practically swarmed him.

"You know y'all have to wait your turn," he'd said, kissing my mom on the cheek.

At the time, I was eight, and Kat was six. Dad had done this every single Friday for as long as I could remember.

He'd draw my mom a bath. Rose petals, plucked off the stems one by one and dropped into hot water, filled the room with a beautiful aroma. Once she got settled, he would come do the same for us. I asked him why.

"Well, Peanut, this is how it should be. You should always be treated like this, by any person you fall in love with. If they don't, they don't deserve your love."

William Dupont repeated that like a mantra. From the baths all the way to something as simple as opening the car doors for us, he never let us believe we deserved any less. Maybe he made my expectations too high. That could explain why I have trouble staying in a relationship longer than a few months, but I'm willing to bet it has little to do with my dad and everything to do with—

"Sadie."

My eyes snap away from the water and toward the one man I'm trying to avoid. "Cole."

"What are you doing here?" he asks, not hesitating to sit down next to me.

I finally release my knees from my chest and lean back on my hands. Giving myself a moment, I study him closely. Despite the hard line of his jaw and his stubble gracing it, his face is soft. He's wearing dark blue jeans and a T-shirt. Something casual. A rarity with Cole. After mirroring my position, he turns his head so he can look at me.

"I needed a break," I tell him, shrugging.

His eyes are conflicting. Not because of any emotion behind them, but because of the way they're warm and icy at the same time. A comfort and a woe all in one.

"Wanna talk about it?"

I press my lips into a thin line. "I don't know if I should. It's not really my business to tell."

"I respect that." He tilts his head toward the sky, gaze unwavering as he takes in the sight before him. "I come here a lot, you know."

"Do you?" I raise my eyebrows at him.

"All the time." He nods. "I like the memories I have here."

Me. He likes the memories he has of me.

No matter how much I fight it, the thought makes my heart race. Leaning forward a bit, I pick at the seam of my jeans, trying my best to ignore it.

"Sadie…" Cole pauses. "Whatever's bothering you, you can tell me. Who am I gonna talk to about it anyway?"

"Valid point." I bite the inside of my cheek.

Stunning blue irises, clear as ice, reflect the bright sunlight from above. Any time we've come here before, it was dark out. Not to mention he's different. His face is somehow more defined, the sharp arch of his eyebrows perfect, and the scruff along his jawline trimmed and styled. Inherently Cole. But not Cole, because I don't recognize this man anymore.

"Kat's pregnant," I say, avoiding his gaze. Returning mine to the water, I sigh and clasp my hands together.

Cole's eyebrows dart up as he purses his lips. "Is that...not good?"

"Not when Mason's the father."

"Oh." He clears his throat. "I definitely did not see that one coming."

I give a short laugh. "He was apologetic at least. And has feelings for her, apparently."

"For Kat. Wow."

"I'm sorry. I shouldn't be talking to you about this. Or at all." I scrunch my face while I scratch my forehead. Resting my hands back on the ground, I inhale the scent of freshly cut grass. Fresh fruit from the picnics around us. Po-Boys. Someone must have gone to Café du Monde, because it smells as if they've opened a bag of fresh beignets.

Warmth spreads through me from my pinky finger to my thumb, making me look down to find Cole's hand against mine. Our gazes meet for the briefest second. Silently, he asks me if this is okay. If his touch helps or hurts.

And somehow, it does both.

"And did you and Mason ever...?"

With a small smile, I say, "Almost. We decided it wasn't worth it."

"Hm." He hums to himself, not moving his hand away as he turns back to the water. "And what was your reaction to them?"

"God, I was pissed. I still am, but it's too late for that. It feels like..." I trail off, unable to find which words I want to say next.

"The two people you care about the most betrayed you?"

My heart twists. It floats upward and gets lodged in my throat as I think of what he's insinuating. *The Incident.* Cole knows exactly what I'm feeling. I put him through it.

"Guess it's karma then, huh?" Chewing on my bottom lip, I take in the area around me.

Families come here a lot. Parents sit at the water's edge, their children frolicking and playing in the background without a care. Oak trees, except for the one Cole and I used to sit under, stand proudly along the bayou, covered in those beautiful, lush green resurrection ferns. God, I miss this. Relaxing on soft grass. People-watching. Maybe even being next to Cole.

His black hair reflects the brilliant gleam of the sun as it sways back and forth in the soft breeze.

"That was a long time ago." He looks down at his lap, a slight slant to his brow. "I'm not mad anymore. All I wanted you to know was that I understood."

"It... It fucking sucks." A miserable chuckle tumbles from my lips.

Cole shrugs. "Yeah."

"She... Kat. She told me that it wasn't about me. That I should stop thinking about myself. And Cole, I lost my shit. As much as I feel bad for it, I also don't. I've taken care of my mom and Kat every day since Dad died. This whole thing is awful. I want to keep my family together, but without my dad, it's almost impossible. We're all keeping things from each other and everything's falling apart, and I don't understand any of it. And here I am, talking to you, of all people, about my family."

My words are quiet when I finish. Admitting all of this to Cole lifts a weight off my chest. It rises through the air and dissipates into the atmosphere as if it never existed at all. This is why I loved him. He helps me without even trying.

"You know, I hate to admit it, but she's got a point." He leans over and nudges my shoulder. "You do, too. Kat should definitely realize everything you do for the family, but this situation is completely different than all of that. She's gonna have to take care of a whole baby. With Mason, of all people. Stress and hormones are real, and maybe it's best to...give her a breather. You should talk to her, Sadie."

"Everything keeps getting stacked." I sigh, scooting my hand over to hook my pinky with his. "My dad, the house, and now this."

Cole's lips part, turning upward. "She's your sister. That baby's gonna be your niece or nephew. Sure, the fact that they did that behind your back sucks, but it happened. You either move on or you don't. Moving on makes things much easier, though."

The warmth of his fingers touching mine sends my heart into overdrive. It should slow after those words leave his mouth, but it refuses. Everything in me is telling me this is right. But if that's true, if this is right, how could things have gone so terribly wrong for us already?

"What would you do?" I ask, scanning over his face.

He smiles. "Well, I would pretend to move on. Pretend like I was fine with losing those two very important people, and then regret it for a long, long time."

I bask in the feeling of his touch, even though I know I shouldn't.

"And from what I recall, anger can be hard for you to control. Especially with all of this. Just know that I understand how it feels, and it'll get easier to deal with eventually."

"I usually have this breathing technique I do." I blush even though he already knows this. "It's worked since I was a little kid, but yesterday was...Wow. It was a lot, you know?"

"I do know." Cole nods.

"What did you mean when you said you understand how it feels?" I ask him.

He pauses, looking down at his lap. "Sadie, when we first met, I think I was at the lowest point of my life. Honestly. Full-swing depression. I always felt like a disappointment to my dad. Like no matter what I did, it wouldn't be good enough. Everything had to be perfect all the time, and it consumed me completely."

Those conflicting eyes meet mine, warmth overtaking ice.

"Before you, I'd never met anyone who could challenge me so easily. The second you punched Mason in the face, I was a goner." He laughs, smile returning. "But in reality, you made me realize all of the things I went through weren't normal. That they weren't the right way, and my dad was expecting things of me that aren't humanly possible. You made me want to get better. To be better. So, when I come to places like this, it reminds me of you, and I really like that. Because it makes me feel the way I felt five years ago when I first saw you."

"Your dad always was a dick." I tap my pinky on his once.

"Oh, he still is." Cole snorts. "But long story short, I guess, I still struggle with feeling...inadequate. Imperfect. And it's something I'll always have a problem with. Trust me when I tell you I understand impulsivity."

I stop for a moment. Hearing all those words come from his mouth sends a spark through me. My heart does something. Skips a beat, races, twists... I can't quite place it. Not yet, anyway.

Until it hits me harder than anything else ever has.

It awakens. Stirs deep in my chest. Beats for the first time since William Dupont died.

I'm damaged.

Cole's damaged.

And somehow, we feel whole only when we're together. As much as I know I need to shut myself off from him, not a single part of me wants to. Right before the dam of feelings breaks, two people come to mind.

My father, who didn't like Cole. Who wanted better for me, since mine and Cole's relationship was doomed from the start.

And Sadie from five years ago. The girl I no longer claim to be after the damage and havoc both Cole and I wreaked upon her.

That's enough. It has to be enough.

"Thank you for the advice." Releasing his pinky, I pull my hands into my lap. "I should get going. It was nice seeing you."

"Of course," he says. "I'm a phone call away. You can see me whenever you want."

I give him a brisk nod before I stand, not responding as I walk away toward my car. When I look behind me, Cole's eyes follow until I turn away again.

• • •

This house is the only thing that feels right anymore. My life has been turned upside down in a matter of weeks, and I'm not sure how to get it back. My dad loved this place and all of the memories we've created inside of it. Mom selling it is a slap in the face to us both.

Mason stands in the doorway of the kitchen as I enter, that guilty look in his brown eyes still present. Ignoring him, I head straight up the stairs. My room is right at the top, but Kat's is down the hall. This journey is complicated for me. Being the older sister has its perks, mostly because it means I'm rarely the one in the wrong.

Knocking on her door, I wait for her confirmation. She's against her headboard, hands clasped in her blanket-covered lap.

"Hey," I say, stepping over to her bed and sitting on the edge of it.

Kat avoids my gaze. "Hi."

"I'm not mad at you anymore," I tell her. Placing my hand on her knee, I give her the best smile I can muster. "I should've realized how hard this was for you. I'm sorry. We'll do this together."

"Thank God." Kat launches herself forward and wraps

her arms around me, squeezing me. "I was so scared you were gonna hate me forever."

I laugh, tears welling in my eyes. "It'll take a lot more than having a baby with Mason to make that happen."

Kat's grip is so tight, it's like she's worried I'll disappear if she lets me go. Dad's death was hard for her. For all of us. The longer we sit here and pretend we're not dealing with the same issue, the more our family will crumble.

I'm the glue, but that doesn't mean Kat's piece isn't just as essential.

By the time Kat responds, she's full-on sobbing.

"This is all so scary," she says, sniffling. "And I really wasn't gonna do it again, and then this happened, and everything is—"

"Kat," I interrupt her, chuckling. "It's fine. I want you to be happy. Whether or not that's with Mason is up to you, okay?"

She pauses. When Kat cries, her dark, emerald green eyes fade to a pale sage, making her that much more beautiful. Her face falls.

"Sadie, I don't...I don't want Mason." Kat glances off to the side.

Oh. Well, that's a little complicated.

"I don't have feelings for him." She shrugs, chewing on her bottom lip.

"Did you tell him that?" I ask.

"After you left yesterday, we talked about what we wanted to do. Like how we were gonna raise a freaking kid. And then he told me he has feelings for me, and it honestly made everything so much worse. I don't want to hurt him. You've always known I've had a little crush on him, but after we slept together, it kinda went away. Like it was an itch?" Kat scrunches her nose up.

Sometimes, I forget that Kat's an adult. She's still my little sister, so hearing her talk like that sends me for a loop. Regardless, I understand.

"So...what? Co-parenting?"

"That's what we agreed on. He said he'd be able to deal with his feelings." She wipes her face, rolling her eyes. "I hope he can, Sades, because this whole thing is gonna suck so bad if he doesn't."

"He's Mason. Believe it or not, he's pretty resilient." I grin at her. "You need anything?"

"I could use one of those juice boxes. And maybe some pickles. The spicy ones."

I have to laugh. Kat hates spicy pickles. "Alright. I'll go grab them."

Heading back downstairs, I find Mason in the kitchen. He makes brief eye contact with me. While I don't have much to say to him in particular, I let it slide. Cole was right. Moving on from the anger will make it so much easier than just pretending like I did.

I almost groan to myself when I realize that I'm no longer hearing my dad's voice in my head to calm me, but Cole's.

"You've had enough heartbreak for tonight." I open the fridge. "It's not my job to further that."

"I really am sorry." Mason sighs, dropping his head into his palms. "This has never happened to me before."

"What? Feelings or a baby?"

He clicks his tongue and gives me a pointed look. "Seriously?"

"Had to make sure." I fight my smile.

"What changed?" he asks. "Not that I'm complaining, but you're...not mad."

Pausing, I debate if I should even tell him. "Impartial third party."

"What does that even mean?" Mason furrows his eyebrows.

I inhale, setting the spicy pickles down on the counter. When I look toward Mason, he stares expectantly. I should tell him. Although, he didn't tell me about Kat, and that is significantly more important than me having a simple conversation with Cole.

"I went to Bayou St. John today." I shrug. "Cole showed up, too."

"Isn't that where you two used to go all the time?" Mason asks.

"Yep." I pop the 'p' sound, cracking open the jar. "I went by myself. It was nice to think about the past. The part of it that wasn't all that complicated."

"Do I need to remind you that everything with Cole was complicated? Did you tell him about Kat and me?"

"See, this is what I mean." I scoff. "You drag him through the mud all the time, but he never does that to you. He's different. Whether you see that or not."

"Different doesn't mean better. You need to be careful."

"I need to be careful? With Cole?" I recoil and cross my

arms over my chest. "You've never been careful a day in your life."

"I'm trying to look out for you." He shifts on his feet.

"Then stop." I clench my fists. "I don't need you to look out for me. Nothing is going to happen between Cole and me because I'm not an idiot, okay? I have more respect for myself than that."

He scrambles for words, mouth opening and closing.

"I need to get Kat these pickles," I say, turning my back on him and leaving him floundering in the kitchen.

None of this makes sense to me. Every external factor is warning me away from Cole. I'm the only one who thinks it may be a good idea, that he's changed in the ways I wished he would've five years ago.

Unfortunately, those outside forces are so much stronger than me. I don't have a choice. My relationship with Cole never should've happened, and it's definitely not going to happen now. Not if the most important people in my life are against it.

Cole

Chapter Ten

FIVE YEARS AGO...

"Sadie, it's thirty degrees outside," I mumble, grabbing her arm to stop her from getting out of the car. "I think we're close enough to the Bayou like this."

"Oh, come on," Sadie teases, a knowing gleam shining in her gaze. "It's my birthday. You have to."

I bite the inside of my cheek to stop my smile. This woman could probably get me to do anything. Birthday or not. "It's cold."

"Please." She pouts. "For a few minutes, at least?"

God, those eyes. They're wide, greener than the ferns layering the trees in the summer.

"Fine. Two minutes."

Sadie squeals, throwing the door open. She's out and

running toward the water's edge. By the time I make it over to her, she turns to me and stares upward, the tilt of her head making her silver hair fall past her tailbone. At the sight of the giddy look on her face, not a single part of me is cold. She eradicates it. Warms me from the inside out, starting from the very veins I bleed from to the lungs I fight to fill when she steals my breath away.

It didn't start out like this. Not really. I never imagined falling for her as hard as I did, and now that I have, I don't want to lose this.

"Your fault you didn't bring a jacket." Sadie giggles, tugging the long sleeve of my shirt. "Come here. I'll keep you warm."

Moonlight dances off her skin, the music of it drowning out every protest I may have had. I pull her close to me. Her chest rests against mine, clouds escaping her lips as she speaks. The frigid air tries its best to swallow me whole, but I can't pay attention to it. Not when she's looking at me like that. Like this is perfect. Like *we're* perfect.

Sometimes, I feel we are.

"I like you like this," she says, reaching up to run her fingers through my hair. "Your cheeks are red. It's cute."

Resisting the urge to grin is futile. "Has it been two minutes yet?"

She fakes a frown. "Not a chance, Cole. You're not getting out of this."

"You sure I can't convince you to get back in the car?" I don't wait for her answer. Leaning down, I press my lips to hers and savor the taste on them.

Hot chocolate. Literally the only thing she'll drink when it's this cold outside. Kissing her is so nice. I'm not sure how else to describe it. Between her hand on the back of my neck and her body molding into mine and the sweet taste of chocolate on her tongue, I can't imagine wanting to be anywhere else.

This is it. She's it.

"You drive a hard bargain." Sadie sighs as she pulls away, pine-green eyes meeting mine. "Can't believe you don't want to stay in the cold with me."

"I'd stay anywhere with you," I say. "No hesitation. Forgive me for my selfish motives of getting you back in that car."

Sadie challenges me. She makes me want to do the weirdest shit, like stay out until the latest hours of the night or go to Bayou St. John when it's next to frozen outside.

"We have to sit by our tree for a little while first," she insists, moving to intertwine her fingers with mine. Leading me toward the giant live oak, her gaze never leaves me, the depth behind it drawing me in faster than a siren's song.

Soon enough, we're both leaning on the wide trunk, staring out at the still water of the bayou. I wrap her up in my arms to make sure she's warm. My heart thunders as I cradle Sadie to my chest, my hands clasped together over her stomach.

Squeezing her gently, I kiss her temple before I rest my head on top of hers. "The shit I do for you."

She laughs. And God, her laugh is something straight off of a music record. Beautiful. Lyrical. My feelings for Sadie have been strong since day one, but it hits me differently today. It must be something about seeing her so happy.

We sit in the most comfortable silence. Even if we didn't, our only audience is the moon and a billion invisible stars.

"I like being here with you," Sadie murmurs.

As if her words travel into the universe, one of those stars floats down from the sky and implants itself in my chest, lighting us up for the entire world to see. I realize, at this very moment, that I needed Sadie exactly when she came into my life. Good things *can* happen. Sadie is a good thing.

"Have they said anything else?" she asks, voice somehow softer than before.

The new light dims as my heart sinks. "No."

I'm lying. She knows it as well as I do.

My parents don't like Sadie. For the life of me, I can't figure out why, but I wouldn't dare press the issue. They tolerate her now, so all I need to do is tread this line. Maybe they'll come around. Or maybe I won't marry Sadie. I'll date her forever instead, so they can't be mad at me anymore.

"Cole, I don't want to cause any problems for you." She clears her throat, shifting forward.

"You don't." I shake my head and cup her cheek. "I don't care what they say. I want *you*, Sadie."

This time, I'm not lying. I *do* want Sadie. But we both know that going against my parents' wishes is something I can never do. Even when it comes to love. I've known for a while that I'm in love with Sadie, but I haven't told her. Too much unnecessary pain will come from it.

Sadie wants to get married one day.

She wants her dad to walk her down the aisle.

Her sister to be her maid of honor.

To plan the whole thing with her mother.

She told me all of these things.

Sadie Dupont is a simple woman. A woman that knows what she wants and when she wants it. She's loud, confident, and can sometimes be abrasive when she's stubborn. All of that makes her who she is, and I love every part.

While I sit with her under this tree, I'm giving her false hope. She thinks I can give those things to her. I can't. And I'm a terrible person for falling in love with her anyway.

Sadie kisses passionately. With every piece of her soul behind it. I savor the minutes that pass with us connected like this until she pulls away, telling me to get in the car with her.

And I do.

Except, she doesn't sit in the passenger seat. She helps me recline my seat back so she can straddle my lap. We've done this so much that my instincts kick in, hands sliding over her hips and pulling her as close as she can get.

"Sadie," I mumble, biting my bottom lip. "What if someone sees?"

"Lucky them." She grins, eyes gleaming.

The moon is her backdrop. A beautiful silver hue outlines her features, accentuating her same-colored hair and the delicate curve of her body beneath my hands. She can't be real. Everything about her is perfect.

Her eyes trail over my face. Moments like these make me

feel like she fell in love with me, too, somewhere along the way. Like she knows as much as I do that everything about us is right.

We're both still frozen to the touch after being outside for so long, but that doesn't stop her from unbuttoning my shirt. Her fingers are so cold, it feels as if tiny icicles are pressing through the fabric. I watch in awe. When I'm with her, it feels like I've never done this before.

I guess, in reality, I haven't. Not in a car, at least.

Sadie groans in frustration as she struggles to push the shirt down my arms.

I sit up to help her take it off before sliding my hands under her shirt, too. We take a brief second to appreciate each other. To look at the bodies we meld together so often. Her hands warm as they trail down my body to the button on my jeans. Goosebumps appear in her wake, leaving every part of me on edge. She chuckles when I push her closer by the small of her back until she's pressed firmly against me.

This would be the perfect moment to tell her I love her.

I don't.

She'll want more.

She'll want what I can't give her.

What my parents would rather die than let me give her.

The air is so dense, so thick with tension, that our chests heave when we haven't even expended any energy. In contrast with the rest of her, her shoulder burns with warmth as I brush her bra strap down. I trace over the soft curve of her breasts until I halt above her heart. It pounds. For me. In tandem with my own.

I see the puff of air clouding from her lips, but her whimper is silent as the pounding in her chest quickens beneath my fingertips. Leaning forward, I press my lips to it. Her body shudders on top of mine.

I tug her close to me and kiss right below her ear. "If only you knew."

It means so much more than she thinks, but it sends a shiver through her anyway. Sadie swallows roughly as I push the other strap down, too.

"I do, Cole. I know."
We fog up the windows.
Sadie leaves handprints on them.
She leaves handprints all over my heart.
Over and over and over again.
Until she makes it hers.
Now and forever.

Sadie's face is the prettiest shade of pink when we're done. While I button my pants, she lifts herself from my lap and kisses me one more time. She falls into the passenger seat and finishes dressing herself.

"You're so gorgeous," I say, reaching into the backseat for my shirt.

She grins at me, cheeks still bright as she catches her breath. "You're not too bad yourself."

The last thing I want is to drop Sadie off at her apartment.

I pull up outside, shifting the car to park before I turn every last ounce of my attention to her. She deserves it.

"Sadie," I say, clearing my throat.

"Yeah?"

Tell her, you dumbass.

"Tonight was...I really liked tonight."

Or not.

She frowns, barely long enough to catch. Her smile returns. "Me, too. I...I'll see you soon, then?"

"Not soon enough," I mutter, gulping.

While the hour approaches three in the morning, people still walk around the French Quarter near where Sadie lives. Over here, it's darker. Quieter.

And then, Sadie sighs. Scratching the top of her head, she looks away from me. "Cole, I didn't just *like* tonight."

"What?" I catch her gaze, eyes wide. Maybe if she says it first, I'll be able to say it back.

"I–I don't know. Nevermind. I guess it doesn't matter."

That look on her face makes my chest deflate. I'm hurting Sadie, even when I don't want to. Getting hurt is inevitable, especially if the hands she chooses to put her heart in are mine.

"Goodnight," I say.

"Goodnight."

Hers is much firmer than mine. I shouldn't let her go like this, while she's upset, but what am I going to do? What good will come of me following her upstairs?

All I've ever wanted was to make my family proud, but how can I when they think she's not an option for me? I sit there, imagining what my life could be like with Sadie. Maybe this is odd, but I like who I am with her. That I'm not scared to be *me*.

I don't get home for another forty-five minutes. Even though traffic is nonexistent tonight, I drive slow on purpose. The longer I'm away from there, the longer I can pretend Sadie is perfect for me. That the life I live doesn't dictate the kind of women I can love.

I'll have to get the car detailed. We made a mess. Grinning to myself, I realize this means a part of her will always be here. A part of *us*. No matter what, at least I'll have that.

By the time I get home, I figure everyone will be asleep. Unfortunately, I'm mistaken. Even though Carter and I live in the guest house, my mother sits at the table when I walk in. I can't deny where I've been, who I've been with, or what I've been doing. My hair is messy. Clothes wrinkled. Shirt untucked.

I deflate. The lecture is coming, and it won't be an easy one to get through.

"Sit down," Mom commands, gesturing toward the seat across from her.

"I'm exhausted, Mom." I shake my head. "Can we do this tomorrow?"

"You think I give a shit about your sleep schedule?" She scoffs. "Sit down."

Sighing, I listen. I close my eyes and rest my head on my palms, trying my best to remember how I felt with Sadie tonight. She'll get me through this.

"You have no respect for us."

I'm silent.

"You keep disobeying the one thing we ask of you. Sadie Dupont is not good for you. She doesn't want you for *you*." Her voice is sharp as a tack, her eyebrows pinched and lips pulled downward.

My mom doesn't know what Sadie wants me for.
Sadie wants me because she...
Well, I don't know.
She just does.
That's enough.

"She wants your money and the respect our family has. You think she really cares about you?"

Yes, I do. I think Sadie cares about me more than either of us want to admit. More than anyone else does.

"Why put yourself in a position to be used? I'm your mother, Cole. I know what's best for you, and she's not it."

She is. She is, she is, she is. Sadie is what's best for me.

"I get it, Mom." I sigh, massaging my forehead. "Please, can I go to bed?"

"Are you at least smart enough to be safe? I didn't find any condoms in your room, and—"

"You went through my room?" I recoil, face blazing.

"This is my house," she says. "Answer the question. Are you being safe?"

"Mom, Sadie isn't using me for—"

"She *is*. And your avoidance of my question makes it obvious that you're being unsafe. If that girl ends up pregnant, we're no longer supporting you. You'll have made your bed. Lie in it." Mom stands from the table, palms bracing on the solid wood.

"I'm being safe," I mumble, jaw tightening.

She pauses. "Good. She's not welcome in this family. If you can't find someone better to screw, at least make sure you wrap it up. There are ways to get that house other than knocking up some girl."

Wow. Mom is satisfied by my lack of response, and she walks out. Someone better? No one is better. Nobody will ever make me feel like Sadie does. It's not about the house anymore. It hasn't been for a long while.

I want Sadie to fall in love with me. To be with me for the rest of our lives, even when things get hard. For better or worse. Hell, if my parents can do it, it can't be that difficult.

After I shower and get ready for bed, I stare at my ceiling for far too long. I can't get Sadie out of my head. Or the way we connected tonight. Sadie likes being in control in every aspect, and I sure as hell let her.

It's ironic. Sadie has control over her life. I don't. Now, Sadie has control over me, too. Grabbing my phone from my nightstand, I see a missed call from her. I frown and call her back. It only rings once before she answers.

"Hey," she says.

"Hi." My heart pangs when I realize I don't want to have a conversation with her. Not after hearing what my mother said.

"I didn't mean to bother you." She pauses. "I wanted to make sure you got home safe."

I smile. "Yeah. Yeah, I did."

"That's good." She clears her throat.

Sadie is my girlfriend. I shouldn't feel awkward speaking to her, but every time Nancy Anderson has one of these conversations with me, the further down the rabbit hole I go. While I love Sadie, my mom makes me question all of it, even if I know what she's saying is untrue.

"Cole… is everything okay?" Sadie asks.

"Of course," I lie. And wow, have I gotten good at lying to Sadie.

"Would you tell me if it wasn't?"

No. "Yes."

Her sigh reverberates through the phone, sinking deep into my chest. The way my heart races tells me I've hurt her again. How do I stop? If all I'm doing is hurting her, why is she staying with me?

"Okay. Yeah. Well, I guess I'm going to bed." A hint of annoyance drifts in her voice.

"Okay."

More silence. I hate doing this to her.

Another sigh escapes her. "Goodnight."

Sadie hangs up.

The line disconnects, and my heart cracks. Sadie isn't the type to allow someone to treat her like this. Like they don't care about her. And while I do care about her more than I'll ever admit, I can't shake the weight of my mother's words off my chest.

I love Sadie.

I want the best for Sadie. What if I'm not it?

Maybe that's the real reason I won't tell her. It could have nothing to do with my parents, and everything to do with the fact that I'm not good enough for her. My parents think she's making me do all these wild things and stay out all night, but that's not true. I've always wanted to do all of it. I never had the courage to.

Sadie gives me courage. She makes me realize maybe... maybe life isn't supposed to be the way I'm used to it.

I want to get better.

For me.

For her.

For *us*.

I want to be what she deserves.

Cole

Chapter Eleven

The sheer force of Sadie's impact on me is knocking me off my feet. Everything about her always has. Seeing her at the Bayou today was an unexpected surprise, especially when she stayed and talked to me. We were open with each other—something we've never done. Not even when we dated.

And while I'd love to spend time being baffled by the fact that Mason slept with Kat and got her pregnant, I can't do that for two reasons.

First, because it's not really a shock. He's Mason. And no matter how much she used to deny it, Kat's always had a fleeting crush on him.

And second, I'm meeting my family for dinner. Mom has been particularly insistent today, so I figured it would be easier to give in and do what she wants for now. They've been so upset since I left Miranda. Appeasing her by going to dinner is the absolute most I'm willing to do.

Miranda is perfect.

At least, she is in my parents' eyes.

They think she's my soulmate. My mother actually verbalized that to her when we first started dating. But it's not true. I met my soulmate already, and it sure as hell isn't Miranda.

Maybe she *is* perfect.

Not for me. I'll stand by that until I take my last breath. No way I'm marrying someone who doesn't excite me.

Miranda likes security. She likes smiling for family pictures and watching me sign checks, which I never had a problem with. It's what I grew up with, something ingrained in me from the day I started comprehending things.

It makes me think of Sadie—of how they never saw her as good enough, but they'll grovel at Miranda's feet because of her family's status. Perfect family, perfect demeanor, perfect *Miranda*. My growing resentment for her probably isn't even her fault, but my family's for so vehemently shoving her down my throat.

The love I had for Sadie was never acceptable to them. Twenty-three-year-old me threw something away in order to *appease* them.

Don't rock the boat, Cole.

Don't upset Mom, Cole.

Don't be anything other than perfect, Cole.

Sadie saw me. She loved me. And somehow, I valued them over her. Regardless, they don't even care about me, not truly, so the idea that someone else did must've sent them over the edge.

Maybe that's why I've missed Sadie so much recently.

And then I walk into the restaurant—expensive, because the Andersons don't do cheap—and see a familiar head of blonde hair sitting at my parents' table. I catch my mother's blue eyes across the way, I run my tongue over my teeth as I think about how the hell I should react to this.

I hate to loathe any woman, especially when this bullshit isn't her fault, but she really needs to learn how to tell them no. Rich coming from me, when I'm guilty of the same exact shit. But not this time. I'm not going back to Miranda, and she knows that just as much as I do.

Chewing the inside of my cheek, I try to hide the scowl on my face as I sit down between Mom and Miranda. Miranda gives me a wide grin, and I feel absolutely nothing. I can't remember the last time I did.

"I thought it was just us," I say, scooting my chair closer to the table.

Mom sighs, sipping her wine. "We figured you could use a little nudge."

"Why not?" I force a smile and reach for my water.

My parents share a glance. Mom quirks an eyebrow, and Dad shakes his head. Their mental communication has always pissed me off, but especially now, when they're doing it on purpose to make it obvious something's wrong.

"Your dad was telling me about the Broussard house." Miranda smiles her perfect smile at me, her blue eyes glimmering under the light.

Miranda is beautiful. *Physically* perfect, but she could not be more different than Sadie. Miranda is taller. Her blonde hair is longer than Sadie's.

"What about it?" I ask.

"Oh, the usual. That he's close to getting it. Did you guys secure the Dupont house yet?"

My jaw tenses at the thought of Sadie. Of her family.

"The last thing Cole needs to think about at this table is Sadie Dupont," Mom retorts.

I cringe. Of course, we're going to get into this. Miranda shifts next to me. If we were on the topic of never talking about exes ever again, Miranda wouldn't be here either.

Miranda swirls her wine glass. "She's the one you dated all that time ago, right? Or was it the other one? Katrina?"

"It was Sadie. Her sister's name is *Katherine*." My mother's voice is riddled with spite. If her words were weapons, I'm pretty sure they're aimed right for the jugular.

Well, it's not just my jaw anymore. My entire body is tense.

"Let's not talk about the Duponts." I fake a small smile. Miranda's gaze meets mine. Hopefully, she reads the room, and she'll stop while she's ahead.

She doesn't take the hint.

"Why not?" Miranda cocks her head to the side, hair falling over her shoulder. "It's harmless. You know they'd never come to a place like this."

I flinch. "Because I don't care enough to keep talking about them."

"Isn't she the one that slept with your best friend right after she broke up with you?" Miranda's voice floods my ears.

My heart twists violently in my chest. Closing my eyes, I silently pray to whatever higher power is listening that I have the strength to deal with this.

I told Miranda that in confidence. Not even recently, either, so she's doing this as a jab. To remind me that Sadie's not good for me, in case I was considering going back to her. Because Miranda is what's best for me. Obviously.

My mother scoffs. "I always knew she was trashy."

"Enough about the Duponts." My voice is loud. Firm.

The three other people at the table look at me in surprise, all sets of eyes wide.

"Just... enough." I look down at my lap.

Miranda's hand grabs one of mine. "Cole, we're only messing around. There's no need to overreact. Sadie was a silly fling of yours almost six years ago. No way this is actually about her."

But it is. It's always about Sadie.

And she wasn't a silly fling. She was the first woman I ever loved. Truly. With all of my heart.

"We told him so many times he was better off without her. He didn't believe us then, but look at him now! Finally making a good decision for himself and his family." Mom reaches across the table and pats Miranda's arm.

"Oh, Nancy, you're too kind to me." Miranda gives her the fakest smile I've ever seen.

"She's right." My dad sets the menu down on the table. "Cole hasn't ever been great at making the right decisions. You've really helped him realize the error of those ways, Miranda. Honestly, I thought we'd moved past that girl already."

"We don't associate with the Duponts. They're not worth our time," Mom interjects. "It's about time he got whipped into shape. I should've hit him more as a child."

I'm going to have to use Sadie's breathing technique in a moment.

"He disappeared with her the other day for a while. I didn't like the way he jumped up one bit," my dad continues, as if I'm not even here.

The anger bubbles. A volcano rumbles in the pit of my stomach, threatening to spill over if someone says one more off-hand thing about Sadie or her family. They don't deserve it. They're good people.

"You disappeared with her?" Miranda looks me up and down.

"He's being dramatic." I pause, glaring at Dad. "We were outside for three minutes. Her dad died, I was making sure she was okay."

"Honestly, good riddance. That man was insufferable." Dad sighs, pinching the bridge of his nose. "We'll be able to get that house from Andrea. She doesn't have a single brain cell left."

"Okay, that's enough." I slam my fists down on the table, making each of them jump.

Bristling, I wait a moment for them to regain their composure. When I stand up, I give them the nastiest look I can muster.

"Regardless of what you think about Sadie, there's nothing wrong with her or her family. I'm so sick and tired of hearing you belittle people because you think you're better than them. You're not. You have a miserable marriage, your children are miserable, and there's not a God damned thing that can redeem you. I'm done. With hearing this shit. Following in your footsteps. Trying to be like you. All of it. Done. I should've done this five years ago, but fuck you."

I don't give them time to respond before I turn my back on them, making my way toward the exit. Miranda will follow me. She'll try to convince me to go back to them, and there's not one thing in this entire world that can do that. I want nothing to do with them. Absolutely nothing.

As soon as I'm out the door, Miranda grabs my arm.

"What the hell was that?" she hisses. "Your dad's going to cut you out of the will–"

"Let him, then." I jerk away from her, trying my best to remain calm.

"What's your issue today? It's harmless banter. You need thicker skin."

"No, what I *need* is for them and you to stop discounting my past. To stop acting like everything's right in the world because I got broken up with by one girl. She's not my life. Not everything I do has to do with her, okay?" My hands fly into the air as I try to calm myself down. Nothing is working.

"Jesus, Cole, nobody said that!" Miranda recoils, taking a step away from me. "Do you still have feelings for her?"

"*No!*" I want to rip my hair out. "I don't need to have feel-ings for her to be pissed off that you told my parents something I told you in confidence. Or that you're shitting on a decent human being. Sadie is so much better than all of you, and you're making fun of her?"

Miranda blinks, staring straight at me with wide eyes.

"I'm not going to let you degrade someone because you're jealous she has my past. That entire situation? Yeah, it sucked. But it made me who I am, and if you don't like that, then you don't really like me." I inhale in an attempt to catch my breath. "My parents don't want the best for me. They want what's best for them. I don't want anything to do with them ever again."

She still doesn't say anything. Processing my words, she takes another step back. "You're overreacting. It's a harmless joke."

"Sadie lost her dad. And if you took a moment to realize that she's anything other than your chew toy, you'd know how devastating that is." I run my hands down my face. "She lost her best friend. And yeah, I still care about her, and that's never gonna go away. I'm sorry, Miranda. I never should've gone along with this arrangement in the first place. Everyone deserves someone who can love them completely, and I'm not that for you. I don't love you."

Her lips part as she recoils in shock. Of course, she's surprised I don't love someone as perfect as her. I expect her to argue. To put up a fight and tell me I'm being ridiculous, but instead, tears well in her eyes and she nods.

"Okay." She takes a deep breath. "I'm done arguing with you, Cole. If you think she's better for you—"

I laugh. "Those words never left my mouth. I'm not

ending things with you to be with Sadie. I'm doing it because I'm not spending my life with someone who doesn't make me happy. You need someone like them." I gesture back to the restaurant, to my parents. "That's not me. I'm sorry."

Even though I shouldn't, I turn away from her and leave her standing alone in the street.

Chapter Twelve

FIVE YEARS AGO...

The one thing I will never tire of in the French Quarter is the constant music. Especially on days like today, where it floods the streets like the strongest of hurricanes. Brass, percussion, woodwind, and string instruments blend together for the smoothest of jazz, although I'm not entirely sure how they do that while walking. I'd be out of breath before the first set of cross streets.

This is the first of many this year, and Dad organized it for my twenty-first birthday. We stand on the sidelines, the parade of people playing seemingly endless. I close my eyes and breathe in the scents of the New Orleans streets, inhaling the melody deep in my lungs.

I've always been able to feel it in my bones—rather, feel

the way it twists into my soul and etches lyrics inside me, carves them into the marrow forever to be found by whomever dares to look.

Every note from the thunderous trumpets and trombones mixes with the sweet, smooth pull of the saxophones.

It's at that moment I realize I want to be this way all the time. I want to bask in the sun and let it melt my worries while someone makes me feel like love songs do. Like my heart will never be broken, like nothing else matters in the world except for this exact moment.

It doesn't take long for a visual to form in my mind.

Someone *does* make me feel that way.

Cole.

It's an existential feeling, really. My heart beats along with the drums, and a wide grin forms on my lips as Gabe finally approaches. Took him long enough. My dad and I have been here for at least an hour. Since Gabe is the only other one in our family who truly appreciates music in all its forms, he comes to these things with us.

My dad dressed casually, in a patterned gray sweater and jeans with his glasses constantly sliding down his reddened nose. He's probably regretting setting this parade up today since the frigid air attacks us with a vengeance. Gabe, on the other hand, looks like he just rolled out of bed. In his defense... he probably did. He's too tall for his sweatpants, his ankles hanging out from his socks and shoes. His black shirt has long sleeves, and even though the sun is mostly covered by clouds, he has sunglasses on.

"Could you have picked a colder day?" Gabe grumbles as he gives my dad a hug.

"It's fifty degrees," Dad deadpans, clapping Gabe's shoulder. "Man up, son."

Instead, he turns to me. "Have you had a drink yet?"

"It's noon." I quirk an eyebrow at him.

"So what?" He scrunches his nose, throwing his arm around me and leading me away from my father. "Leah's there. She might even give you one for free."

I roll my eyes at him. "Gabriel, you're gonna make me miss my parade."

Gabe shushes me, and though the bar is only half a block away, I continue to grumble about it. This will be the first legal drink he buys me, so that has to be the reason he's insisting. We grew up together. He's always been an older brother to me, and Hell would have to freeze over to change that.

Besides him and Kat, Leah is my only other friend. We work together at least once a week, so we've become pretty close over the past few years. Behind the bar, she wears a tiny pair of jean shorts and a familiar black crop top. Not many people are here yet, so she notices us as soon as we walk in.

"I thought that parade was something your father would put on." Leah grins, leaning forward with her head on her palms. "I can card you if you want."

While my attention strays, Gabe tells Leah what to make. I get something mixed with Coke, which I recognize as Malibu once I sip from the plastic cup. Gabe sits in one of the stools, spinning back and forth like a child.

Leah smirks at me. "Was your birthday up to your expectations?"

It was two days ago, but the memory of that night with Cole sends a swift blush to my cheeks. Gabe stops spinning, glancing between Leah and me.

"What *did* you do for your birthday?" Gabe asks.

Your friend.

"Um, not much, really. I went to the bayou." Clearing my throat, I look down at my drink. "We should get back to the parade."

"You went to the bayou *by yourself*? For your twenty-first birthday?" Gabe narrows his eyes.

"She went with—"

"Leah." I cut her off, glaring.

Realization sets in, and Gabe groans. "Oh, motherfucker."

"No, actually, I think she's your cousin." Leah fakes a frown, trying hard not to let a smile break through. "And from the sounds of it, she did indeed get her world rocked."

"Oh, my God." Mortification burns my face as I bury my head into my palms.

When I look up at Gabe, he's blinking vacantly at the wall, eyebrows raised. After a few moments of undeniably awkward silence, he pinches the bridge of his nose. "And I needed to know that, why? That's the last image I want burned into my eye sockets, Leah."

"She wasn't gonna tell you." Leah shrugs.

"Sadie, what the hell?" Gabe says. "Cole? Seriously?"

"I like him, okay?" I push his shoulder. "Leave it alone."

Gabe pauses for a second, his chest rising but never falling. He shares a look with Leah before he turns back to me, indifference taking over the shock on his face.

"I literally would've preferred you screwing Mason," he deadpans.

"Mason?" I laugh. "Mason's with a new girl every week, and you think Cole's bad? What do you have against him? He's your friend."

"He—" Gabe cuts himself off, finally releasing his pent up breath. "At least Mason would have enough respect not to fuck you at a damn bayou."

Unsettled, I shift in my seat. "Not that it's any of your business either way, but it wasn't *at* the bayou. We were in the car. And believe it or not, it was my idea."

Leah stands behind the bar, pursing her lips as she watches the scene unfold in front of her. Once I'm on my feet, I grab my drink and poke a finger at Gabe.

"I can do whatever I want with whoever I want, so you may as well accept it because it's been going on for a while." Frowning, I nod toward the door. "He's a good guy, Gabe, and I have a parade to get back to, so if you'd like to stop being an ass about someone who's supposed to be your friend, I'd appreciate it."

I walk out, my grip so tight on my cup, I'm surprised the liquid doesn't slosh over the sides. Trying to hide my annoyance as I take my place next to my dad again, I watch the people stomp by us in perfect sync.

"You okay, Peanut?" Dad asks.

"Yeah, Gabe's being Gabe," I reply. "He'll get over it eventually."

He begins pointing out everyone he knows, leaning closer to me so I hear him properly. He tells me little stories about all of them, I laugh, letting my anger at Gabe fade away. He stayed in the bar with Leah, probably fuming at her and trying to get more details out of her.

Dad jokes with me, twirling me around a few times every now and then to make a smile appear on my face. Somehow, he always knows when I'm feeling off. If I'm in a bad mood or if something's wrong.

He's there for me whenever I need him. A lot of times, I forget how real my support system is, and how he's at the center of it. He'd never get mad at me for what I do, and he genuinely wants to help. Those things slip my mind way more often than they should. At the end of the day, my dad would never leave me to fend for myself, so if I really needed to talk to him about my Gabe problem, I could. But right now, that would mean bringing up Cole, and that's not a can of worms I'm willing to crack open.

Gabe appears once he's had time to calm down, and he gives me a nuanced look before silently agreeing not to speak another word of it. It'll be easier for us both if we don't.

When the parade comes to an end, I finally check my phone. Cole texted me thirty minutes ago to let me know he's at my apartment. I inadvertently blush at him being there by himself, but I message him back and let him know I'll be there soon.

As the three of us are about to part, my dad gives me a big hug.

"God, you kids grow too fast." He lets out a long sigh. "You better start coming around more. I'm getting too old."

I snort. "Dad, you're not old. I'll come see you this weekend, okay?"

"You'd better." Dad's eyes narrow. "And you should bring that boyfriend your mom said you've been hiding from me."

For the millionth time today, my cheeks heat up. I hope the chill of the cold air stinging them hides it.

"I'm not hiding him," I say. "He's busy. Working with his parents or whatever."

Gabe scoffs.

"It's just new. I'd've scared him off if I brought him around any sooner. He'll be there Saturday."

"Alright, Peanut, I trust you." My dad holds his hands up in mock surrender.

I give him one last hug. "Everything's great. Thanks for everything today, I loved it."

"Of course." He grins.

"It was alright," Gabe says, earning a push from my father. Laughing, he raises an eyebrow at me. "Do you want me to walk you home? I don't work for another couple hours."

"Nope. All good." I turn on my heel and start down the street before Gabe can argue. Thankfully, he doesn't follow me. He'd probably have some choice words for Cole if he found out he was already upstairs.

At the end of the day, I don't want to doubt Cole. Gabe has known him a lot longer than I have, but I wonder what his reaction truly means. And if it were *that* important for me to stay away from Cole, why wouldn't Gabe just tell me why?

I shake the thought from my head as I make it to my apartment, tossing the door open with a sigh. Cole's smile immediately turns into a frown when he sees me from where he sits on the couch.

"That doesn't sound good," he says.

"'Not good' doesn't even begin to describe it." I make my way over and practically dive into the cushion next to him. "So, I told Leah about the other night, and she let it slip in front of Gabe, and he may or may not have put this all together. And my mom told my dad that I have a boyfriend, so now he's demanding to meet you."

Cole stays quiet for an entire minute before he says anything. "Um, okay, so I'll meet your dad."

I lean away from him, frowning. "What?"

"Sadie, it's been three months. And I would've done it before, but you know I've been busy. Tell me when, and I'll be there." He shrugs, as if this is something I expected him to say.

Cole is a lot of things. He's sweet and caring, almost to a fault at times, but when it comes to family—specifically his family, or meeting mine—he quickly shuts down and talking to him is like talking to a brick wall.

Brick Wall Cole isn't here today, and I'm about two seconds away from asking him to pinch me.

"What'd Gabe say?" Cole intertwines his fingers with mine, staring down at them as his thumb drags across my skin.

"Oh, you know. Just that he'd rather me be hooking up with Mason." I snort. "*Mason*. I really don't know what his problem is."

"He'll get over it once he realizes this is real." He reaches up and cups my cheek.

"Is it?" I ask. "Is it real?"

"Sadie, I waited forty-five minutes alone in your apartment for you to get here. This is the realest thing I've ever had." He tugs me closer to him, warmth radiating from his body into mine. "I can show you, if you want."

Even when his smirk sends warmth to my cheeks, a short laugh escapes me, and I shake my head. "Ever the charmer. Not the best time for that, though."

"Okay. Pick something to watch, and I'll make popcorn." Cole grabs both my cheeks, pressing a quick kiss to my forehead. "And if you're worried about Gabe, don't be. I'll talk to him."

I breathe a sigh of relief as he stands and walks toward the kitchen. Gabe will have to understand. Cole and I aren't going anywhere anytime soon, and he'll have to get used to it. All I have to do is believe in Cole.

Believe in him, in us, and how the way he looks at me makes his words undeniable. Easy enough, right?

Chapter Thirteen

My brain is reeling from dinner. The first thing I did when I left Miranda was call Carter. He showed up at my house within an hour, more than ready to help me deal with any backlash I'd more than likely created.

When he arrives, I'm halfway through packing the last of Miranda's things in a box. She took most of it when she left, but I've found a few miscellaneous things lying around.

"What's going on with you?" Carter asks, eyes wide. "You told Dad to fuck off?"

"Wow, they didn't hesitate to tell everyone, did they?"

"Cole, this is not funny," he snaps in response. "Not anymore. What are you gonna do if he decides to cut you off?"

I lift my hands in the air and give him a dramatic shrug.

"No clue. Nor do I care. Come on, Carter, do you really think this shit is worth it?"

He pauses, massaging his forehead as he takes a long, deep breath.

"They're not worth it. Miranda's not worth it. None of this has ever been worth it." I slide my fingers through my hair. "I've spent my whole life trying to make them happy, and I never could."

"That's not true." Carter grabs my arm to stop me from dropping a frame into the box. "Think about it. Are you sure this is the route you want to go? I can't help you with this."

"Miranda's on her way to pick this shit up," I tell him, blinking. "I made my choice already. The least you can do is wait and get me through seeing her for the last time."

Carter's the youngest, so he's been dealing with mine and Clark's shit for as long as he's been alive. As his older brother, I probably need to be a better role model for him. Maybe it's too late for that, considering he's well past the point of needing anyone, let alone me.

"His word is not *law*." I close the box. "We don't have to sit here and bend to his will just because he says so. You're a grown ass man. You don't need him. Honestly, you never did. I learned that too late, but that doesn't mean you have to, too. Get out while you can."

"This has nothing to do with him," Carter replies. "He knows that, Mom knows that, everyone knows that! You're turning into someone you're not, like what happened when you were with Sadie last time. Don't embarrass us again."

"This is not about Sadie." I point a finger at him. "It's not like I spend every day with her. I've seen her three times in the past few months."

"Three more times than you've seen her in the past five years," Carter mentions.

Nothing I do will ever be enough to convince any of them. They think I'm throwing everything away for Sadie, but I know better. Miranda was a mistake. I won't be spending my life with her.

"Is it impossible to have a change of heart for any other reason?" I frown. "None of this is anyone's business, anyway. The only reason they care is because they think it's about Sadie. You know they go out of their way to berate her in front of me? Like she deserves that? Like *she's* the one who screwed up?"

"Get it together." Carter turns away from me. "I've seen you get through everything else, this can't be any worse than what you've already been through."

"Being the family disappointment isn't easy. Someone's gotta do it though, right?" Sighing, I drop my head into my hands.

"Family disappointment is a bit dramatic, don't you think?" Miranda's voice drifts from the doorway, and I fight hard not to roll my eyes.

"Oh, joy," Carter says.

"Here's your box," I reply dryly. "You can leave your key on the table over there."

I walk over to her and set it down by her feet. When I meet her gaze, it's frozen, not an ounce of feeling behind it.

Ah, this is the Miranda I've known all along, despite everyone else's varying opinions on her.

"Your key." She smacks it down on the table before reaching into her pocket and thrusting her hand toward me. "Your ring."

I glance at it once, cringing as it sparkles in the light. "Keep it."

"What?" She recoils.

"It's all you wanted, isn't it? The money and the pretty things. Sell it, keep it, I don't care. Do whatever the hell you want as long as it doesn't involve me." I nudge the box closer with my foot. "My family's going to ask you to come back. Tell them no."

"Why would I do that?" She tilts her head, blonde hair falling gracefully off her shoulder.

"For one, you have more self-respect than to go after a man that wants nothing to do with you. Not to mention I just told you to keep a ring worth more than three years' worth of your salary. Take it, be happy, and leave." I fold my arms over my chest, waiting for her next move, aching to anticipate it. With her, I never really know how.

"I loved you," she says.

"You didn't." I press my lips into a thin line. "If you ever did, it was conditional. Take your things and go."

"Cole," Carter scolds from the side. "At least be civil."

"This is as civil as it gets." I don't remove my stare from hers. Ever since I met her, there's been a power imbalance between us. She held the favor of my parents, and with that, she kept me under her foot.

I don't need any of them. I never did.

Watching her leave, I don't close the door until she's in her car and pulling away down the street.

Saying goodbye to Miranda isn't as simple as it seems. With her goes the weight of the world. My family acts as if letting them go is the worst thing I'll ever do, but to be without them is to be without an anchor.

No longer will I sink.

Chapter Fourteen

FIVE YEARS AGO...

Cole pulls into the driveway, car moving so slow I'm almost certain he'd rather not be here. He's meeting my family today. While that shouldn't seem daunting, it absolutely is. This was supposed to happen months ago, and after begging my mother to stay silent, I don't need to hide Cole anymore.

Hiding may be the wrong word. My dad, who I love to death, is the single most protective person I've ever met. One hint that someone may be in my life, and all bets are off.

William Dupont being blissfully unaware that his daughter is falling in love with a man he's never met may not be a bad thing.

He shifts to park, taking a deep breath as he settles back into his seat.

"You okay?" I ask, quickly scanning his face.

His jaw is taut when he turns to look at me. "Yeah, Sadie. I'm okay."

No elaboration, I guess.

I have to be fine with it. Cole doesn't elaborate, and I'm starting to think he never will.

We've been dating for three months. And, honestly, I've never lived a shorter three months in my life. Time is nonexistent with him. Moments like these, where he seems utterly indifferent to everything around him, aren't my favorite by any means. But then, I think of Cole at the Bayou. Cole in my apartment. Cole anywhere else except around other people.

He's kind. Sweet. *Loving*.

Cole Anderson hasn't told me he loves me yet, and the fear slowly sinks in. I could be in way over my head. Maybe I'm falling in love with a man who is incapable of reciprocating.

Sure, I've only been in one real relationship before Cole. I was sixteen when I met him, and we broke up nine months ago. Cole's not that much older than me, but the experience I have with him is so completely different from my previous one. I want to ask him if he's ever been in love before. Maybe if he's had his heart broken, he'd have a reason for not loving me yet, for continuing to date me even if he doesn't.

I do wild things with Cole.

We go to the bayou a lot. My birthday was last week, and it was the best night I've ever had. If love was conveyed through physical touch and intimacy only, I'd be convinced Cole was in love with me.

When he touches my hand with his own, encasing it with his warmth, my attention is finally snapped back to him.

He clears his throat. "I'm nervous."

"Nervous?" A smile fights its way onto my face. "The almighty Cole Anderson is nervous about meeting a family like mine?"

"Yeah, actually." He nods, not betraying a single emotion on his face.

"You don't have to be." I shift so I can link my pinky with his. "Pinky promise."

Cole bites back a grin. "That only works if both parties are willing."

He's beautiful like this. Smiling at me. Hand so dangerously close to mine. As much as I want to reach out and touch his face, we're not in the best place for me to do that. If Cole's nervous to meet my family, we should keep the physical touch to a minimum, even if that's the only thing that makes me feel loved by him.

I haven't ever felt like this before.

My dad, the wonderful man he is, taught me what to expect from anyone I date. Cole does those things. And more. Sometimes, I get ahead of myself and think about what life could be like with Cole. If I could spend the rest of mine with him.

"Sadie," Cole says, tightening his grip on my pinky.

"Yeah?"

"Should we go inside?"

"Sure."

He doesn't let go. Keeping his gaze on me, he traces shapes on my palm. "What do they know about me?"

"Not much." I frown at him, giving him a slight shake of my head. "You met my mom. Kat is already obsessed, and all she knows is your name. The only thing my dad knows is that we're dating."

He nods. "Okay. Let's go."

An odd feeling settles in my stomach, but I shove it away. The last thing I need is to doubt Cole.

He leans across the car and kisses my cheek. My face blazes from it. We've done that—and more—many times, yet it still feels new. He smiles at my reaction before getting out.

Cole walks around the front and opens my door for me, holding his hand out. His skin is already red from the cold. Taking his hand, I allow everything around me to disappear as he helps me out of my seat.

As soon as I open my mouth, sounds from inside the house catch my attention.

Music. Loud, *live* music.

"Those shits started without me." I gasp, dropping Cole's hand as I rush to the house. "Come on!"

Childlike giddiness rises in me as I throw the door open. The music room is right inside the house, barely down the long hallway. When I enter it, my family stands in formation, Dad with his trumpet, Mom in the center waiting to sing, and Kat with her saxophone. Their smiling faces find me.

William Dupont has what would be my natural hair color. His green eyes shine under the brilliant light of the music room.

My mother, Andrea, is blonde, hair ending right past her shoulders. Her eyes are gray, much like the downcast weather of New Orleans after a summer rain. Kat could be mistaken as my twin. The only difference is her hair is slightly lighter than mine.

"You're late, Peanut," my dad says, beckoning to me.

My heart skips in excitement. With a wide smile, I rush to the piano bench and sit down. The sheet music is already open, but I know the song they picked like the back of my hand.

Fly Me to the Moon, one I've heard at least once a week for my entire life.

I barely realize Cole leaning on the doorframe as we play through the song the first time. The lyrics falling from Mom's lips sound angelic. I join in at the chorus, and for the life of me, I can't keep the smile off my face.

The high, brassy tones of the trumpet mesh together with the smoothness of the saxophone and piano.

This. I cannot imagine life without this. Without them.

When I meet Cole's blue eyes, he doesn't try to hide his grin—one that rivals my own. Dad and Kat put their instruments away as I walk over to Cole. I put my hands in the back pockets of my jeans, suddenly feeling shy at the thought of him hearing me play.

"That was amazing," he says, quietly and only for me. "Really."

"This must be the boyfriend your mother's met." My dad approaches us, Kat right behind him.

Cole looks away from me, meeting my father's gaze. And

while his smile still seems genuine, Cole puts up fronts. I noticed how much he changes based on situations. Like the first night he met me, the charm switch has been flipped. He plans to use charisma to win my father over. I'm not entirely sure something like that could work on him. I have my doubts that simple charm will work on Dad.

"Cole Anderson, sir." Cole holds out his hand.

Dad shakes it, frowning. "William Dupont. Sir is fine."

I try not to snort and roll my eyes, but my natural reaction to my father trumps any sort of effort.

"Anderson, you said?" Dad quirks an eyebrow.

Kat peers curiously over his shoulder, glancing at Cole up and down. Giving me an approving look, she purses her lips. I scoff. This girl is ridiculous.

"Yes, sir." Cole nods once.

"As in Isaac Anderson?"

"That'd be my father." Cole blinks, zero movement on his face other than his eyes and lips.

Dad pauses, glancing over to me.

"Um," I interject, pushing myself closer to Cole. Turning my head upward, I raise an eyebrow at him.

"Andrea, do you mind taking the girls into the kitchen?"

I almost groan, ready to open my mouth and argue when Cole nudges me. My mom and Kat exit the room, Mom's hand brushing my arm on her way out.

"I'll catch up in a minute," Cole says.

Frowning, I contemplate staying anyway. Both men stare at me, both telling me silently to walk away. If I know anything about the two in front of me, it's that arguing is futile, especially when my dad has that look on his face.

My mother shuffles around the kitchen as I take the seat on the stool by the island. Kat sits next to me, folding her arms over her chest.

"Sadie, he's cute," Kat says, frowning at me. "Why's he with you?"

I don't even look at her. "Because I'm cute, too, you bitch."

"Sadie." My mom clicks her tongue, giving me a disapproving glance.

"I'm twenty-one years old, Mom. I can say bitch." Glancing back toward the hallway, I wonder what my dad and Cole are talking about. Shaking the thought from my head, I slide off the chair and walk over to the fridge. At least my parents still stock my juice boxes.

As soon as I close it, Cole's on the other side of it, a small grin on his face. I jump in surprise before placing my hand over my heart.

"Christ, you scared me." I nudge him. "Don't sneak up on me like that."

"He didn't really sneak. You're just oblivious." Kat's stool screeches on the floor as she slides it outward.

I give Cole a pointed look. "I told you. She's a nut."

"Still not seeing the trouble times six." Cole purses his lips in mock thought, chuckling as I set my juicebox on the counter.

"It'll get worse." I wait for Kat and Mom to leave the room before I slide on top of the island. "What'd my dad say to you?"

"Nothing I'm going to tell you about."

We both forget we're at my parents' house. He walks closer to me until he stands directly in front of me and between my legs. Resting his hands on my thighs, he studies my face.

"That's not fair," I grumble, leaning back on my hands. "You have to tell me. Those are the rules."

God, those eyes of his leave chills as he looks me up and down. Like little icicles pricking into my skin everywhere.

He squeezes my thigh. "Sucks."

I drop my head back and groan.

"If he wants you to know what he said, he'll tell you." Cole shrugs, taking a step away from me. "Until then, you'll have to be clueless."

"You know I'm a control freak."

"Oh, do I know that." He quirks one of his perfect eyebrows, a teasing glint in his eyes. "Pretty sure I benefit from it more than not, so you won't catch me complaining."

I slide off the counter. "Aren't you so lucky? C'mon, I'm sure they're waiting for us."

My mom and Kat seem to get along with Cole well enough. Dad, on the other hand, is indifferent to his presence. He doesn't hate Cole, but I wouldn't say he likes him. If anything, Dad is protective. After he realizes Cole's not going anywhere, he'll relax a bit.

Once we're finished with dinner, I give Cole a tour of the house. Really, I use it as an excuse to show him my room.

The walls are painted like a faded sky, as they have been

since I was a young girl. Cole is hesitant to walk in, like he's unsure if he belongs. He does. He belongs anywhere I am.

Nothing covers the windows. I used to like waking up with the sun. A solid oak dresser sits against the wall, directly across from a matching desk. My queen-sized bed is in the middle of the room. Silk the color of chiseled stone drapes over the sides, blocking most of it from view.

Cole leaves the door open and slides his hands into his pockets.

"You have a gallery, right?" he asks.

"Yeah, it connects all the way down to Kat's room."

"Did you know builders in Louisiana made windows the entrances and exits to galleries because of property taxes?" Cole rocks back and forth on the balls of his feet.

I chuckle, tilting my head at him. "You're in my bedroom, and we're talking about property taxes?"

"What else would we be talking about?"

"Something other than property taxes, I'm assuming."

He sits on the edge of my bed, pulling me to him. Sighing, he rests his hands on the back of my thighs right below my butt.

"Anything." He nods, angling his gaze upward to look into mine. "I could really listen to you talk about anything. Your voice is so pretty. I should've known you could sing, too."

"Not really." My face heats up. "I don't do it often. Unless it's that song."

Cole smiles. "You should."

He doesn't elaborate much. Ever. He says things, and if

they're cryptic, that's how they stay. I trace my finger along his jawline to enjoy the way his skin feels.

"I want to hear it all the time," he says, a deep breath wracking his chest. "You. All the time."

Looking into his eyes, I take notes of the colors in them. They remind me of Lake Pontchartrain. More precisely, where water meets skyline on the far horizon. Where the waves disappear into the sky and meld together, becoming one in a world that demands they be separate.

Forever close but never truly touching.

Sometimes, I feel as if we're the same way.

Cole is my first real love, yet at times I'm unsure I know him. The real him. He keeps part of himself hidden. From me. From everyone. And I'm right next to him, completely lost to who he is.

His lips jolt me from my thoughts, a gentle brush lighting a spark. I let out a sigh and watch those beautiful eyes flutter shut. His kiss is magic. One of his hands leaves my thigh, gripping my shirt at the small of my back instead.

I like when he holds on to me like this. Like he needs me. Like he's not willing to let me go.

And I know one thing for sure about the part of Cole he buries deep.

He's *scared*.

When we separate, I rest my forehead on his, meeting his stunning gaze. Silently, I beg him not to be afraid.

And silently, I tell him he's safe with me.

At that moment, he tightens his grip on me, bringing my mouth back to his.

I think he heard me.

"Sadie," Cole whispers, tapping my spine.

"Cole."

"I..." he trails off, a sigh escaping his lips.

Is this it? Is this the moment he tells me he loves me?

"This is the only place I want to be. With you."

I smile. He loves me. In his own way, he told me that.

"It's getting late," he says, turning his head toward the uncovered window. "We should get going soon."

Resting my head on his shoulder, I nod. He wraps both his arms around me tightly, squeezing me into his chest as much as he can. His hand caresses the back of my head. The warmth he brings is unrivaled. Nobody else sends these soothing sparks through my body quite like he can, and I wonder how I'd ever handle being apart from him.

"Stay with me tonight?" I ask.

Cole plants a kiss at the base of my neck. "I'd love that."

I love *you*.

Those words almost slip carelessly out of my mouth, but I choke them down at the last second.

Cole has stayed at my apartment many times since the first night. Lately, he's always had a reason not to. While I know it has nothing to do with me, and everything to do with his parents, it hurts knowing they don't like me that much. They don't think someone like me is worthy of their son. Honestly? They might be right.

We say our goodbyes to my family, and as we're walking out, my father requests I stay back for a moment. Cole says he'll wait for me, and he heads out to the car.

Leaning on the doorframe, I cross my arms over my chest.

"I trust you." Dad shifts on his feet, a sigh falling from his lips. "I care about you, and I'm worried he might not have the best intentions."

I pause, contemplating what he's saying.

William Dupont is a kind man. He wouldn't say something like that without good reason.

"I'll be careful." I hug him. "See you soon?"

"Of course." He nods once, patting my back. "Love you, Peanut."

"Love you, too, Dad."

Once I'm back in Cole's car, I stare into the windows of my parents' house. The lights are on inside, and the curtains drawn. I can see inside the music room. As we pull out of the driveway, my dad walks into view, a record in his hands. If I had to guess, I'd say it's Frank Sinatra. He's Dad's favorite.

"You okay?" Cole's hand lands on my thigh, his eyes never straying from the road ahead.

"Yeah, I'm okay." I intertwine our fingers. "I'm happy you're staying with me tonight."

His hesitation makes my heart sink, disappointment clawing at its strings.

"You're staying, right?" I frown at him.

"Sadie..." His grip tightens on the steering wheel. "I want to. But my mom said we're doing something in the morning. She called while you were inside–"

"I was inside for less than a minute, Cole." I scoff. "Can you be honest with me? For once? And maybe I finally won't feel like shit when you leave?"

He recoils. "What do you mean?"

"I guess I just feel stupid." I shake my head. "You act like all you wanna do is be with me. If that's the case, then why do you...check out? It's like you change your mind constantly."

My breath catches in my throat, but I continue anyway. Under the uncomfortable weight of his gaze, I roll my eyes.

"Sometimes, it feels like all you want me for is the physical stuff."

His chest deflates. "Sadie, that's ridiculous."

"My feelings aren't ridiculous." I tap my fingernails on my palm. Anything to stop the tears from falling. "You were all over me at the bayou. And then you went home, and everything changed. Again. And in my room today, you told me that there's nowhere else you'd rather be. Damn it, you're giving me whiplash. This isn't fair."

"I have responsibilities," he says. "I can't spend every night with you–"

The spark churns in my stomach, igniting into a full-on flame in seconds. "Every night?"

"Sadie–"

"No! You haven't stayed with me in *weeks*, Cole. I get that your parents don't like me, and you don't want to disappoint them or something, but at this point, isn't this just cruel? Take what you want and go. Please." I fold my arms over my chest, furrowing my eyebrows.

Cole lets out a long sigh. He wracks his brain for something—anything—to say, and finds nothing. Or I assume he finds nothing, because he doesn't say another word. I'm not sure what would hurt more. The silence, or a truthful answer of what he wants from me.

My dad's words echo in my head, planting another seed of doubt. Right next to the one that was already budding.

We pull up outside my apartment, and he puts the car in park. When he turns it off, I frown at him.

"What are you doing?"

"Staying with you."

"Bold of you to assume I still want you to."

His eyes meet mine, and I notice the unquestionable difference. Sky and water are no longer a comparison to the color, not when the emotions swirling in them are so vastly different than his normal fear. Instead, sadness. Pure, unadulterated sadness. Still the same almond in shape, yet irises as dark as night.

"I want *you*," he says. "If I didn't, I wouldn't be here, okay?"

I sigh. "That's a shitty explanation."

"Please. Do you want me to come in or not?"

Desperation rises, and any effort to fight it is futile. "Okay. Yeah. I want you to come in." At the end of the day, I know I should be stronger than this. Stronger than a few words leaving his lips.

Reluctantly, I get out of the car. He follows me up the stairs, rocking on the balls of his feet as I unlock the door. But as soon as we're alone, cut off from the outside world, he's my Cole.

"Come here," he says.

Someone like me can never deny someone like him.

He's too powerful. Too beautiful. Maybe even too sad.

I approach him. As soon as I'm within arm's reach, he pulls me to him. Usually, Cole's heartbeat is steady. I've only heard it pound a few times, and those times typically occur after we've been physical.

Not today. The saddest part of tonight, of hearing the beautiful, uneven sound in his chest, is that it's enough to convince me he does want me. That he loves me, even if he won't say it out loud.

"I'm sorry, Sadie," he whispers, pressing his lips to the top of my head. "I want you. In every way and all the time. I promise."

And even though his words ease me further, that little voice in the back of my head warns me this will happen again.

Chapter Fifteen

"Need anything, KitKat?" I call up the stairs, tapping my foot impatiently as I await her answer.

"I'm coming," she grumbles, finally appearing at the top.

First trimester pregnancy is not doing her well. She's exhausted all the time, has the weirdest food aversions (along with the weirdest cravings), and apparently, her fingers are swollen. Not the best advocate for having kids, honestly.

She's twelve weeks along now. Her belly is barely visible, but the sight of it brings me joy. At the end of the day, this baby is the one good thing on the long list of things going on in my family post William Dupont.

Mason walks through the front door as Kat reaches the bottom step. Without acknowledging him, she walks toward the kitchen. A sigh escapes his lips, but he regains his composure after. I quirk an eyebrow at him.

"It's nothing." He shakes his head and purses his lips. "She's mad at me."

"Wow, really?" I widen my eyes, feigning a gasp.

"Ha, ha." He glares at me and sets his keys down on the table in the foyer. "We have... different ideas on parenting, I guess. She didn't like my idea."

"While I'd love to talk about all of this," I tell him, gesturing toward Kat and the kitchen. "I have a parade to catch. Or to start. Anything I have to worry about while I'm gone?"

"Sadie, she's already pregnant. We can't make it any worse."

"Is that supposed to be reassuring enough for me to leave you with my sister?"

He gives me a pointed look. "She's not going to the parade?"

"Her feet hurt." I shrug, refraining from rolling my eyes.

Sure, pregnancy is hard. But losing your father is also hard, and sometimes, it seems as if Kat's indifferent. While I've seen her break down enough to know she's not, it doesn't help that she never wants to go out and do anything, even in his honor.

Mom still hasn't been the best at getting out of bed. And honestly, I get it. I don't want to get out of bed either, but life has to go on. Yes, I miss my dad every day, more than I thought possible. He's gone. That grief is stuck so far deep into my lungs, I can barely breathe. My heart hurts with each passing second, and that'll never change. Andrea Dupont lost the same person, but she lost her life partner. The one she was supposed to grow old with and love forever, even when the grays started to settle in. Dad's never had the chance to.

I invited Mason, but he told me he had things he needed to do today. No elaboration. Gabe has to work a normal, typical job, so, in the briefest moment of weakness, I invited Cole. He accepted without hesitation. Kat, Mason, and Gabe are supposed to be the people closest to me, and they know how important my dad was to me, it hurts that they couldn't help me with something like this.

I didn't tell them about Cole.

I'm not sure when he'll arrive or how long he'll be there, but he's the only one. He'll be the only one supporting me in my time of need.

Today is a positive event. Not to think of my father in death, but in life. The parade is running down the length of Frenchmen Street, where everyone he's ever played with will be performing. When I brought up the idea, they all loved it.

I needed something good. Something happy. A way to distract myself from all the negativity swarming his death. Everything about it makes the weight on my shoulders grow, I figured the best way to try and heal is to celebrate him and his life.

The parade starts and ends right outside my aunt's bar, at the corner of Decatur and Frenchmen. I went back to work a month after Dad died. Being a manager means I don't have to do much on the floor. I do a bunch of paperwork in the back and schedule payroll, which allows me private time until someone from the staff needs something. Which isn't often. The bartenders are pretty resilient.

I wasn't expecting it to be so hard seeing all these people here for him. Since I barely know any of them, I feel alone. Like I'm drowning in a mass of everyone my father's life has touched with no clear end.

Until I see him.

Cole saw me first. I try to hide the instant sigh of relief leaving my lungs. With his hands in the front pockets of his jeans, he makes his way over to me. His pants are dark, and the deep blue of his shirt accentuates his eyes.

Something feels different today. I can't quite place it, but when I look at him, I remember him from all those years ago. The look in his eyes has changed. They're not dark as night, but they're also not Lake Pontchartrain.

As he gets closer, I forget I wasn't breathing, I crane my neck up to see him.

Cole is the only one that showed up for me. He hasn't talked to my father in over five years, so I have to be the reason he came. Mason didn't come. Kat didn't come. My mom wouldn't even get out of bed.

"Hey," he says, rocking on the balls of his feet. "The turnout is great."

"Thanks."

I pause, fighting the smile on my face.

"And thank you for coming. Kat and Mason are...doing Kat and Mason things, I guess. And my mom is probably still in bed. I really appreciate that you came here for me."

"I was happy to get an invite, Sadie." His chest rises. "You look pretty."

Oh, my God.

My heart skips. Cole Anderson is standing right in front of me, giving me the same compliments I used to swoon over five years ago. Face red, I look down at what I'm wearing. A simple A-line lavender sundress speckled with white flowers.

I clear my throat. "Thank you...again."

"I figured someone should tell you." Cole shrugs.

"Um, I should tell the band to get started. Wait here?" I blink up at him, awaiting his answer.

"Of course," he replies.

As I go toward the band, I take a deep breath to regulate myself. Cole is still Cole. I have to stop thinking about him. Falling for silly compliments. Honestly, it's embarrassing.

The music starts, and I head back to Cole. He walks by my side as we move forward, his arm brushing mine with every step. For the first block, we're silent. We listen to the music flowing through the air and use it to distract ourselves from the obvious—that he shouldn't be here.

Everything disappears when *Fly Me to the Moon* starts. Cole smiles, and I wonder if he's thinking of the same memory. He holds his hand out to me, and I respond with a head tilt.

"Dance with me."

"Dance?" I ask, recoiling.

"Yep. Dance." Cole nods. "We can dance and walk at the same time."

I chuckle. "Who are you, and what the hell have you done to Cole Anderson?"

Hesitantly reaching over, I place my hand on top of his.

The warm, constant crackle of sparks between us makes my heart race.

"You should sing." He spins me once, watching as the skirt of my dress flows outward.

"Oh, no." I shake my head at him. "Pick one. Dancing or singing. I can't do both."

He laughs. "Excuses, Sadie."

The parade halts at the corner of Decatur and Frenchmen when we make it back. *Fly Me to the Moon* continues to play, and nearly everyone finds a partner to dance with. Cole twirls me once more before he pulls me to him. Every last breath leaves my body when his chest is against mine.

"One of these days, I'll hear you sing again."

I don't have time to respond. His hands find my hips, and he lifts me into the air for another spin. I'm laughing so hard by the time he puts me back on the ground, I have to lean on him for support.

As I calm down, I realize he's laughing with me. I get an overwhelming urge to kiss him, to feel those sparks everywhere instead of only my palm. My eyes move on their own accord, darting down to his parted lips. More heat swarms me, and this time, it's not from the Louisiana summer. It's him. Always him.

And then, I'm pressed to his chest once more. Scrambling for something to say, I remember the last words that came out of his mouth.

"You heard me sing one time over five years ago."

"You have no idea what I'd give to hear it again."

"Cole–"

We're interrupted by the mass of people coming up to me. Most of them filter out after saying their goodbyes, and finally, the last couple gets into their car and drives off. An awkward silence ensues. Being left alone with Cole is daunting.

My heart buzzes. Here I am, swooning over Cole like I did five years ago, when he's probably doing this just to be nice. To pity me in the wake of my dad's death.

"Sadie," Cole says, fingertips brushing my arm.

I clench my fist at the feeling of our sparks. "Yeah?"

Even in the burning temperature outside, his touch leaves an undeniable chill behind. I shy away from him before he sees the goosebumps. Brushing my hair off my shoulders, I run my fingers through it in an attempt to distract myself from everything he is.

"Are you alright?" He clasps his hands together, gaze grazing my movements.

"Why wouldn't I be?" It comes out much too quickly.

Cole pauses. A bewildered smile plays on his lips. "Are... Are you doing anything today? I've only seen you a couple times recently, and if you're okay with it, we should catch up. Figure out what we've missed."

Shock rings through every single vein in my body. The times I've seen Cole have all been random except for today. And now, he's standing in front of me, asking if he can see me for the rest of the day, regardless of how bad of an idea it is.

"You and me?" I raise my eyebrows.

"Uh." He clears his throat and puts his hand on the back of his neck. "Well, yeah. I get it if you don't want to, but it's been a while. And I want to hear how life has been besides... recent events, I guess."

"Well, I—"

In the distance, a loud clap of thunder echoes. Cole and I have a mere moment to share a shocked look before rain begins to pour over us. It takes seconds for it to soak us. Quickly, Cole starts to pull me onto the sidewalk by my aunt's bar, under the awning that covers the entrance.

The rain slams into it, making it nearly impossible to hear anything. When I look at Cole, my breath catches in my throat. He's beautiful. His shirt sticks to him, outlining every muscle in his upper body, and his hair is slicked to his forehead, small drops of water falling from it. When I meet his eyes, he's already looking at me.

Let me preface this by saying I believe in ghosts. In the supernatural. In people sending messages from the afterlife. And this? This has to be a message from my dad. He's pissed I'm here with Cole.

"I have to go home!" I shout. "I'm sorry."

"Are you kidding? It's next to a hurricane out there, Sadie. Wait it out a little bit." His grip stays firm on my arm.

"I can't." I shake my head and pull my arm away from him. "This...I can't be alone with you."

A pang of hurt flashes across those iridescent blue eyes. "Be alone with me? You're not gonna get anywhere with the rain like this." A slight pause. "I don't want you to get hurt. Please."

Sighing, I look at the bar next to us. The bar we met in. I deliberate for a moment if I can trust myself to do this.

"What is it about me that makes you hate me?" he asks, eyebrows furrowed as his gaze begs me for answers. "Tell me. I'll do whatever I can to change it."

My heart sinks into the depths of my stomach. "Hate you?"

"That's what this is, right?" He pushes his hair back, the wetness acting like gel. "You hate me so much that you can't stand the idea of being alone with me?"

"Cole, what are you talking about?" I blink at him, almost forgetting the chill of the rain sinking into my bones.

"Look around," Cole says, gesturing to the empty streets. "We're literally in the middle of a damn storm, and you'd rather drown in it than spend a little bit of time with me. What am I supposed to think?"

God, does he have it all wrong. I don't trust myself around him because I'm scared of rehashing old feelings. Old feelings that everyone knows are a bad idea.

"I don't hate you." I sigh and turn around, trying to find my keys in my purse. Once I do, I unlock the doors of the bar. "We can wait it out in here."

Cole follows me in, hesitant himself. I take one look in the mirror behind the bar and groan. I'm a disaster. Well, at least I finally look how I feel. My hair is stringy, the soaked strands sticking to my back. The dress is ruined, fabric bogged down and water-logged.

"Um." I avoid Cole's eyes. "Did you...want a drink or something? We have a full bar."

He laughs. "If I recall correctly, you have shitty tequila."

"Nope. I gave you the shitty stuff on purpose." I send a teasing glare toward him, which he takes with a small smile.

"I usually drink whiskey now."

"On the rocks?" I ask, making my way behind the bar.

"Neat."

I scrunch my face and fake a gag. "Gross. Only old men drink whiskey neat."

"Not true." Cole approaches the bar and leans on it. "I'm not old."

The excess water has dried from his skin, but his clothes still stick to him in a way that makes me curious. I wonder if he still looks the same. If his body is sculpted the same way it used to be. Biting my lip at the thought, I pour his whiskey quickly to get the image out of my head.

"You okay?" he asks, accepting his drink.

"Yeah. Um, the employees leave extra clothes in the back. And we have a dryer if you...if you want something to change into." Heat swarms my face, so I pour my own drink. "Not that you have to, but I assume the wet clothes are uncomfortable. I mean, you don't look uncomfortable, I just—"

"Sadie," Cole interrupts me, sipping his whiskey. "You're rambling."

I clear my throat after swallowing the burning liquor. "Am not. Answer the question."

"If you have something that fits me, that'd be nice." He stares down at the bronze liquid in his cup, swirling it.

"Yeah. Give me a few minutes. I'm gonna go find it." I disappear into the back room, yanking my fingers through my newly tangled hair. The duffel bags are in the corner. I grab mine first, deciding it'd be better to change before finding something for Cole.

I lay the shorts and shirt out on the table before I slide the straps of the dress down. How unfortunate that today is the day I figured I'd be okay not wearing a bra. Circumstances change. Note to self, always plan for everything.

"Sadie, I—" Cole opens the door behind me, freezing in his tracks.

Gasping, I grab the shirt and cover my chest. I meet his gaze. He grips the door handle tightly, shock evident on his face as he blinks at me. My heart thuds and twists as his gaze sweeps over me. The action is fast, near nonexistent, but it makes red-hot embarrassment course through my veins.

"Can you close the door?" I snap at him, clenching fabric in my fingers.

He slaps his hand over his eyes. "Yeah. Oh, my God, Sadie, I'm so sorry."

It slams shut. My chest deflates as I let out a pent up breath, and I quickly pull the T-shirt over my head. Embarrassment floods my body as I drop my forehead to my palm. I knew this was a bad idea.

Pulling the shorts on, I grab a bag of clothes for Cole. I take a deep breath to prepare myself. When I walk out, he's sitting at the bar, staring into his now empty glass. He looks up at me, only to hurriedly avert his gaze, gulping.

"I, um." He scratches the top of his head. "I didn't know you'd be—you know. I'm an idiot. Sorry."

"Here." I set the bag on the bar and push it toward him.

"For you to change. Back's all yours. Come out when you're done, and I'll throw your clothes in the dryer."

"Okay. Thanks." Cole shoots up from his seat, almost knocking it over in the process.

He bolts into the back without another word. Sighing, I try not to think about what happened. Cole's seen me naked before. It shouldn't be a big deal. But it's been five years, and I've changed in a lot of ways. I hate wondering if he's attracted to what he saw.

I'll stay far away from that stupid room until he comes back. If I see any part of him, it'll be burned into my memory, and I absolutely cannot risk that.

Cole Anderson saw me mostly naked. And I'm about to spend God knows how much time with him until the rain lets up.

Lucky me.

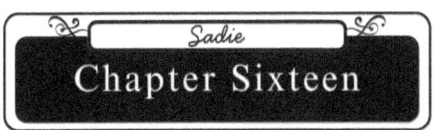

Sadie

Chapter Sixteen

FIVE YEARS AGO...

E ver since Cole and I started dating, Mason has made sure to drag me out with them. So not only is he forcing Cole out of his house, he's forcing me out of my apartment. I barely get alone time with Cole. Especially lately. Mason is a stage-five clinger, which is...surprising, considering he's never done anything other than casual sex.

Somehow, we ended up somewhere with loud music and hundreds of people dancing. Cole's not usually into this scene unless it has to do with Mason, so I had to beg him to dance with me. Although, I shouldn't say beg. It didn't take all that much convincing.

"Sadie." Cole's breath is warm on my ear, sending a chill down my spine that I'm sure he feels against his fingertips.

Instinct takes over, and I lean my head back so he can kiss my neck.

"Yeah?"

"Maybe we should go." He tightens his grip on my hips and pulls me as close as he can. "I have no idea where Mason is, and I'm dying to take this dress off of you."

"You've been dying to take everything off me for the past six months, Cole." I raise an eyebrow at him.

He pauses, his eyes snagging on every inch of bare skin he can see. "I want to take off whatever you wear for the rest of fucking time."

Putting my hand on the back of his neck, I slide my fingers into his soft hair. When he says things like that, I can't help but want to leave too. He looks at my lips. His gaze is hooded, shameless, as if his thoughts are as dark as mine.

Without another word, I pull him to me, connecting our lips in a beautifully passionate kiss. His tongue slides across my bottom lip. I try to remember we're not the only ones here, but when his hand moves and squeezes my ass, I give up. Everything is Cole, and I love it.

"I need you," he whispers. "Can we please get the hell out of here?"

"If we piss Mason off, you're dealing with it."

"Works for me."

Cole grabs my hand, leading me toward the exit. We push our way through throngs of people, and I look over my shoulder once and find my eyes meeting with Gabe's behind the bar. He's not accustomed to me being with Cole, nor does he approve of it. Once we're closer to the door, Gabe leans down to say something to Leah, who nods.

As soon as we're out in the open, the heat swarms me. I know Frenchmen Street well, and it never fails to amaze me. Endless lights, all sorts of music blaring into the streets from different bars, lost souls looking for any sort of interaction. The humidity in the air sticks to my skin. A thin sheen of sweat forms as we walk further down the road.

Cole and I started dating in the dead of winter, and now, the brilliant heat reminds me of how long he's been a part of my life.

"Come on. I parked over here." His palm finds the small of my back instead.

"Are you sure this is a good idea?"

"It'll be fine, Sades. He probably already left with someone."

Cole's car is on one of the more secluded streets, meaning it's dark and kind of dreary. Puddles from yesterday's rain gather in the uneven road.

"Where the hell are you going?" Mason's voice startles us both.

We turn around, Cole's hand clenched into a fist as he holds me close to him. Gabe follows closely behind Mason, a deep furrow to his brow.

"We couldn't find you, so we figured you left," Cole explains.

"Seriously?" Mason scoffs. "Like, all of this is a fucking joke, right?"

I recoil in shock, looking between Cole and Mason. Cole

runs his hands over his face and shakes his head, sighing. Gabe seems relatively indifferent, his expression unmoving.

"Can we not do this tonight? You're drunk, and I've got to get Sadie home–"

"When are you going to tell her?" Mason narrows his eyes. "It's been six months. What? You're gonna lead her on forever?"

At this point, even Gabe is sending a questionable look Mason's way. My heart sinks. I take a step away from Cole, frowning at him. "What is he talking about?"

"Don't listen to him. He's got no idea what he's saying," Cole tells me. "Get in the car, Sadie."

"I don't know," Mason says, throwing his hands in the air. "Would he really put you in the car if he was so sure that I'm lying?"

"Sadie, please." Cole looks at me, scanning over my face.

"Yeah, not gonna happen." I cross my arms over my chest and lean back slightly. A fire sparks in my gut, but it's soon masked by the feeling of uncanny pressure on my spine. I need to know. My mind is going a hundred miles per hour.

"He's been lying to you." Mason glares daggers at Cole.

"Mason, do yourself a favor and stop while you're ahead." Cole jabs a finger in his direction. "You don't know shit about what's going on."

Gabe steps closer. "Actually, I'm pretty fucking curious myself. What have you been lying about? Did I not warn you about screwing around with her?"

"I can handle myself!" I shout at Gabe, returning my attention back to Cole. "What the hell is he talking about?"

"Do you think I know?" Cole's eyes are wide, attention snapping between Mason, Gabe, and me. The frantic look on his face tells me he knows exactly what Mason's talking about.

"He's using you! And you're too blind to see it. If he really wanted you, wouldn't he be bringing you around his family? Or, I don't know, maybe he would've told you that he knew yours before he ever met you?" Mason stares right at Cole as he says it. "God, Sadie, the *house*. You think he'd be with you if his parents hadn't placed him at the right place at the right time?"

Oh, my God, I might throw up.

My dad recognized his last name. Cole knows my dad. And somehow, neither of them told me this.

"Look, I get you're pissed off, but this isn't the way to handle it–"

"I'm more than pissed off, Cole. Sadie's a good person. She deserves better than bullshit and lies. It's screwed up," Mason cuts him off.

"The night we met." I pause, closing my eyes. "Did you know who I was?"

"Sadie..."

"Cole! Did you know?"

"I knew." He sounds small, weak. Like he regrets the detail as much as I'm beginning to. "Not until you told me your name. But...yes, I knew."

My stomach churns. That night flashes through my head —to when he told me Gabe wasn't the reason he'd feel bad for being with me—and it all makes sense. Everything pieces together.

Gabe stomps past Mason, a look of anger in his eyes I've never seen before. Without thinking, I put myself in front of Cole, blocking Gabe from getting to him. He halts, hands tightening into fists.

"Sadie, move."

"This is my relationship," I reply, holding my ground and pointing at him. "You don't get to intervene like this. I can handle myself." It's the second time I've said it tonight, yet somehow, I mean it less.

Gabe glances upward, his jaw tightening. He takes a few steps back, but he's still close enough to reach Cole if he changes his mind.

"What else?" My voice is barely loud enough for Mason to hear it. "Anything else you'd like to bring to my attention?"

"You're fooling yourself by staying with him. I know you, Sadie. You want to get married and settle down, and he can't give that to you. He won't. There's not a chance in hell he's going against his parents' wishes. They don't like you, and that's the only reason he's with you. To fucking stick it to them." Mason's face is red, hands clenched into fists and eyebrows slanted further.

When I look at Cole, guilt and shame prick on his face. For some reason, this hurts worse than if he tried denying it.

"Is it true?" I breathe out, tears welling in my eyes.

He's silent, even when he looks at me.

"God damn it, answer the question." I take another step away from him.

"He won't." Gabe shakes his head. "It's been six months, Sadie. He doesn't love you. If he did, he wouldn't treat you the way he does. You of all people should already know that."

"Sadie." Cole's voice is strained, his chest rising and falling. "Please, just get in the car."

"You can't even deny it." I scoff, dropping my arms to my sides and nodding slowly.

"I'll explain when you get in the car."

"No," I say. "No. What? I get in, and you spew a bunch of lies, and I fall right back in?"

"It's not like that–"

"Bullshit," I snap. "Do you even know me? At all?"

"Are you serious? Of course, I do." Cole recoils, shoving his hands in his pockets. "You're actually listening to him?"

"I'm serious, Cole."

I pause, clenching my fists and trying my best to calm myself down. "I know so much about you. You suck at directions, for one. You're *so* fucking bad at them, it's kind of annoying. And any time you're up past midnight, you go outside because you need fresh air. Your jokes are stupid as shit, but for some reason, your laugh is my favorite sound in the Goddamn world, and I can't help but laugh, too. I know so many things about you, and you can't tell me one thing about me. Do you even know my favorite color?"

More silence. Neverending, perpetual silence.

"That's what I thought." I look at Mason. "Thanks, I guess."

Turning away from both of them, I stomp down the street. Frenchmen Street is close enough to where I live. I'm not getting in that car with Cole, no matter what he says to me. One of my heels snaps on the cobblestone.

"Sadie, come on." Cole grabs my arm, stopping me from falling and turning me toward him. "It's too late for you to walk alone."

"Don't touch me." I yank myself from his grip, glaring at him as I take my shoes off. "You really think I want to get in that fucking car with you? After everything Mason said?"

"Please, don't do this right now. At least let me take you home."

"Why?" I hiss, throwing my hands into the air.

The lump in my throat becomes too much to bear, and my voice breaks along with the dam holding my emotions back.

"From where I'm standing, all of this is some fucked up joke to you. Something to throw in your parents' faces. I'm *so* glad I can be that for you, that I'm so disappointing you use me as fucking cannon fodder. Everybody was right. This whole thing was a mistake."

Cole reaches up to wipe my tears, but I smack his hand away.

"Don't touch me."

"I can't lose you. This is all so much, I can explain—"

"Do you not understand? I don't want you to explain! I want you to leave me alone. We're done, Cole. I respect myself too much to let you keep doing this to me. Go. Please." I sniffle, trying hard to make my voice strong.

All he has to do is say it's not true. Three words.

"Sadie..."

"Go." I point back in the direction of his car. "If you feel even a *shred* of guilt for what you're doing, turn around and *go*."

The cells in my body are at war, half demanding I beg him to stay, half demanding I let him go. He closes his eyes and nods as if he's working up the courage.

"Okay," he whispers, voice rough. "Fine."

He turns away from me.

Away from us.

And against both our wishes, he becomes just another one of those faces I see on Frenchmen Street. How stupid of me to think he could ever be anything but.

He drives off. Mason has disappeared, and Gabe tries to make it to me before I lose it. The only thing I can do is scream, pick up a bottle off the ground, and throw it as hard as I can against one of the buildings.

I shatter with it.

W hen Cole comes out of the back room, he's using one of the hand towels to dry off his hair. The pants I gave him seem to fit, but the shirt may be a bit small. My gaze moves over him on its own accord, taking in the way the sleeves hug his muscles and how the midnight-colored fabric makes his blue eyes pop.

"I hope this is okay," he says, holding up the towel. "It was back there, and my hair was pissing me off."

"Yeah, totally fine." I clear my throat and head behind the bar.

He stays away from my half of the building. Sitting down on the floor, he rests his head back on the wall. He watches me as I go into the back to throw our clothes in the dryer. When I come back, I try to find something to do.

"Sadie."

"Mhm." I don't look over at him.

He pauses. "Are you okay?"

"Me?" My voice comes out higher than normal.

"Yeah. You."

"Why wouldn't I be?"

"I..." he trails off, a sigh escaping his lips. "I didn't see much."

"Oh, my God." I massage my forehead and clench my eyes shut. "Cole... let's forget that happened, okay?"

I grab his empty glass and fill it. As I approach him, he looks up at me, his gaze piercing me like thousands of tiny needles. I hold it out to him, my other hand fidgeting with the bottom hem of my shorts while I wait for him to take it.

Once he does, he brings it to his lips. "Thanks."

I turn around to go back to my half of the bar, but he reaches out to grab my wrist. The warmth of his touch makes me realize how cold I am. Heat runs from my wrist through my veins, spreading throughout my body. This is Cole. The same man I knew five years ago, but different at the same time. Familiar, but not.

"Sit with me."

"I don't think that's a good idea," I tell him.

"Do you hate me, Sadie?" he asks, his eyebrows furrowing. "For everything that happened between us?"

My heart thuds on my ribcage. "Why are you so sure I hate you?"

"Because I did shitty things," he says, releasing my wrist and shrugging. "I didn't treat you right. Hurt you. I don't know." His voice gets quieter, as if he's not supposed to speak those words into the open.

"You did hurt me," I confirm. "But I hurt you, too. Actually, if anyone should hate someone, you should hate me."

"I couldn't. Not even if I tried." Cole sips his whiskey.

After a brief moment of hesitation, I sit on the ground next to him. I cradle my knees to my chest and rest my head on them.

"I don't hate you," I tell him. "Honestly, we both did some shitty things. So, I say we call it even and move on."

"That's the thing, though. I was pissed. For a long time, I was pissed. You did one thing, but I put you through so much in six months. I dealt with that one thing, and you dealt with hundreds of things. You can hate me if you want." Cole worries his bottom lip.

Shifting back, I meet his gaze. "Do you remember the first time we went to the bayou?"

"Like I'd ever forget."

"I felt like that was the first time I ever really saw you." I pause. "Whenever we were alone, it was like you were a completely different person. You were...open. I learned a lot about you there."

"We learned a lot about each other at the bayou." Cole swirls his glass. "It's still my favorite spot."

When I don't say anything, he continues.

"I guess I did use you in a way." He frowns. "It's still not the right word. I really cared for you. I wanted to be with you, and I'd never known anything with such certainty before. I've spent the past five years wondering how you were doing. Hell, I even went as far as asking Mason."

"You asked about me?"

"Sometimes, yeah. He'd always give me some kind of... beat around the bush answer. And then tell me to leave you alone."

With my heart pounding in my chest, I stare at him. In awe, in shock, in disbelief, *something*.

"Some part of me always knew you wanted me." I look up at the ceiling. The panels are supposed to be white but seem to be turning beige. I should have them cleaned. "I saw it in your eyes. The way you looked at me, I mean. I would always tell myself that you don't look at someone like that if you don't want them."

"I did. But I wasn't ready for...any of it. When we went to the bayou on your birthday, that's the first day I realized how much I was hurting you. And I was selfish. I thought that as long as you put up with it, it was okay. It was a little surprising you never said anything. I was so bad."

"I'm surprised, too." I nod.

"That night, I decided I wanted to get better. And if there's one thing I could take back, Sadie, it's when I decided to do that at your expense. I hurt you over and over because I needed your energy to feel better. You're this...ball of happiness and spontaneity. All the time. I tried to take that from you, and I'm really sorry for that."

I let his words sink in. They float around in my chest before wrapping around my heart and squeezing it with the close precision only Cole has.

"We were...pretty wild back then."

"Yep. We have all these adult responsibilities these days."

For a moment, I look at his face. I watch as he sets his glass down on the floor. It hasn't taken long for me to realize Cole's changed substantially on the inside. Regardless, he's still the same man I fell in love with all those years ago. His eyes have evolved from the darkness of the night and Lake Pontchartrain, but underneath this new layer the old Cole still exists.

And here we are, meeting again like skyline and water.

Forever close but never truly touching.

He catches me staring and raises an eyebrow.

Chewing on the inside of my cheek, I shrug. "You already had adult responsibilities at twenty-three, Cole."

"Sure, but not the same ones I have now."

Talking to him brings back the memories. The fun. The love. It makes me remember it all.

"You okay?" Cole frowns, tilting his head.

"What? Of course." I nod, giving him one of my expert fake smiles. He shifts, a sympathetic look overtaking his features.

I almost forgot it was raining since it was muted by our conversation. After we fall silent, all I hear is it slamming mercilessly, relentlessly into the building. It'll be hours before it stops.

"Hey," he says. "You don't have to hide from me."

"I'm not hiding."

"You are. You can talk to me, you know."

I talked to him at the bayou when I found out about Kat

and Mason. Since I already trusted him with something like that, why should my feelings toward our situation be any different? I'm not shy by any means. Cole deserves the truth, too.

"I keep thinking about what my dad would think about this. About me being here with you." I pick at the loose threads of my shorts, giving them all my attention.

Cole turns away from me, hands fidgeting in his lap as he stares out the windows. "He wouldn't like it."

Rain cascades around us, but I swear I still hear the breath catch in his throat. I wonder if he regrets The Incident like I do. And while we only dated for six months, I fell in love with him in a way I've never loved anyone else.

"He would not," I concur, nodding and pursing my lips as I follow his stare outside, watching the downpour on the pavement.

"You remember the first day I met your family? When he wanted to talk to me?" Cole asks, looking back at me and raising an eyebrow.

"Yeah, I remember."

"It's probably fitting to tell you what he told me." He pauses, a smile gracing his face as he shifts his gaze to his lap. "He, very graciously, said that you were his favorite person in the universe. Those were his words, Sadie, not mine. And he warned me that if I ever hurt you, used you, anything, he had a shotgun with my name on it. Classic Southern dad, I know. But he loves you. No matter where he's at."

I gulp, fighting hard with the lump in my throat. "He said all that to you?"

"Oh, yeah. He came to my house after we broke up, too. Without a shotgun, thankfully. But he said I made a big mistake. Because life without you wouldn't be a life at all." Cole stops, a short laugh escaping his lips. "He was right."

"Wow." The twist in my chest is so hard, I swear a rib cracks. Thoughts of my dad swarm my mind, forcing my eyes shut as I see his face.

"I'm sorry I wasn't honest with you at the beginning." Cole taps his fingernail on his glass. "Maybe if I'd told you everything about my family and how we knew yours, we'd still be together."

Cole's hair is beginning to dry. I've only seen it imperfect a handful of times, especially back when he was twenty-three. Every muscle in my body screams for me to move, to run my fingers through it and tame it the same way I used to. It should take more than a few words for him to make me rethink every bad thought I've ever had about him, about our breakup and the things that happened right after, but he makes it so easy to forget the negatives.

"Cole, I..." I trail off, scanning over his face. Strong cheek-bones. Tense, clenched jaw.

"You don't have to say anything. I lied to you and let you believe all of those things Mason said." His chest rises as he inhales, but he doesn't exhale.

"They weren't true?" I can't manage anything over a whisper.

Cole chuckles. "They weren't true. I was an idiot. You had every right to believe what he said. I didn't exactly defend myself. And...I never told you this back then, but I was in love with you. I should've fought harder. Honestly, I've never been the best at confrontation, and I panicked. I'm not used to people arguing with me, I guess."

"I did, too." I swallow roughly. "Love you, I mean."

Good God, the way my heart's racing makes me think I still might.

"I know." He smiles.

"We call it The Incident." I try not to look at him. "Mason and me."

"Fitting title." He turns his smile toward me and leans his head back on the wall.

"And... since we're being honest, Mason and I never slept together. I told you that because I wanted to hurt you, and I knew—or hoped—that it would." While it's freeing to have those words fall from my lips, I can't shake the feeling that I'm the world's biggest bitch. But he deserves the truth as much as I do.

Cole rests his hand on top of mine. I almost flinch from the sparks, my eyes flicking between his and his hand. He still feels them, too. My proximity to him would make me sweat if it wasn't so cold in here.

"I know that, too."

"How?" I furrow my eyebrows, settling my gaze on his face instead of the hand that's still engulfing mine. Still warm.

"Mason told me. A couple years ago." Cole chews on his bottom lip. "I wanted to go see you, but he told me not to. He said it'd be a bad idea."

"It would've been." I nod in agreement. "I was the same

person. We would've ended up in a cycle neither of us could break. We did the right thing."

"I guess we did. But we're different now."

He's so close. This is why I dreaded being alone with him in the first place—everything else has left my brain except how easy it would be to kiss him. I can't control myself around him. A desperate urge to feel his lips on mine takes over, and as soon as the thought crosses my mind, it looks as if it crosses his, too. This is Cole. Our bodies have always been in sync, regardless of if our minds were, too.

I can't hear the rain anymore. Instead, I hear only the pounding in my ears and my blood flowing through my veins. Cole gulps. His eyes dart down to my mouth for a split second, but it's long enough.

My breath shudders as he leans closer to me. This is the closest we've been in years, and he's not stopping there. His hand leaves mine, gently brushing my hair behind my ear before cupping my cheek. No words are spoken. There's nothing to say. Only kissing to be done, and hearts to set on fire. Every thought about the past, about Mason, my dad, *everything* is gone.

But oh, my God.

My dad.

My dad didn't like Cole. He didn't want that for me, and I swear the storm outside is directly from him in the afterlife.

The hot *zing* of a spark passes when his lips brush mine. Tensing, I shoot up from my spot. I slap my hand over my mouth and put as much distance between us as possible before I look at him. He runs his fingers through his hair. I pace. We don't talk.

I try to find something, anything to do with my hands, so they end up gripping the edge of the bar top as if I need some sort of support. I sigh in relief when I see the rain has slowed to a light drizzle. Good. I can get the hell out of here and far, far away from Cole.

And then it hits me. Regardless of how much he changed, he's still Cole. The man who tried to take everything from me, who ruined me in the process and made me into someone I never thought I'd have to be.

"I didn't mean to freak you out." He takes a step toward me.

"My *God*, Cole! We can't do this." I drop my head into my hand.

Cole sets his glass down behind the bar. "Why not?"

"What do you mean why not?" I recoil, hating how much hope flares in my heart, wrapping it in the warm embrace of his earlier words.

"You're right to be worried, but I...I know I screwed up. I'm not the same person," Cole says slowly, sighing.

"I'm not either," I breathe out, barely audible.

"Do you want to know why I left Miranda?"

I only realize then that I've never heard her name before. Curiosity gets the best of me. When his eyes meet mine, I see Pontchartrain. Water and sky. Sadness and fear.

I nod in response.

"I thought I'd...I don't know, that I'd come to love her eventually. My parents loved her, and she was perfect to them, but she's not you. She never made me feel like you do. Like I need to work hard to deserve you. Like time is fucking nothing, and the only thing that matters is each other."

"Cole..."

"I don't think I ever stopped loving you, Sadie."

The breath catches in my throat. I would've crumbled to the floor if he hadn't caught me in his arms. Simple touches were doable. The sparks from his fingers are nowhere near as intense as the sparks from the rest of his body. They send a steady hum of electricity coursing through my bloodstream. I want this. Him.

"I can't." My voice breaks as I bury myself deep in his chest. "I'm so sorry. He doesn't want this for me."

Even though I feel him deflate, he kisses the top of my head. "Hey, it's okay. I get it. I'm not mad at you. But it'll always be you."

And for me, it will always be him.

I wish I could tell him that. For more reasons than one, I can't, and he knows it.

"The rain slowed," I whisper, sniffling. "You should go."

With my head pressed to him, the sound of his heartbeat reaches my ears. Even our hearts are in sync. Our minds.

"Okay." He takes a deep, shaky breath and steps back, putting his hands on my arms.

I look at him through tear-filled eyes, and for a brief moment, I see us how we were. In love. No cares in the world. I challenged Cole, and he grounded me in ways no one else could.

Cole looks me up and down, an unrecognizable gleam in

his eyes. He chews on his bottom lip before he works up the courage to turn away from me.

Away from us.

From all of the things we could be if I didn't care so much about everyone else.

"Goodbye, Sadie. I won't bother you anymore." His chest rises.

"Bye," I choke out, closing my eyes. The urge to grab him and pull him back to me is greater than anything I've ever felt, but for both our sakes, I need to let him go.

As he opens the door, the bell chimes. Finally, I look. Cole pauses in the doorframe, hand gripping the handle until his fingers pale. His head drops.

"It was blue."

I recoil in confusion. "What?"

"Your favorite color. It was blue."

Paralyzed, I'm stuck to my spot. My heart shatters all over again as I watch him leave the same way he did five years ago.

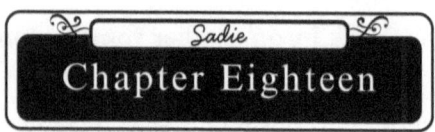

Sadie

Chapter Eighteen

FIVE YEARS AGO...

Ba y the time I make it back to my apartment, I'm in shambles. Every inch of my body itches. My walk was a good twenty minutes, but I'm still furious. My body shakes, my stomach churns, and my mind refuses to stop reeling. I strain to remember the breathing technique my father showed me as a young girl. My efforts are futile.

I let myself fall in love with a man who couldn't care less about me.

He walked away.

My heart in hand, he left me behind in the darkness of the French Quarter.

As much as I want to collapse on my couch and cry until my ducts are dry, I can't. It reminds me of him. God damn it, everything reminds me of him. With a shout, I yank the cushions off of it and throw them as far as I can possibly manage. The lamp wobbles, ultimately falling off the side table and crashing to the floor. Like the bottle in the street, like *me*, it shatters on impact.

In a fit of blind rage, I swipe my arm over the counter and knock everything off it. I clutch my hands to my chest, over the spot where my heart is meant to reside, and crumble to the floor. The gaping hole in its place only widens, spreading to cover every inch of the apartment already saturated with his presence and memory.

I cry so hard, I'm sure I'll flood my living room. Sitting there, I realize how obvious it all was in hindsight. I think of how he's had me in every inch of this place. That alone makes me want to burn the building to the ground before selfishly taking the rest of the world with me.

The sickest part of all of this is how I still try to make excuses for him.

I need to remember what I've been taught. If he loved me in the way he should, I never would've felt otherwise. I spent so much time here with him, proving to him I loved him. He gave himself to me the same way, yet never the one piece I truly wanted. Never his heart.

My body still shakes from anger. Or maybe it's from the remembrance of his touch, the warmth I'll never feel again.

I should've got in the fucking car. At least then, I'd still have him. Even if it wasn't in the way he had me.

No, Sadie, I think to myself, shaking my head. *You did the right thing. He's not good for you.*

But it felt so right. So beautiful, and overwhelmingly like fate.

I need to know.

If what Mason said was true. If Cole has been lying to me this whole time. And since I can't go to Cole, the only person left is Mason.

Mason will tell me.

Mason is my last hope.

Please, *please* tell me it wasn't all a lie.

●　●　●

When Mason opens the door, he does a double take, like I'm the last person he expected to show up at his house. It's comical, really. He blew up my entire relationship with Cole in a matter of five minutes. And, oh boy, does he look guilty about it. His eyes cloud with that concern I've only seen from him a handful of times now.

"Sadie." Mason clears his throat, looking around like Cole might be with me. "What are you doing here?"

"I don't have anywhere else to go," I tell him. While I like to tell myself that's the truth, we both know it's not. I'm a mess, and at this rate, Mason knows it's all his fault. Well...that's not true. Cole did this, Mason just exposed it. Mason did the right thing.

"Your apartment? Your parents?" he offers.

"It's not the same." *That's* the truth. "I go to my parents, and what? Tell them they were right?"

He inhales, his eyes closing as he pats the frame. He'll

regret this, I know that from the look on his face. His eyebrows are furrowed, lips pulled together in a thin line.

"Fine."

It's one word. But of course, it's *that* word. The word that Cole said the first night I invited him into my apartment. The word he said when I was too stubborn to listen to his explanation earlier.

Mason steps back to allow me inside. Blinking back tears, I cautiously step into Mason's house. *Mason's house*. God, what the hell am I doing? Logically, I know this is the last place I should be, and by the way he's standing by the door, he knows it too.

His living room is small with dark oak floors and off-white walls. The kitchen is separated by an 'L'-shaped counter, three lights dangling down to shine on the granite. A TV is mounted to the wall by the door, and his couch is in the middle of the room, the fabric a faint sky blue. Not much, but inherently Mason.

"You...Um, you want something to drink?" Mason asks.

"I don't think so." The only other time I've been in Mason's house was with Cole.

"Right." He anxiously taps his foot. *Tap, tap, tap.* "Sadie, I don't really have anything to say to you." *Tap, tap, tap.*

"Was it true?"

Tap, tap, tap. Mason pauses, eyes flicking between me and his stupid feet, one *still tapping the floor*.

"For the love of God, Mase, I'm gonna cut your damn feet off." I roll my eyes at him and cross my arms over my chest.

"Can you be normal for five seconds and answer my question?" Thankfully, the tapping finally stops.

"I don't know," Mason says, closing his eyes. "Honestly, I was drunk and pissed and said what I felt was true. That's something you'll have to ask him."

"You're his best friend. You know him better than anyone, and you're telling me you can't say if his feelings for me are real or not?" I scoff.

Furrowing his eyebrows, Mason takes his bottom lip between his teeth. "I don't know what kind of idea you have about men...but we don't talk about feelings. Girls. Not in that way, at least."

I sigh. What else can I do in this situation? Besides, Cole is Mason's best friend. I doubt he'd tell me even if Cole *did* talk about me. Slumping onto his couch, I drop my head in my hands and let the last six hours replay over and over in my head. And while Mason confirmed my literal worst fear (regarding my relationship with Cole), it's better that I found out. After six months, and not a year. Or six.

I'm shocked when Mason lets out his own sigh, joining me on the couch. He sits on the other cushion, about as far away from me as he can get. Now *I'm* tapping *my* foot. I know why I came here, and suddenly, I'm not too sure that's what I want anymore. I fell in love with Cole. I still love him, so there's not a chance in hell I'd do something like this to him.

Shaking that thought from my head, I remember Cole never loved me. Not at all. Not even a little bit. I almost scoff all over again as I think about what he wanted me for. To use me. To shove something his parents didn't like in their faces. I'm not a pawn, and I won't let him treat me as such.

"Look, Sadie." Mason puts his hand on my knee, garnering all of my attention. "I didn't mean to hurt you tonight. Not you."

Not me. Cole.

I gulp. "I changed my mind. Do you have any whiskey?"

"Be serious." He frowns. His voice is sharp, protective.

"You didn't care the last time I was here." I meet his gaze and blink at him once. Twice. I'm still acutely aware of the warmth of his hand on my knee.

"That was under different circumstances." He wets his lips. "We weren't alone. And you weren't heartbroken. I really do care about you."

It's hard to hide the chill that runs through my body, but if Mason notices, he doesn't say a word. His frown softens to the point where his eyebrows are barely slanted. I stop shaking my leg. His index finger taps my skin, eyes scanning me as if it were physical touch.

"Who cares?" I mutter, watching the minuscule shake of his head.

"I do. He would."

Our topic is invisible. Intangible. Neither of us dares to say what we're talking about out loud. Mason knows exactly what I came here for, and for someone who used to try and charm my pants off all the time, he doesn't seem too keen to do it at the moment.

"Mase..."

"I'm serious."

"He hurt me."

Mason's jaw tightens, full lips pressed into a thin line. His touch is no longer warm—it's blazing, like lava slowly tracing up my leg.

"He lied to me. Hell, he lied to you, too. He hurt both of us, so what does it matter if we find comfort in each other?" I shuffle a bit closer to him, my movements making his hand shift to the middle of my leg, fingers hanging loosely over my inner thigh.

"He's my best friend." It doesn't sound like Mason is talking to me anymore. He's looking right at me, but his voice is distant while his eyes flutter shut.

"Look at me," I say.

He does.

"After all of that...do you really think he deserves your loyalty? Mine?" I don't believe any of the words coming out of my mouth. I love Cole. I want the best for Cole, but there's a part of me that wants to tear the world down around him and make him suffer.

That part wins. It's not even a real battle, if I'm being honest.

"I already fucked him over tonight," Mason says. "Sadie, I've been attracted to you since I met you, but...I care about you. I don't care about many people, but I care about *you*. And Cole, even if he's being a dick."

I'm not sure what else to say. His gaze and touch are betraying what he wants, contradicting every word leaving his lips. I debate whether or not I should reach out and touch his face. Convince him that this is okay. But it's not my job to make him want me, though if he does, he can have me.

"I can't do that to him."

"Who said anything about him finding out?" I raise an eyebrow at him.

Mason jerks his hand away from my thigh and clasps his hands together in his lap. He laughs nervously. "Any other circumstances and this wouldn't be a question, Sadie. It's just..."

"Just what?" I sit up a little straighter.

"I don't want to hurt you." His tone makes the words seem simple when they're anything but.

"I'm already hurt." I laugh. It's a sad, almost pathetic laugh, but it seems to do the trick. He narrows his eyes for a moment.

"That's...not what I meant. At all." Mason gulps, the intensity of his stare so different, yet so much weaker, than Cole's. Is it fair to compare them? Mason and Cole are different. They always have been, and they always will be. The only thing they have in common after tonight is *me*, and how much of me they have.

"Then what?" I cross my arms over my chest. His eyes flick downward before his jaw clenches.

"I can only give this to you once," Mason whispers, squeezing my leg. "I don't date, and I'm not gentle. I'm not like him."

My throat is dry, and there's suddenly a heat between my

thighs that causes me to clench them together. Good God, I can't fucking breathe anymore. I'm glad he said it too—that he didn't want a relationship with me—because I certainly don't want one with him. He watches me closely, the weight of his gaze making me realize exactly what I'm about to do.

I can't come back from this. Cole would never forgive me for something like this.

But then, I realize it's not Cole's forgiveness I'm looking for. It's mine.

"Perfect. I don't like it gentle."

Mason practically lunges across the couch, lips meeting mine with a fervor only someone like him could be capable of. I dig my nails into his arms, heat swarming every inch of my body. He guides me backward on the couch. My back presses into the cushions.

I can't shake how wrong this feels. Mason's touch doesn't leave those beautiful sparks Cole's does. He kisses rough, in complete contradiction to the way Cole was always soft and sweet with me.

Mason's hand slides beneath my shirt, and my entire body tenses. Sitting up, he stares at me, his chest heaving.

"What are you doing?" I ask, lifting myself on my elbows.

"Seriously, Sadie?" He stands and runs his fingers through his hair. "We can't do this."

"Why?"

"The idea of me touching you makes you freeze. You're clearly not comfortable. I'm not...I can't do this." His hand rests on his forehead as he massages it.

I sit up and bring my knees to my chest. "I'm sorry. I...I

just want him to hurt the way I do." I avert my gaze from Mason.

His kiss doesn't tingle on my lips like Cole's did. After I clear my throat, I tap my fingers on my knee.

"You can still stay," Mason says. "If you don't want to be alone."

"I don't want to bother you." My voice is unrecognizable, grated by the sandpaper in my throat.

"If you bothered me, I wouldn't let you stay." Mason touches my arm, all previous remnants of our brief kiss gone.

No matter how hard I fight it, the tears start welling in my eyes. He sits next to me and pulls me to his chest. His hand rubs on my back.

"I'm sorry, Sadie. For what I said."

"Don't be. I needed the truth. Better now than wasting any more of my life on someone who doesn't care about me." I drop my head on his shoulder.

"I could've done it differently, though." Mason sighs. "Come on. You should change and get some sleep."

Nodding, I let Mason lead me toward his room. His hand grips mine loosely as he leads me down the small hallway to the back of the house. The door squeaks as he opens it. Stone gray paint covers the walls, but the flooring is consistent throughout. One dresser. One bed. Nothing else will fit.

He pulls one of the drawers open and hands me some of his clothes to change into. After he leaves, I put them on. The shirt swallows me whole, and the sweatpants slide down even when I tie them. I sigh to myself and play with the strings.

Climbing into his bed, I stare up at the ceiling. It's so tall.

Fourteen feet is standard in New Orleans, I'm pretty sure. Cole told me it was a pre-air conditioning standard, and most of these houses were built long before it. Whenever he would get nervous about something, or awkward, he'd always tell me a little real estate fact. Property taxes, iron lace railings, room height, and even romeo spikes.

I hate blinking. Every time my eyes close, I see his stunning blue ones. His pleading face when he asked me to get in the car. The utter defeat when he realized his efforts were futile, and I was never going anywhere with him ever again.

And then, the thoughts change. Instead, I begin thinking about how he looked at me before that. When we were alone. When he touched me all over. The vulnerability in that gaze made me think he might be in love with me, too. No greater heartache exists than this, I'm sure, than figuring out the man you thought may love you forever never truly loved you at all.

"Mason," I call out to him.

His footsteps echo down the hallway before the door squeaks. "Yeah?"

"Can you stay with me? I can't be alone." Forcing the words out makes them quiet, maybe even pathetic.

I'm scared I'll regret asking for Mason for comfort. We both know this is the last thing I need. Maybe I deserve to wallow in the wake of what Cole left behind, to be heartbroken since everyone warned me this might happen.

My heart wrenches, and a shuddering breath escapes my throat.

"Of course," Mason says, walking toward the bed.

I'm drained. Empty. Unfeeling, especially as Mason

climbs in next to me and adjusts to get comfortable. He pulls me to his chest, but his warmth does little to comfort me. I move closer. He kisses the top of my head.

"I'm sorry, Sadie."

But he doesn't have anything to be sorry for.

Cole did this.

● ● ●

Unsurprisingly, I wake up alone.

I sit up and stretch. Every muscle in my body aches. Mason's bedroom door is cracked open, so when I hear two voices in the kitchen, I freeze.

Mason and Cole.

Cole's here. With Mason. In Mason's house.

I could get up and go see him. Talk to him. Maybe he'd have a different explanation for me today than he did last night. But Cole walked away from me. He left me alone with barely an argument.

Cole doesn't care about me, so why should I care what he thinks about me being at Mason's house?

Two things could happen when I see Cole.

One, I could absolutely crumble into a puddle of tears.

Or, I could seem indifferent, and maybe hurt him the way he hurt me.

Nerves gnaw at my stomach when the door squeaks on my way out. I stop at the end of the hall. Cole sees me first. His eyebrows furrow as he recoils, looking between Mason and me. Mason closes his eyes and sighs, running his fingers through his hair.

Cole scoffs. He rests his hands on the edge of the countertop. "Sadie."

"Cole, it's not—" Mason begins.

"I'd rather not hear it," Cole interrupts, lifting a hand. "I mean, honestly, what did I even expect? How long has this been going on?"

"What do you mean *this*?" I question, taking a step closer.

"Seriously?" Cole snaps. "Mason blows up our entire relationship last night, and suddenly, you're coming out of his bedroom the next morning?"

"Mason didn't do shit." I clench my fists at my sides. "You did. You blew up our relationship, Cole. That's not his fault. At least own up to your own bullshit."

Cole laughs. To the point where his head leans back a bit. "*My* bullshit? So, fucking my best friend the same night you break up with me isn't considered bullshit?"

I should correct him. Let him know that Mason and I didn't really do anything last night. But I see the look in his eyes, and it makes me want to continue hurting him in the same way he hurt me.

"What I do and who I do it with is no longer any of your business." I cross my arms over my chest and lean on Mason's fridge. "You lost that right when you all but admitted you never cared about me in the first place."

"You." Cole points at Mason. "This is what last night was about? You wanted her for yourself?"

"That's ridiculous." Mason shakes his head.

I know why I'm not denying it—but why is Mason going along with this?

Mason walks around the counter toward the door, opening it and staring at Cole like he's waiting for him to leave. I look between the two of them. Cole's perfect eyebrows are furrowed, but I can't tell if his eyes are shiny or not.

"You should go." Mason's jaw tightens as he grips the door knob.

"After everything you did, you had to make it worse, didn't you?" Cole takes a couple steps toward him.

"Everything I did?" Mason scoffs, running his tongue over his teeth. "I didn't piss her off so bad that she needed to blow off steam—"

Cole's fist connects with Mason's face. A mix between a gasp and a scream leaves my mouth, and for a moment, I think Mason's going to retaliate. He doesn't. All he does is gesture outside and clench his jaw.

Cole brushes off his shirt—finally, a wrinkle in the perfect fabric—and leaves.

As soon as Mason closes the door, he curses under his breath and touches his face. I rush to him, tilting his head in the light to see how bad it's going to be. He sits on the couch, fidgeting restlessly with his hands. I go to his freezer to find something to put on it.

"Sadie, it's fine," Mason says. "He doesn't hit that hard."

"Mase." I make my way back to him. "I'm so sorry. I never thought he'd—"

"It's not your fault." He gulps.

I grab his hand. "You didn't have to go along with that."

He moves it away from mine. "You're too good for him. If it keeps him away from you, it was worth it."

"Thank you."

"You're my friend. I told you I care about you."

Another difference between Cole and Mason.

Mason isn't a liar.

Cole

Chapter Nineteen

Walking away the second time should be easier, right?

Dead wrong.

I should've fought harder. Then and now. Sadie always did, and still does, deserve better than what happened between us, than me in the state I was in back then. Talking to her today and being honest about everything lifted a weight from me I hadn't known I was carrying.

When I make it to my car, I sigh and run my hands down my face. Sadie is almost the same on the outside. She changed her hair color, but everything else is exactly as I remember it. On the inside, however, I've never seen such change in a person. I didn't know it was possible. She still struggles with impulsivity, that much I can discern from her actions today, but her sending me away proves she can control it.

But even when we were younger, she was so much better than me.

I can't find the energy to open the damn door. Resting my head on top of the metal, I try to close my eyes and see anything but Sadie. No matter how hard I try to force her out, it doesn't work. Maybe I'm an idiot for holding onto her for so long, even if I haven't exactly been waiting for her.

"Cole, wait."

My heart stops in my chest, and I look up to catch that pine-green gaze I never stopped loving. Frozen in place, I wonder if she changed her mind. If she wants me, too. The drizzle patters on the cobblestone I left her on all that time ago. It soaks into my clothes, leaving a cold chill on my skin as I await the only true warmth I've ever felt—*Sadie*.

By the time she makes it to me, I realize I still haven't said anything. Wide, doe-eyes look up at me, and I have to wonder if this is the last time I'll ever see them. Her chestnut hair reaches right below her shoulders, the slight gust of wind sending it behind her back.

Here we are, standing at the all-too-familiar corner of Decatur and Frenchmen, cutting the final tie that holds us together.

"Your clothes," Sadie finally says, sliding the bag off her shoulder and handing it to me. "They...They should be mostly dry."

"Right, thanks."

When I take it from her, I don't mean to brush her fingers.

Her eyes well before she shakes her head to snap herself out of it. "I'm sorry."

"Don't be." I force a smile. "I had my chance, and I blew it. That's not your fault."

"Not just that." She pauses, gently chewing on her bottom lip. "For everything. For lying to you about Mason, and for not realizing how hard things were for you back then. I didn't mean to make it worse."

I look her up and down one last time. "Regardless if things were hard or not, I was so bad to you. I took all your love until you had nothing left to give. And then I walked away. You shouldn't forgive me for that."

"I forgave you a long time ago," Sadie says. "I want the best for you, Cole. Truly."

I'll never have it. Not when the best for me is her.

After a moment of hesitation, I nod. "You, too." I clench my fist to stop myself from touching her face. "And...you never made anything worse. You were the only good thing I've ever had. You made me realize I needed to be better. That I *wanted* to be better. So, thank you."

"If only you'd realized a little earlier." She shifts on her feet. "I'm proud of you for doing better for yourself."

I blink at her. The world around us—the dark, dreary, wet streets of New Orleans—fades to background noise. Nobody has ever said that to me before. I've never made anyone *proud*. Somehow, her words part the clouds and sunshine beats down on my skin.

Warmth.

Sadie's warmth.

Proud.

Sadie is proud of me.

Sadie.

The only girl I've ever truly loved.

Without thinking, I pull her to me and wrap my arms around her. A small gasp leaves her lips, but she hugs me back.

"Thank you," I breathe out.

Sadie relaxes in my grip and buries her head in my chest. I don't care if she hears how hard my heart is pounding. Everything is out in the open. The past, the truth, and every hardship in between.

"Thank you," I say again, pressing my lips to the top of her head. "You have no idea how much that means to me."

"I'll see you around, okay?" Sadie sniffles. She pulls away from me and wipes her eyes.

"I hope so."

She walks backward a couple steps before she turns around. At that moment, I think of how easy I had it the past two times being the one to leave. I didn't have to watch her form retreat farther away from me. Nor did I have to look at all of the emotions on her face—regret, sadness, longing.

I didn't have to let her go.

Now, I do.

I thought the past five years without her were my punishment for being so bad to her. Never in my life have I been so terribly wrong.

Sadie stops in front of her bar, hand on the door when she looks at me. Her eyes trail over me before meeting mine. The rain has all but stopped, tiny drops dripping down my arms and leaving goosebumps in their wake.

I nod at her.

She goes inside.

And finally, I understand just how much I broke her all those years ago.

I park outside my house and sit there for a while. Almost like I need to work up the courage to see anyone in my family before walking in. The curtains are closed, leaving everything inside a mystery. Since my dad died, I've never felt so far from him. I can't feel him. To be completely honest, I haven't felt him since that day.

I believed the storm earlier may have been a message from him. Now that I'm home, thinking of everything that transpired today, I'm beginning to think otherwise. If his presence isn't here, why would I think he sent the storm?

And he'd probably do the opposite of sticking me alone in a room with Cole for hours. A storm wouldn't do that.

The first thing I do when I go inside is change my clothes. Putting on something comfortable after the day I had is necessary. After I put leggings and a different T-shirt on, I run a brush through my hair. Sighing, I look at myself in the mirror.

My hair is mostly dry. The humidity mixed with it being soaked earlier makes it curly and frizzy. I can't imagine Cole looked at the person I'm looking at and wanted to admit he was still in love with me.

Running my hands along the top of my head, I fail to straighten out some of the baby hairs. I groan in defeat instead.

Everything feels distant. I miss my dad, Kat, Mom, Mason, and even Cole. Kat's pregnant and focused on too many things to spend much time with me. Mom isn't handling Dad's death well, not that I assumed she would. She barely gets up. We're lucky if we can convince her to take a walk with us. Mason...Mason is different. Ever since I found out about him and Kat, it doesn't feel right for him to be my best friend. With that logic, I don't have anyone.

Not even Cole, considering I sent him away.

One thing resonates in my mind—one way for me to feel closer to my father. I haven't played piano since he died. Avoiding it was simple. I'm used to hearing him sing along or play another instrument as I work the keys. But when I can't bear the space between Earth and Heaven, it's the only thing I can think of that'll bring me closer to him.

If I could break the veil separating us, I would. No matter the consequences, and no matter who else got hurt in the crossfire.

Missing someone who's here is easy.

Missing someone who's not is impossibly difficult.

When do the subtle things that used to bring me closer to him stop hurting so damn badly?

Playing piano, singing, being in this house...when does it end?

Like the center of gravity is in the music room, I'm drawn to it. Pulled with such undeniable force, I'm sure it's not *just* a feeling. My dad pulls me toward where I belong—where I've always belonged.

Right by his side in the room we spent so much time in together.

Already blinking back tears, I take a shuddering breath as I spread the curtains apart. The front yard is less daunting from the inside. Live oak tree leaves create canopies, leaving a beautiful array of shadows on the ground below. The heat of the sun drifts through the window.

No sign of the storm remains. The sidewalks have since dried, and the grass stands tall and proud. Resurrection ferns cover the branches, stretching further this year to cover the bark than they ever had before. If only the name were real. If only my dad could be resurrected through the greenness of the ferns fervently clinging to the trees.

I haven't accepted he's gone yet. Somehow, I think I'll see him behind me when I turn around.

He was supposed to turn fifty this year.

One day, I'll get married, and he won't be there to walk me down the aisle.

He'll never know Kat's baby. His first grandchild.

How am I meant to accept something that never should have been reality in the first place?

Clenching my eyes shut, I sit at the piano bench. I make sure to scoot over far enough to give him enough room. In case he's here. Looking up to the ceiling, I silently ask him for the strength to get through this. No matter what, that's what he is. My strength.

I take a deep breath, straighten my back, and position my fingers on the keys. *Fly Me to the Moon* will be too hard for me at a time like this. I'm not entirely sure what song I plan on playing. My mind takes over.

The first tear falls when I play the first note.

And then, a waterfall—both tears and music, both flooding the area around me like a hurricane.

Let It Be floats through the room, the melody gentle and soft as silk. As I open my mouth to sing, I swear I catch a glimpse of him in my peripheral vision. I choke on the words. Regaining my composure, I shake my head and wait for the chorus.

The longer I play, the clearer he becomes. I feel his warmth I've been so desperately grasping for. My hands shake. I yearn to look over and truly see him, but I know he'll disappear the moment I stop.

And if this is what brings him to me, I will never, ever stop.

A voice joins mine, and my heart shatters further, taking the lyrics straight from my mouth and leaving me with my piano.

Mom.

She walks over to the bench and sits in the spot I left for Dad, and, for the first time since he died, I don't feel alone.

Andrea Dupont has the voice of an angel, and part of me is convinced that angel is William Dupont himself.

When she wraps her arm around me, I have the strength of a thousand suns. I have transformed the weight on my shoulders from storm-hardened rocks to gentle clouds filled with the light she shines through me.

As the final notes play, I'm smiling.

I don't have to be the glue. Dad still is.

"I'm so sorry, Sadie." Mom sniffles, wiping her eyes. "I've been so unfair to you."

I lean my head on her shoulder. "You're grieving."

"Not any more than you are." A sigh wracks her chest. "I heard you playing, and I realized how terrible all of this must have been for you. Honey, I...I don't want to make this worse for you. I don't want to add to your pain."

"What are we gonna do?" My breath hitches, and I tighten my grip on her.

"I don't know," she says, sliding her fingers through my hair. "I'm sorry I don't have more answers for you. None of this makes sense for me, either."

"Everything's happening at once," I whisper. "Dad, Mason, Kat, and I saw Cole again today."

"Even I was surprised by Mason and Kat." Mom chuckles, twirling my brunette strands.

She pauses for a moment.

"Cole, huh?"

"It's nothing," I say. "We were catching up."

Thinking about him sends a pang through my heart. Mom notices my quick answer, and she leans away so she can look at my face. Her eyes are identical to clouds right before a storm—deep, deep gray that only grows darker with every emotion.

"Sadie," she begins. "What's going on there?"

I shrug. "I don't know. He was there when I needed someone, I guess. It's not like anything happened, either. Today, he came to the parade, and we got caught in that storm. We resolved a lot of issues. Old ones I never thought I'd get the answers to."

"For someone who got answers, you don't seem too excited about them." Mom runs her fingers along the piano keys.

Contemplating, I chew the inside of my cheek. I'm not excited about them. Not at all. When I thought Cole never really loved me, it was much easier letting him go. At least then, I didn't feel guilty for the things I did.

"Sometimes, we get the most comfort from the people we least expect." Mom presses a few random notes. "Fate works in mysterious ways. You should never be ashamed in your healing process, no matter who it includes."

I blink at her, seeing my own grief in her raincloud-colored eyes. "He...He told me he still loves me."

"Oh." Mom's eyebrows raise, but she makes no other movement, offers no other thoughts.

"And obviously, I told him I couldn't."

"But you want to?" Her head tilts.

I furrow my eyebrows, turning my attention back to the piano. "No."

She gives me a pointed look. I used to hate having these

conversations with her, but today, I'm grasping onto any source of normalcy I can get.

"Okay, yeah, maybe. I can't, though."

"Why not?"

"We're not good for each other. We weren't back then, and we're still not now. Dad didn't like him, and I can't do something that'll disappoint him." I purse my lips and sniffle.

Mom brushes my hair behind my ear. "He wouldn't be disappointed in you for something like that. If Cole's been supportive and good to you when you've seen him recently, and you think you have feelings for him, your dad would be happy for you."

When I don't respond, she slides off the bench.

"Why don't you go up to Kat's room? I've got something for the two of you." She gives me a small smile.

Nodding, I follow her out, watching as she goes toward her bedroom while I go upstairs. Standing outside Kat's door, I don't mean to eavesdrop on her conversation.

"Ew, absolutely not." She gags.

"Come on, it's not that bad," Mason grumbles.

For the first time since I found out about them, I smile at the thought. I knock on the door, waiting for Kat's confirmation before I come in.

"What's not that bad?" I ask, sliding my hands into my pockets.

Both of them are sitting on her bed, Mason toward the foot and Kat by the headboard.

"Mason wants to name our baby Barbara." Kat sends a

glare his way before looking at me. "*Barbie*. Can you tell him he's ridiculous?"

"You're having a girl?" I tilt my head.

My heart swells in my chest at the thought—Kat and Mason being girl parents fits so well. Maybe she'll teach Mason a thing or two.

"Yeah." Kat nods, fighting the smile on her face. "I found out this morning."

Seeing them both in this context—both happy with the future laid out for them—makes me realize how much I've missed them. Maybe it wasn't that they weren't there for me, and more we weren't there for each other. I climb onto her bed next to her and wrap my arms around her.

"I'm so happy for you, Kat. Really." I lean on her shoulder, eyes flicking up toward Mason. "You, too. I guess."

IIe chuckles, looking down at his hands in his lap as he fidgets. "Thanks, Sades."

"Ugh, this is so stupid," Kat whines, wiping her face in frustration. "I swear, these hormones make me cry at fucking everything."

"Oh, no. You've always been a cry baby. Don't blame my niece." I laugh and poke her side.

"Barbara." Mason nods, looking between the two of us.

"Absolutely not." I scrunch my face.

"Not a chance in hell," Kat says at the same time.

The door creaks open, revealing Mom's form behind it. She carries two envelopes in her right hand, the left bracing the frame as she watches us.

"Mom." Kat's voice shakes and more tears fall down her

face. "God damn it." The last part is under her breath, her eyes rolling.

I scoot over and let Mom climb in between us, both of us looping our arms through hers. She gladly takes our affection.

"I can leave you guys alone." Mason shifts to get up.

"Don't be ridiculous." Mom shakes her head. "You're bound to this family by blood. Just as much one of us as I am."

I've never seen a look on his face like that before. His eyebrows are furrowed, but his eyes are hopeful. He settles back in his spot.

"So, a few years ago, your father had this wonderful idea." Mom squeezes us both. "He wanted to write you guys letters for when you got married. After your grandfather died, he got really sentimental." She laughs, but tears well in her eyes.

"Those are Dad's letters?" I look at them, clutched to Mom's chest, and feel all sorts of things rushing over me. Right there, in my mother's hands, are the last pieces of our father that we'll ever see. The tiniest part of his soul, imbued in ink and paper.

"They are," she says, voice weak. Sniffling, she hands them to us. "You can wait to read them if you'd like, but I think you both need to see the truth. How proud he was of you both. How much he loved you, no matter what happened. There is nothing in this entire world you could do that would change that."

My hands shake as I stare at the envelope. I look over at Kat. She's gripping her letter so tightly that it's beginning to bend. When I turn my gaze to my mother, she's smiling at me, her thumb rubbing my arm.

"And...I'm sure you're both curious as to what's going on with the house." Mom pauses, taking a deep breath and leaning back on the headboard. "I'm not selling."

"Oh, my God." I gasp, clasping my hand over my mouth.

"It's not mine to sell," Mom says. "Cole was right. It's your house."

My heart twists at the mention of his name. I realize, at that moment, the only person I'm excited to tell this to is Cole. The urge to call him or show up at his house or even to *see* him and tell him all of the good things happening today is overwhelming.

I catch the worried gleam in Mason's eyes, but it dissipates as soon as I do. He smiles at me. Since he has no clue about what happened at the parade, I'm not sure he understands the weight of it all. Mason and I haven't been as close as we usually are.

"I'm signing it over to you, Sadie." Mom pats my knee. "I'm looking for other places. I still can't stay here, but I know how much it means to you. It was selfish of me to not consider that at first."

My fingers fumble around the envelope, aching to rip it open and see what my dad wanted to say to me. His handwriting—while terrible—is such a comfort, staring at it warms me.

"I think I need to read this." I nod, pursing my lips. "Thank you. I love you guys. Even you, Mason. And you're a shithead."

I hug Mom and Kat first, and then I make my way over to Mason. His grip on me is tight, and he breathes a sigh of relief.

"We love you, too, Sades." Kat smiles at me as I separate from Mason.

I look back at the three of them when I make it to the door. Our family will never be whole again. Without my father here, that will always be impossible. But now, looking at some of the most important people in my life, I realize this is as close as we'll ever be to *complete*.

Mom, Kat, and Mason are my family.

I make it back to my own room taking in the details of it. Not much has changed. The canopy is still gray, the walls are still blue, and not a single piece of furniture has been moved.

My mind lingers heavily on Cole. After hearing about the letter and the house and having my mom back, my first thought was to tell him. Because he'd be happy for me. He would support me.

I sit on the edge of my bed, unable to wait any longer to read it. Careful as to not rip the envelope, I unseal it with my finger. With a pounding heart, I unfold the paper. The pages are stiff, crinkling in my grasp as I take in his handwriting. To be honest, it's barely legible. But I would spend years discerning it if I have to.

Peanut,

Today, you're getting married. Ever since you were born, I've imagined walking you down the aisle. Leading you into a new start of your life that you've yet to experience. Sadie, as I write this, you're barely twenty-three years old. Throughout those twenty-three years, I've seen you love fiercely. Live wholly. Get your heart broken and bounce back from it.

And since I'm writing this early, I have no idea who's going to be lucky enough to marry the strong, confident woman you've become. Your mom and I have done our best to prepare you for a life on your own, but that doesn't mean we're quite ready to let you go.

This will be long-winded. When you receive it, I imagine you rolling your eyes and giving me that look that says I've overdone it (again). But, that's the thing—I will always overdo it when it comes to my girls.

The day you were born was the happiest day of my life. Holding you in my arms felt like a success. Like I finally made an impact on this world. You were the most beautiful baby, and you've grown into an even more beautiful woman.

I hope you continue to grow, to love freely, to speak your mind. No matter what, you'll always have me. Whether I'm here, away for the weekend, or gone forever, I will always be right by your side. Your biggest advocate. Your biggest supporter.

Whoever you're walking to at the end of that aisle has my full approval. I don't need to know who they are, only that you trust them enough to give them your life. Your heart is pure, and it won't lead you in the wrong direction. I've taught you what to look for. How you should be treated. You know, and that means whatever you decide, whoever you choose will be the right choice for you.

I've never seen someone glow as bright as you, Sadie. Whatever you do, the only request I have for you is to never let someone dim that. Knowing that this is your wedding day, I won't say too much. You're a bit of a cry baby, and you'll kill me for ruining your makeup.

So, I'll keep the end of this short and sweet.

I am so proud of you. Everything you've accomplished, what you've done for yourself in the short life you've had so far, and how wonderful you are to everyone around you. Never give up music. Your dreams. Anything. If there is one thing I know for sure about you, it's that you'll always accomplish anything you set your mind to.

I love you, Peanut. I can't wait to walk you toward the rest of your life.

- Dad

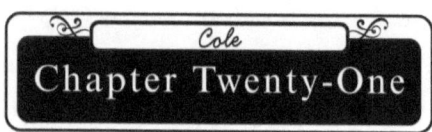

Chapter Twenty-One

"Yeah, Clark, I got it." I sigh, massaging my forehead. "Yep, he's pissed. What else is new?" After twenty minutes on the phone, I'm ready to throw it into the damn bayou.

"Come on. This isn't a game anymore. Breaking up with Miranda was a mistake. She's gonna find a way to tear this family to the ground—"

"A mistake for who?" I recoil. "It was a mistake *not* marrying a woman I didn't want to marry?"

"You proposed to her," Clark points out. "You had to think you wanted to marry her at one point."

This conversation is going nowhere. Clark fails to realize that I couldn't care less about what my father thinks. I wasn't kidding when I said I was done with them—Miranda included. She's as bad as the rest of them.

"Maybe, and then I decided I didn't want to marry someone just like our mother."

"I mean, the timing seems convenient—"

A knock sounds.

"Speaking of convenient timing, someone's here. Gotta go." I hang up before he can say anything else.

Sighing and shaking that conversation from my head, I walk to my front door and open it. Mason stands on the front porch, shifting on his feet and fidgeting with his hands. After everything with Sadie, we've stuck to public gatherings, so it's safe to say this is an unusual occurrence.

"Can I come in?" he asks.

"Well, you're already here." I frown, walking further into the dark-floored living room.

Up until a few weeks ago, Miranda's things were everywhere. Her artwork. Small things like hair ties, bobby pins, and everything else symbolizing a woman lived here. Every last trace is gone, and I'm the happiest I've been in three years.

The gray walls seem to close in on me the longer I wait for Mason to speak. A million thoughts run through my head. Did Sadie tell him about the bar? That we finally told each other the truth after five years of believing otherwise?

"Do you want a drink?" I clear my throat, sticking my hands in my pockets. "I have beer. Or whiskey."

"I won't be here long." Mason shifts on his feet.

"Alright, then." I lean on the wall, crossing my arms over my chest and waiting for whatever the hell is about to happen.

Mason sighs and scratches his forehead. "What's going on with Sadie?"

"Sadie?" I frown at him. "Nothing's going on with Sadie."

"Cole, I'll be honest, I don't like you two together." Mason shakes his head. "You're bad for each other. Nothing good is going to come from any of this."

"I have no idea what you're talking about, but if you've come here to tell me I'm not good enough for Sadie, we've been down this road before." I run my tongue over my teeth, holding back the twinge of anger I feel.

"What's your goal here? Show up for her until she falls in love with you again?"

I scoff. "That's really funny coming from you. Considering you got her sister pregnant." I shift and stand straight. "I've been showing up for Sadie because she deserves to have someone do that for her. Not for me. And if you'd actually been there for her at all, you'd know what happened. She would've told you."

"The look on her face when her mom brought you up... She was *guilty*." Mason narrows his eyes at me. "If you cared about her at all, you wouldn't want that for her."

"Stop saying shit like that. You have no idea how I feel about her."

"Can't you see this is a repeat of the last time you two were together?" Mason asks.

"Stop."

"No, I'm serious. She's only entertaining you because you're there. You think if she hadn't—"

"Mason, I walked away from her. We talked about things,

and then we left it at that. She told me she couldn't go against her dad's wishes. I respected that. So, if that's all you're here for, know your spot in her life isn't threatened."

Mason recoils. "You think that's why I'm here?"

"What else?" I lift my arms in exasperation. "Yeah, I did some fucked up things five years ago. I admit it. Sadie deserved so much better than that. But if you can't see that you're the catalyst of all these events, then I don't know how to help you. You yelled at us in the middle of Frenchmen Street about how I didn't care about her—when you *knew* that wasn't true. You knew I loved her. And then this whole thing with Kat? Who's really the one not good for Sadie?"

"Kat and I are figuring everything out." Mason crosses his arms over his chest. "And Sadie's happy for us."

"Maybe now, sure. But do you know who she talked to about it? Who told her that you and Kat were adults that can make adult decisions? She didn't come to that epiphany on her own, jackass."

Mason's jaw tightens, and I think back to five years ago.

To how I told him I was in love with Sadie.

Before the explosion on Frenchmen.

The past is the past for a reason. Part of my healing process for both Sadie and every other thing going wrong in my life was forgiving things I never would have otherwise. I no longer hold a grudge against Mason. At the end of the day, it probably was best for Sadie and me to take some time apart.

But he's here, telling me I'm still not right for her.

That I'm still going to hurt her.

But I know that's not true.

"Cole, you were bad for each other then. What makes you think things will be better now? She's going through a lot." Mason pinches the bridge of his nose, chest deflating.

"I don't need to prove myself to anyone, Mason. Least of all you." I give one firm nod and an unimpressed look.

"She's my best friend."

"*I* was your best friend. For years, actually. Forgive me if I don't really think you care all that much about your best friends. You told Sadie I didn't care about her when I actually told you not even a week before that I was in love with her."

"Do you not see the issue here?" Mason scoffs. "You dated her for six months and never told her that. Can you actually remember a single good moment between the two of you?"

I recoil. "You're kidding, right?"

"No."

All of them. Or, almost all of them. Obviously, I'd change some of them if I could—if I could go back in time, I'd tell her I loved her at the bayou on her birthday. That's when I knew.

"I've done...a lot of shitty things in the past. That's not a secret by any means. But Sadie and I had a lot of good times. A lot of them. You weren't there. I don't expect you to understand, especially not when you've screwed anything that could walk for the entirety of your adult life." I close my eyes and lean my head on the wall.

He doesn't say anything. While he stands there, I'm sure he's attempting to seem brooding. Or scary. Nothing he says would keep me away from Sadie. *Sadie* keeps me away from

Sadie. She told me she wanted to respect her father, and in no way would I ever ask her to do the opposite.

"How do you feel about Kat?" I ask.

He shifts on his feet, gaze leaving mine. "Doesn't matter."

"But it does, Mason. You're telling me it's not gonna break your heart to see her with someone else some day? That she's carrying your child, and the fact that she doesn't want to be with you isn't tearing you up from the inside out?"

"We're not talking about me," he says firmly.

"Why not?" I shrug. "You're so quick to talk about my relationship with Sadie—something you know nothing about—but the second I bring up Kat, you want to shut down?"

"I'm worried about them both, okay?" Mason throws his hands up in defeat. "Sadie won't even talk to me anymore. Kat only talks to me because of the baby. Then I hear from Andrea that Sadie's talking to you, and it's throwing me off."

"Oh, so you know how I felt five years ago, is what you're saying?" I raise my eyebrows, trying my best not to laugh. "How do you think it felt to lose both of you? That my best friend purposefully wedged his way between me and the girl I loved? Years, Mason. I dealt with that for *years*."

Mason gulps, his chest rising as he takes a deep breath. "I didn't think about it like that."

"Obviously not."

"I was worried about both of you. More so Sadie, I guess." Mason shakes his head. "I mean, she was so...engulfed by you, in everything you wanted to do. She never thought about herself. And then you weren't exactly being great to her. You both needed some time."

"We did. Trust me when I tell you I've taken that time and more. Sadie told me she couldn't be with me, and I'm respecting that. Like I said I would. I'm not going to bother her anymore."

"I'm sorry," Mason says, looking down at his feet. "For getting involved in something that was none of my business. I should've talked to you directly, or chosen a better time. It's not just that I saw the issues, Cole, I was jealous of both of you."

"Jealous?" I frown.

"Yeah. You two had each other. I was still...doing my own thing and dealing with everything on my own. When I saw the way she looked at you, I wanted something like that. Not with Sadie, but in general."

A long, silent pause ensues, as if Mason's working up the courage to say what's coming to his mind next.

"I thought I'd get that with Kat. Or at least maybe she'd want to try to be with me. It's so off the table for her, like I'm the last person she'd ever consider dating."

"Those Dupont women." I snort, smiling. "Gotta work your ass off for them."

"Pretty sure they both hate me." Mason purses his lips.

"I thought Sadie hated me. Maybe she did for a while, but she doesn't anymore. She's probably confused, Mase. It doesn't help that all of this is happening right after everything with their dad."

Mason and I have never had a conversation like this. He's typically closed off. Secretive. And while I'm not much better,

I've come to terms with emotions being an everyday experience.

"I want to be a better friend to both of you," Mason says. "I've been so shitty to you these past few years. And putting you through all of that with Sadie wasn't that great either."

"I haven't been mad at you in a long time. You should talk to Sadie. She's not nearly as mad as you think she is." I shift from the wall.

"I came here to yell at you, and you're comforting me." Mason furrows his eyebrows. "Maybe you have changed."

"Thanks, I guess." I roll my eyes. "Too little, too late, it seems."

"You're right, though. I'll talk to both of them and try to figure out what the hell's gonna happen." Mason scratches his forehead, gazing blankly at the wall.

He doesn't stay much longer. After he leaves, I find myself in bed, staring at the ceiling. Sadie appears at the forefront of my mind. Our memories are all I have left to cling onto, all I'll ever have of her.

I want her to look at me the same way she used to—like I grabbed a star from the sky and brought it down to Earth just for her. It sparkled in her eyes every time I caught them.

I told her, all that time ago, how I thought the world was evil. Chaotic. How, if things were innately good, half of the planet would cease to exist.

"The world's not evil, Cole. If it were, it never would've brought us together."

Hindsight tells me it is.

Because the evil act was not bringing her into my life, but taking her out of it.

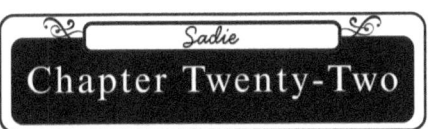

Chapter Twenty-Two

Time is frozen for the rest of the night. I reread the letter over and over again, trying my best to discern the things he wrote. Leaving my brain to its own devices at a time like this is the worst possible thing, but doing this—staring between the wall and his horrible handwriting—is the only thing keeping me sane.

The sun has long since set, leaving my sky blue bedroom soaked in orange and red hues. I sit on my bed, leaning against the headboard, and the cast of rays reaches me, warm to the touch, as if they're tangible and not a magnification from the glass.

Although I shouldn't, I look straight into that glob of light in the sky. It stops hurting my eyes after a minute, and I pretend the rest of the world has stopped. Even me. My heart no longer beats because it doesn't need to, my lungs no longer fill because at this moment, oxygen isn't necessary.

What's the point of all of this? The painted walls, the creaky hardwood, the canopy draped over my bed... My imagination has ceased to exist. For once, it's only me, the sun, and silence. Complete and utter silence.

It's beautiful. Golden, even.

Playing not only brought me closer to my father, but the endless melodies that were once Cole's words spoken to me in this very room. Part of me wonders what Dad would think about this—about me, lingering on Cole even after all this time.

After all the heartbreak.

But then, as I blink for the first time in who knows how long, I realize in some way shape or form, he must've known I would end up here. Or that Cole would come back, and my brain and heart would be at war like this. That's William Dupont, though. He knows everything, always.

A rap on my door unpauses the world around me and plants me back on my feet. I look up, eyebrows raised as my eyes adjust to the change in light. Gabe leans on the frame, his feet crossed at the ankles. He glances between me and the letter sprawled out on my bed, a solemn look on his face.

"Hey," he says. "You've been sitting there for a while."

"Yeah," is all I offer, along with a shrug.

"You alright?"

"Alright is relative, I think." I chuckle. "What are you doing here?"

"Kat asked for help putting together a crib or something." Gabe fidgets with his hands.

Kat has been chronically early for everything since the day she was born. It doesn't surprise me that she'd want to build her baby's crib when it's not due for another seven months. A sigh escapes before I stop it.

"Mason can't help her with that?" I ask.

"He's busy or something. She didn't want to wait the two hours until he gets here, not that he would've been all that good at it, anyway. I don't think Mason's very handy." He laughs to himself. "You two are the worst at following rules, you know? And my friends are also really fucking bad at it."

I smile, shaking my head. "Oh, come on. You know better than to tell Kat or me no. We'll do the exact opposite."

"Sadie," he starts, hesitating as if he shouldn't even be talking about what he's thinking. "You can still talk to me about anything. I've been hard on you a lot, lately and over the past few years, but you'd better know that I love you. And I want you to be comfortable talking to me like you were before Cole."

I open my mouth to speak, but my voice catches in my throat. As much as I'd love to deny it, I did stop confiding in him as much as I used to.

"I do get why, though." Gabe nods, chewing the inside of his cheek. "It was never my goal to shut myself out like that. I should've been better about it."

"It's okay," I reply, patting my bed on the opposite side of the letter. "Join me. I'll show you what's weighing on my brain today."

A half-grin forms on his face as he makes his way over, climbing up and sitting criss-cross applesauce. I put the pages of the letter in order and give it to him, waiting patiently while he reads it. A mix of emotions crosses his face, from pain to a quick laugh to watery eyes from a stray tear or two.

"Ouch." He clears his throat. "What do you think about that?"

I wager with myself if I should be honest right now. If it's worth seeing if Gabe meant what he said about being better about his reactions regarding Cole.

Picking at the seam of my jeans, I swallow hard. "It makes me think of him."

I don't need to specify the *him* I'm talking about. Realization settles on Gabe's face as he nods slowly with his lips pressed into a thin line.

"Have you seen him recently?" Gabe asks. "Is that where this is coming from?"

"I invited him to the parade. And we got stuck in the storm and had to wait it out in the bar."

"Did you—"

My glare stops him mid-sentence.

"Okay, okay, next question." He holds his hands up in mock surrender. "Would you like my honest opinion, or do you want me to be supportive?"

"Oh, like you've ever held back an honest opinion before. Let's hear it." I cradle my knees to my chest and rest my head on them.

"You gave him a choice before, Sades, and he walked away. He didn't choose you." He pauses, as if pondering his next words. "You deserve someone who will choose you all the time, no matter what. That's what I want for you, and I don't think he's capable."

"Maybe not." I take a deep breath. "But that was five years ago. We were both...awful back then. I never used my brain, and he had undying loyalty to shitty people. It was bound to be a disaster."

"What changed?" Gabe asks. "Seriously. What about him has changed to make you think he doesn't depend on his family anymore?"

"Honestly? He told me he thinks he still loves me. And this probably sounds so dumb to you, but I believe him."

Gabe wets his lips. "There's a difference between being in love with someone and being what's good for them. That night was awful, and he's not the one who had to pick up the Sadie-sized puddle in the middle of Frenchmen Street. What did you even do that was so bad?"

"You don't want to know." I snort, scratching my head. "We're both over it now, so it doesn't matter."

"Look, I won't tell you not to do it this time, but I might kill him if I see you go through that heartbreak again." Gabe massages his forehead. "And as much as I don't want to admit it, you probably know him better than I do. All I ask is that you be careful."

I reach over and nudge his shoulder. "C'mon, Careful's my middle name."

He sets the letter down next to us and leans forward to hug me. "You wouldn't know careful if it hit you upside the head."

After that, I go 'help' Gabe with the crib. Which actually consists of Kat and me watching him and laughing. The directions must be confusing, because he's still trying to put it together by the time Mason gets here.

The two of them get it figured out within an hour, and then we leave Kat alone to get some rest. In the kitchen, we sit around the island, each of us with a beer despite the fact I don't have much of a taste for it. The late night air is almost stagnant. I consider opening a window before I hear the air conditioning kick on. That should fix it.

Everything is reminding me of Cole now. Seeing Mason and Gabe chat away like the old friends they are, it makes me wonder if they're not in Cole's life because of me. And then I wonder if he has anyone at all.

But the longer I think about it, the quicker I realize he dug that hole himself. He had the chance to be honest back then, and he wasn't. He may be different now, but that doesn't change the past.

While Kat sleeps upstairs, Gabe, Mason, and I talk and joke and laugh for the next few hours. I use it as a way to get further from those treacherous Cole thoughts.

They don't leave until well past my bedtime. When they've gone, I walk back into the kitchen and let out a sigh. The lights spill against the ground outside, illuminating a small rectangle of gold in its wake.

Without Gabe and Mason, this room begins to feel like a black hole. The hum of electricity floods my ears, and the floors creak under my feet. This house is my birthright. It's mine. Yet, somehow, even after the promise of legal paperwork to sign it off to me, it's as if it's still being tugged away from me.

Tapping my fingers on the island, I inhale. Something—what, I'm unsure of—prevents me from exhaling.

It's more than *home*. It's family. Love and revelations and warmth.

If I close my eyes, memories in this very kitchen swarm behind my eyelids. Beautiful memories that should haunt my every waking moment with loss, but instead, they make me smile. That's what Dad would've wanted, and for him, I'd do anything.

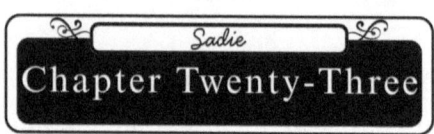

Sadie

Chapter Twenty-Three

S t. Louis Cemetery No. 1 is vast.

Of all the places I thought I'd end up today, in front of my family tomb was not on the top of the list. I brought him flowers. It's not much, but what else do you bring the dead? He won't actually see them.

The slab of stone with his name on it sends a pang through me. As much as I know it's real, all of it sinks in far too often for comfort. I set the flowers down, sighing while I brush my hair behind my ears.

Where do I even start?

Hey, Dad. Don't be disappointed in me, but I think I still have feelings for Cole Anderson.

Hey, Dad. I know you hated Cole for all of the shit he did five years ago, but he's changed. Really changed.

No, that won't work either.

"You said you trusted me, remember?" I finally say, tracing the tip of my finger along the grooves of his name. "I wonder if you meant that, or if you were saying it to make me feel better about my choices."

I laugh softly, dropping my hand to my side and rocking on the balls of my feet.

"He's the only person I wanna talk to. Well, I wanna talk to you, but you're not here. He's...second best, you know? Mom told me she wasn't selling the house, and the first person I wanted to tell was Cole. I really think he's changed. It's been five years. How different can he be in *five years*? But I guess I did, too. I'm so confused. My brain says one thing, and my heart says another. This is what I need you here for. The voice of reason.

"Were you surprised about Mason and Kat? I definitely was. And a little mad, Mason's supposed to be my best friend."

I should've brought a chair. Something tells me I'm going to be here for a while.

"I'm telling you this because I'm only half-convinced you can hear me, so if you can, and you don't want to, then plug your ears. Okay, you know I've dated after Cole. It's just... none of them made me feel the way he does. Which is also weird because we weren't even...we weren't that great. He told me yesterday he still loves me. Whenever I'm around him, I get this odd sense of calm. Like I'm supposed to be with him.

"Dad, I feel like everything is falling into place. Is that a bad thing to say? Think about it. The letter, the house, Cole...

all of it feels right. And I'm not that much of a cry baby. I can't believe you would call me out like that."

After a while, I run out of things to say. He hasn't truly missed any of what I'm telling him about. Not if he's here like I think he is. I sit with him in silence for so long, I don't even realize the sun setting on the horizon until the orange hues cast shadows upon his name.

Making sure the flowers are placed properly, I take a step back. The more I think about the letter, the more I realize something about my dad—if Cole had come back when he was alive, everything would be okay. Dad trusts me, whether it's about what songs to play or who I bring into the family.

"I love you, Dad." I wipe away a stray tear. "Thanks for listening. Unless you plugged your ears, because that's so mean."

I laugh at my own joke.

"Seriously. Thank you for everything you gave me when you were alive. For being the best dad anyone could've asked for. I'll come visit more often. Until next time."

Once I make it back to my car, I realize the last place I want to go is home.

I want Cole. The comfort and warmth he brings.

Gretna isn't that far. I still remember the way to Cole's like the back of my hand. Almost as if it's muscle memory. Their property is daunting. The long, winding driveway, two houses —one a miniature version of the other—standing side by side. Cole and his brother, Carter, live in the smaller one together.

Both homes are huge. White pillars jut from the porch up

to the respective galleries. Black accent paint coats the windows and doors. The Andersons aren't shy about the amount of money they have, especially when it comes to things people can see.

I stop my car in front of the guest house. It takes me another ten minutes to work up the courage to go knock on the door. Cole's on the other side of it. Even though I know his feelings toward me, my body shakes.

Finally, I climb the wooden steps and ring the doorbell instead of knocking. If they're not downstairs, they won't hear anything other than that. Observing the porch and the forever unused rocking chairs adorning it, I wait for what feels like hours.

Carter answers. He recoils in shock at the sight of me. His black hair is a mirror image of Cole's, but Carter's eyes are so dark, they're almost black.

"Sadie."

"Hey." I clench and unclench my fists. "I don't mean to bother you guys, but I'm looking for Cole."

Carter blinks at me in confusion. "For Cole?"

"Um, yeah." I clear my throat. "If he doesn't want to see me, that's fine, I'll go—"

"No, that's not what I mean." Carter chuckles, sticking his hands in the pockets of his black pants. "He doesn't live here anymore. Not for the past three years."

A sharp inhale almost makes me choke on my own air. "Oh, wow. Well, this is... awkward. I really shouldn't have come then."

"Do you wanna come in? I don't know his address off the

top of my head, but I can find it if you give me a minute."
Carter steps aside.

"Sure." I fidget with my hands as I enter.

The foyer reminds me of my own, with a long hallway divided in half by a staircase. When Carter closes the door, I stand in front of it with my hands clasped behind my back. Heels click on the stairs, and a woman with ebony hair comes into view. She's putting pearl earrings in.

"Carter, what time is—Oh, hello." She raises her eyebrows at me, freezing on the bottom step. "Who are you?"

"Oh, um—"

"Sorry, Lana, this is Sadie." Carter walks toward her—Lana—and puts his hand on the small of her back.

"Sadie, as in Cole's Sadie?" She narrows her eyes at Carter.

"That'd be the one."

"What's she doing here?"

"Um," I cut in, scratching the top of my head. My face is red hot. "I should...go. This was probably a bad idea."

Carter holds a piece of paper between two of his fingers and hands it to me. "That's what you're looking for. And if he asks how you found out where he lives, you can tell him it was me. I could use some brownie points with him."

"Not sure they'll be brownie points." I chuckle nervously, taking it from him.

"You've left quite the impact on him," Lana says, finally moving down off her step. "Carter would never tell his parents to fuck off for me."

"What?" I frown.

"This poor girl is so out of the loop." Lana sighs and clasps the other earring. "When Cole broke things off with Miranda—his ex-fiancée, sorry—his parents were talking about your house. I don't know exactly what happened, but Miranda told me he told his parents to fuck off and said you were better than all of them."

There I go, choking on my own air all over again. "Interesting."

"Lana," Carter says, laughing to himself. "She probably didn't need to know that."

"I'm just saying." Lana holds her hands up.

Clearing my throat, I shift on my feet. I hold up the piece of paper. "Thanks for this. I'm gonna go."

As soon as I'm outside, I take a deep breath. Fresh air feels so much better than being back in that house. I head to my car and plug the address into the GPS on my phone. Once I read it, I realize how close he's been this whole time.

Bayou St. John.

He lives in Bayou St. John.

The drive is short. Strong, blue lights on my radio tell me it's almost 9:30. The sun has long since set, leaving me in the overwhelming darkness as I arrive at Cole's house. When I stop in front of it, I pause.

It doesn't seem like somewhere the Cole I knew would want to live. The Cole I knew wouldn't have ever moved out of that guesthouse. Taking in the details of it, I notice the dark blue exterior blends in with the sky. The moon is a sliver, waning ever-so-slowly from its vast distance. Soft music emanates from my speakers, the delicate melodies not doing much to quell my nerves, for once.

And then, for the second time tonight, I knock and wait for Cole.

He opens the door, and it's safe to say that I'm the last person he expected.

No words are spoken. He allows me inside, watching as I step past him. This place is much different than where he used to live. Not as fancy. It suits him more, I think.

I stop. I'm standing in Cole Anderson's living room. After everything my dad said in that letter, I'm relieved I'm not wracked with guilt. This feels right. Being in Cole's presence leaves behind warmth.

Cole not being perfect is, oddly enough, perfect. His black hair is a little messy, kind of like he hopped out of bed to answer the door. And I don't think I've ever seen him in sweatpants, but he's wearing them tonight. Chewing the inside of his cheek, he slides his hands into his pockets and shifts on his feet.

"Hi," I finally say, gulping.

Cole looks down at his feet. "Hey."

I hate this awkwardness. When I saw Cole last, we almost kissed. We were so close, it brought back the memories of how his lips felt and how electric every touch was. After all this time, I remember it clear as day.

"This is hard." I shift, fidgeting. "I don't know how to do this. Or even explain why I'm here."

"I think you made yourself pretty clear the last time."

I shake my head. "I don't think I did."

Cole stares at me, gaze unwavering. His lips part as if he's going to say something, but he closes them before anything comes out. He sways back and forth.

"I don't know what's happening to me," I whisper, clenching my eyes shut. "I don't want this. Or maybe I do, and it's everything we talked about...God, Cole, I'm so confused."

"Your favorite song was *Fly Me to the Moon*."

I frown, shooting my head up so I can see him.

"And you never explicitly told me that, but you were always humming it. You used to do it so much that I still catch myself doing the same." He pauses, his chest rising. "I always loved watching you listen to music. You would tap the beat onto your thumb with the rest of your fingers. Tap your feet. Whenever there was music around, you couldn't stop yourself. It's like it's a part of you."

It's my turn to be speechless. I have no idea how to respond to that.

"You like cooked vegetables but absolutely hate raw ones. And God, you're the most frustrating, stubborn person ever when you want something. You create attachments. With people. With inanimate objects, which is how I know you still have that bookshelf."

He's right. I do still have it.

"Cole..."

"I don't have a lot of regrets in life. Barely any, if I'm being honest. The biggest one was walking away from you."

Nothing. There's absolutely nothing in my head besides the image of Cole standing in front of me. He's tall, strong like a pillar. And in reality, that's what he's been for me. At first, when I saw him at my dad's funeral, I was so angry with him. With my dad. With everyone. It took me so long to realize (until now, I mean) I wasn't mad Cole was at the funeral. I was mad he didn't come back sooner. That he didn't make amends with my father before he died.

Maybe if he did, I never would've felt guilty in the first place.

"It kills me knowing you believed all those things for so long. That I didn't love you, or that you weren't important to me." Cole chews on his bottom lip, black eyebrows furrowing. "I never stopped thinking about you. But whatever you choose, I'll respect that. We've both changed, but that doesn't mean we're right. Missing someone doesn't make them perfect for you."

"If I'm being completely honest..." I trail off, fighting to keep my eyes on his. "I don't know if I want this because I need someone or because I need you. And sure, that's shitty, but you're familiar, Cole. You made me forget every negative thing in my life when we were together, and I need that."

"I can't lose you twice. I can't do this again without knowing it's what you really want. Sadie, I loved you. And I know I could love you the right way now if you'd let me." He inhales.

So many things rush through my head at the moment. He continues to stare, awaiting my answer. Irises of ice seem to be melting under the dim lighting until he decides to continue.

"It doesn't matter if you need someone or me. I can be both."

My heart falls into my stomach. Of all the times and places I could be to make this decision, this is probably the worst of them. I'm in his house. It's late.

Removing every last worry from my mind, I gulp and take a step toward him. He's not too far from me. I crane my neck upward to see him and put my hand on his chest. His heartbeat is strong. Steady.

And God damn it, we're *alive*.

We need to live.

Cole's thinking the same thing I am. I'm not sure how his heart is so calm, especially when mine is raging hard enough to break a rib. His fingers brush my face.

"Someone...or me?"

His words make something click inside me. For the first time in months, everything is clear. I know what I want.

"You. Always you."

Since the night we got rained in, I've craved the feeling of his lips on mine. I had so many questions. How many people has he kissed since we've been together? Does he kiss differently?

It doesn't matter. Not when it feels exactly the same, still as magical as it was five years ago. A floodgate opens, and we melt into each other in a way we haven't in so, so long, it has me holding onto him for dear life.

Cole turns us around and presses my back to the wall. Emotions pour through every touch, and his fingertips ghost along my skin.

"I want this." He closes his eyes and drops his head on my shoulder. "I need you, Sadie. I really do."

Shallow breaths fan across my neck. Cole's hold on me is tight, as if letting me go would ruin everything. His kiss tingles on my lips.

"I'm here," I tell him. "I need you, too."

He pulls my mouth back to his, and I relish in the taste of fresh mint. With my hand on the back of his neck, I hold him as close as possible. His touch caresses my hip, sparks shooting from the feeling of skin-on-skin.

Like every other time I've been around him lately, a dam breaks—no, it *shatters*. I arch into his body, grasping onto him and pulling him to me like I can't get enough. His hand snakes further under my shirt. He explores every inch of me he can reach.

I pull away from him and let my head thud against the wall.

"Sadie," he says, swallowing roughly. "We shouldn't. Not tonight."

"Right." I nod, despite every nerve in my body standing on edge.

"We need to talk about this. And work all of it out." He kisses the base of my neck. "I want to put all the cards on the table before we even consider it."

"Look at me." I drop my hands to his shoulders.

He listens.

"This...Does it feel right to you, too?"

"More than anything." He pauses, brushing my hair behind my ear. "We're gonna get it right this time."

"I got some good news today." I smile at him. "You were the only person I wanted to tell."

"Please, tell me."

Neither of us recognize how close we are—not when it's been so long since the last time. If I move forward an inch, his lips will be on mine. He doesn't stop touching me. His hands are beneath my shirt, running his fingertips along the curve of my spine.

"Mom's not selling the house. She's signing it over to me."

His movements halt, and relief plasters across his face. He grins, pulling me closer to him into one of the tightest hugs he's ever given me.

"That's amazing," he says. "And it makes me so happy that you wanted to tell me."

"Kiss me. Please."

The words barely have the opportunity to leave my mouth before his lips connect with mine. He parts them easily, his tongue dancing with mine. His nails drag along my skin, leaving goosebumps with every slight movement. When he trails them down my spine, I shiver and whine.

My phone vibrates in my pocket. A puff of air escapes his lips and fans across my neck as he pulls away from me.

"Terrible timing," I mutter under my breath, arching to grab it.

Kat's name flashes on the screen.

"It's Kat," I tell Cole, taking a deep breath. I answer. "Hello?"

"What are you doing? It's almost eleven, and you're not home." She shuffles with something in the background. "Mason's talking my ear off about the whole Barbara thing again—for the love of God, Mason, I will throat punch you if you eat my pickles—anyway, we miss you. Where are you?"

I laugh. "Um, I'm at Cole's."

"Oh." She pauses, taken off guard. "Did I interrupt something?"

Humor sparkles in Cole's eyes as he smiles at me.

"Of course not." I trace along his jawline, falling right into a trance. "What could you possibly have interrupted?"

"Well, if y'all are anything like I remember, then—Ow, don't pinch me! I wasn't gonna actually say it!"

"Okay, can you two stay alive until I get there? I'll leave soon." I'm talking to Kat, but I can't seem to avert my gaze from Cole's.

"By all means, take your time." Kat chuckles. "Mason might be dead by the time you get here, anyway."

"Alright, KitKat. Be nice to him, okay? If you kill him, my niece won't have a dad." Most times, I'm obviously the voice of reason.

"I'll try. He keeps trying to eat my pickles. But yeah, I'll see you when you get here. Love you."

"Love you too." I hang up.

"Glad to see she's as much trouble as she used to be." Cole backs away from me, face slightly red.

"I'm sorry," I say, rocking on the balls of my feet. "She doesn't usually call me."

"Don't be. I'm glad you guys are okay after all the Mason stuff." Cole fidgets with his hands.

"You know, if you could forgive me for the shit I did, I can forgive them."

I pause, taking Cole in. He runs his fingers through his hair to tame it, his jaw tightening as he looks at me. The sleeves of his T-shirt are snug on his biceps, and his sweats are hanging loosely on his hips. Curves of muscle strain the fabric of his shoulders. He's beautiful. If it weren't a terrible idea, I'd stay. I'd reestablish our relationship right where we left off, and we'd never look back.

"You didn't actually do anything. You only said you did," Cole says.

"That's gotta be worse, though, right?" I furrow my eyebrows. "I'll never forget that look on your face, Cole."

"I promise you, whatever you did was minuscule compared to what I put you through. You're here, and for some reason, you want me again. The past doesn't matter here. We do. Right now." He wets his lips and sighs. "But we definitely need to talk about all of this before you really decide what to do. You should go to Kat."

"I'll see you soon?"

"As soon as possible." Cole gives me a smile as soft as silk.

I close our distance one last time and kiss him. For a moment, I contemplate never letting go. If we stay here, like this, with our lips connected, nothing could ever separate us. We'd be a monument. Made of chiseled stone ingrained with exultant melodies.

We needn't say anything else. Today, we're not walking away from each other. Not truly.

Not when we have a prospect of tomorrow.

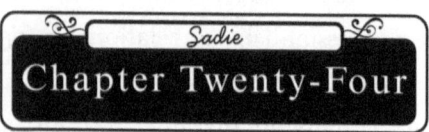

K at convinced me to watch a movie with her last night. We ended up falling asleep in her room (Mason included), and none of us woke up until noon. Hours pass, yet I've heard nothing from Cole. He lingers heavily on my mind the entire day, up until six when we order pizza.

Mason walks away to go to the bathroom, and a floodgate of questions open.

"So, Cole?" Kat takes a big bite of her slice.

"Kind of, I guess." I shrug.

"Did you have sex with him last night?"

"My God, Kat." I almost choke on my water. "No, I did not have sex with Cole."

"I don't know." Kat's eyebrows dart up. "You sounded kinda breathy on the phone."

"The things you can get away with because you're pregnant." I shake my head at her, snorting.

"Sex isn't a bad thing, Sades." Kat pats my shoulder. "Plus, Cole's like...fancy and hot."

"Fancy and hot?" I can't stop my laugh.

Kat sips her Pepsi, shrugging. "I don't make the rules. Or the words. I just say them."

We both fall silent when Mason and Gabe come in the room. They notice. Mason has been around us nonstop for the past five years—he knows us better than we'd care to admit. He grabs a juicebox from the fridge and pops the straw in it.

"What's going on in here?" Gabe quirks an eyebrow.

"Sadie slept with Cole last night."

"You slept with Cole?" Mason's eyes nearly bug out of his head.

"Oh my God, *no*." I run my hands down my beet-red face.

Mason looks between Kat and me, like he's not sure who he's supposed to believe, and Gabe massages his forehead.

"Mase, she was probably naked with him when I called her. She sounded—"

"*Kat*," I groan. "You're projecting."

"Look, apparently men don't want already-pregnant women." She grins.

Mason chews the inside of his cheek and sips his juice, avoiding Kat altogether. My heart pangs at the sight. Mason must still be struggling with his feelings, even if he's supposed to be over her.

"Um, I should go." Mason swallows hard, his eyes finding mine.

"What?" Kat stands straight. "Why?"

"I haven't been home in over twenty-four hours, and I don't think this is a great conversation for me." He clears his throat, bringing his straw back into his mouth.

Kat sighs. "Mase, it was a joke."

"Yeah, but it won't be one day. So, best to distance myself now, I guess." Mason's bluntness takes me off guard. He grabs his keys from the counter and says his goodbyes. Before we have time to process what he's said, he's gone.

Kat's lips press into a thin line, and she sniffles. "God damn it. These stupid hormones." She aggressively wipes her eyes and groans.

"Everything alright?" I ask her. Gabe steps toward her and throws an arm over her shoulder. Out of the three of us, Gabe has always been the one to go right to comforting us, whereas I'm more prone to... anything else, believe it or not.

"Obviously not," she replies, shifting on her feet. "He said he'd be able to deal with his feelings, but I don't think he can. So, I don't know what to do. I can't...force myself to like him."

My phone has a magical way of interrupting me during serious situations. Every single time.

This time, Cole's name is on the screen. I breathe a sigh of relief before I remember Kat, and how she needs me. Looking between her and my phone, I watch a smile spread across her face. Gabe doesn't share the same enthusiasm. Something more along the lines of indifference and disappointment. Maybe slight irritation.

"Sadie...answer it. You've been waiting for him all day."

"All day is a bit of an exaggeration," I mumble, answering the phone anyway. "Hey."

"I'm sorry I took so long," he says, baritone voice rumbling through the phone. "I've wanted to call you all day, but I...I don't know. I'm outside. Can I come in?"

"Here? My house?" I look at Kat and Gabe with wide eyes, but the only response is a thumbs up from the former.

Cole chuckles. "Yes, Sadie. Your house."

"Yeah, of course." I nod even though he can't see me. "We're in the kitchen."

"Okay, I'll see you in a second, then."

He hangs up, and my palms are already sweaty. I look at Kat. "Am I a mess right now?"

"Not any more than you usually are." Kat laughs. "Relax. If he liked what you looked like yesterday, this is honestly a step up."

"Damn, okay." I scrunch my nose and brush my shirt off.

My brain is short-circuiting. Cole. My house. Me. Together?

We hear the front door open, and I swear, Kat looks like a kid on Christmas. As if this is the moment she's been waiting for since I saw him at Bayou St. John.

Cole steps into the kitchen, and all I can think about is the last time he was here. When my mom tried to sell the house. When I broke down and unwittingly let him back into my life. Kat glances between us.

Gabe and Cole share a moment of eye contact before they

give each other slight nods. Not approval, but at least some respect.

"We'll leave you two alone. I should go find Mason, anyway." Kat grabs her things, loops her arm through Gabe's, and heads for the front door, stopping to wait for me. Cole stays put while I approach them.

"I'll start the car," Gabe grumbles, taking the keys from Kat and leaving before anyone can say anything else.

She lowers her voice so only I hear her. "Whatever you decide...Dad won't be mad. He'll love you no matter what, okay?"

"When did you become the big sister?" I sniffle, rolling my eyes to stop the tears as I pull her into me and kiss the top of her head. "Drive safe. Love you, KitKat."

"Love you too, Sades." She smiles, and then she's gone.

When I make it back to Cole, my hands are in the back pockets of my jeans. I rock on the balls of my feet. He braces himself against the island.

"So...are Kat and Mason having trouble?" Cole raises an eyebrow.

"Honestly? I'm not sure." I laugh, shrugging. "They've already decided on co-parenting, so I think it's hard for Mase that the one girl he likes doesn't exactly like him back."

Cole doesn't say anything else. He looks like he wants to spill the contents of his heart onto the counter, and I can't honestly say I'd hate it. I want that from him. After our kiss, I realized how hard it would be to let him go.

"But you didn't come here to talk about Kat and Mason, did you?" I tilt my head.

"Definitely not." He grins with that familiar, playful gleam flashing in his irises. "I know it's so selfish of me to want you at a time like this, when you've already gone through so much...but I don't think that love ever faded. I'm still in love with you, Sadie. I wish there was a way for me to turn back the clock and fix everything I broke. Or at least to give myself enough courage to come back before all of this."

Cole takes a deep breath, tapping his fingers against the granite. I place my hand over his. I know he has more to say.

"And I wouldn't hate you if you sent me away. I fucked up my chance, and I'll take full responsibility for that. I wasn't your dad's favorite, and I know respecting his memory is the most important thing to you. But, *God*, I need you. I need us and how spontaneous we were and how well we worked. You're everything to me, Sadie. And if I have to spend the rest of my life proving that to you *and* your dad, I will."

"I don't want to send you away, Cole," I whisper, taking another step toward him. "You're right. You weren't my dad's favorite, but when he was alive...if you'd come back when he was alive, he would've loved you. He would've because I still do."

Cole's gaze shoots to mine, blue eyes wide with hope. Tightening his grip on my hand, his lips part as if he's going to say something, but he closes them.

"I want you forever this time." He inhales sharply, pulling me closer until there's less than a foot of space between us. "No games. No lies. No Mason getting in our way. You and me."

"I'm so mad at myself for believing what he said for all

these years," I say, gulping. "I don't know how I couldn't see it."

"Even if it wasn't the truth, it made sense." Cole shrugs, looking between me and our hands shooting off undeniable sparks.

And then, we can't get any closer. I'm not sure who made the final move, but he's so close to me that I can feel his warmth radiating off his skin. His hands move to grip my arms, thumbs rubbing against me. His chest rises and falls against mine, both of us arrhythmic yet in tune only with each other.

"I love you, Sadie. I have for a long, long time."

"I love you, too, Cole."

Words have never been more freeing. A weight is lifted off my shoulders. It completely disappears. Evaporates. Another pang of hope flashes in his eyes as they look down at my mouth. My breath catches in my throat, needing to feel the sensation of his lips on mine.

"I need to kiss you," he says, furrowing his eyebrows. "Can I?"

I nod, closing my eyes as he obliterates the rest of our minuscule distance. Gripping the fabric of his shirt, I melt into his grasp as we connect. Everything around us simply becomes background noise, leaving me to relish in the heat and softness of his kiss.

Cole pulls away so he can lift me onto the counter. He's back in a split second, his tongue parting my lips with ease and hands exploring beneath my shirt. I wrap my legs around his waist. He groans, scratching up my sides. A chill follows his fingertips.

"Sadie," he whispers, breath warm on my ear. "I want to do this right. Tell me if this is too much tonight."

I shake my head, bringing my hand to the nape of his neck. "Take me upstairs, Cole."

"Same room?" he asks.

"Same room." I smile, nodding at him.

I'm not expecting him to carry me up the stairs—not in a house like this—but he slides one arm under my knees and the other around my shoulders. Squealing, I wrap my arms around him.

"I've got you," Cole says, his words reverberating all over my body. "I won't hurt you."

And regardless of our past, our history, I believe him so easily. Cole finds my room quickly as if he still has the path memorized. He sets me down. While I sink into the mattress, I watch him as he runs his hands up my thighs.

"This is enough for me," he says. "We can stop here, and I'd still be happy. Don't rush into something if you don't want it."

"It's been five years. No part of this is rushing." I sit up, legs hanging off the edge of the bed. Grabbing his arms, I pull him closer until he's pressed against me, heat rolling from his body into mine. Or maybe it's the other way around, I can't tell where I end and he begins. He closes his eyes for a second as he squeezes my thigh.

"I promise you, Sadie, I will never do that to you again. It still feels like I don't deserve this after everything, after I let you walk away thinking I was using you." Cole takes a deep breath, fingers digging through my jeans.

"We both put each other through a lot," I remind him, playing with his shirt sleeve. "If you don't deserve it, then I don't, either. We'll play it by ear."

He laughs quietly, reaching up to touch my face. "I guess we will."

Cole smiles because he knows the old Sadie would never say something like that. The immature Sadie who said she slept with Mason to get under Cole's skin is gone, and she's never coming back. I smile because I know the old Cole is gone, too. The man before me isn't hindered by his pride. He loves freely.

And while we've both loved and lost, we're ready to restore everything that's been broken for so long.

Cole's strong hand guides me back onto the mattress before he climbs over me. It feels so good to have his body on top of mine, to be engulfed by his natural heat. He kisses me. His lips take my own and deliver the most passionate, yet gentle, kiss I've ever experienced in my life. My heart thunders in my chest as I start working on the buttons of his shirt.

"You're beautiful, Sadie."

I drop my head on the bed, sighing when he moves down to my neck. The words resonate. Sink into the depths of my body and soul. Nothing else exists anymore, not when Cole's tongue drifts across my skin with undeniable precision, like he remembers every spot that used to make me tick.

Finally, I lose the last button on his shirt and push it from his shoulders. He takes it off, and the muscles in his arms flex as he throws it to the floor. I've been craving his bare skin against mine, so I gasp when his hands slide under my T-shirt and squeeze my breasts. I meld into his touch, arching my back to press into him as much as I can.

"Glad to see you still like the same things." Cole chuckles, his eyes shining.

"And some new ones," I say, breathless. "Wanna find out?"

"Thought you'd never ask." He winks, removing my shirt. It joins his on the floor.

Pausing, Cole wets his lips as he takes in the sight before him. He rolls his hips with enough force to make my breath catch in my throat. This is perfect. His movements are perfect, especially when he keeps a steady rhythm after I pull his mouth back to mine.

The heat between my legs only grows for him, spreading through my entire body until I start to shake from need. Cole notices. I dig my nails into his shoulders as he pops the button on my jeans, fingers trailing the hem of lacy fabric beneath. His touch still sparks on my skin even after so long.

"I love you."

"I love you, too." It's easy for me to say it back.

His hand is so warm it leaves burns, melting my skin as he delves into my underwear. Everything about Cole is precise. He moves slowly. It makes the pleasure so much more intense when he slides two fingers inside me and watches my face. His eyebrows furrow, and his eyes are hooded with arousal. Lifting myself on my elbow, I tangle my hand in his hair and pull his lips back to mine, grinding down the best I can. I need to feel more of him.

He retracts his fingers, making me whine at the loss and slump back to the mattress. Cole grins, face flushed. "I fucking love that sound."

I don't have time to respond before he's tugging my jeans down my legs. With my help, we make quick work of them. Every nerve in my body is on edge, craving his touch all over again.

Cole teases me over my underwear before they end up with my jeans. This is the only time I've ever seen him impatient, and I love that it's because of me. He takes his pants off, gulping as I unclasp my bra and throw it. His hands travel down my legs until he finds my knees, slowly pushing them apart so he can get a full view. He tightens his grip, and I know his patience is waning.

"Sadie, I'm gonna fucking lose it." His voice tumbles from his lips as if it was caught by sandpaper on the way out, rough and deep.

I raise an eyebrow at him and tilt my head. My hair falls from my shoulder and his nails bite into my skin. "Do it."

In the blink of an eye, his boxers are on the floor, and he's pushing inside me. Crying out in a mix of surprise and pleasure, I arch my body to mold it to his. I never want to separate from him. I want this, all the time and forever.

"Fuck," Cole groans, dropping his head on my shoulder.

For a moment, we lie there, connected and breathless. His chest heaves against mine. He moves his head from my neck to join our mouths together. I sigh into his kiss, relishing in the idea of being together in this way. In every way.

When he pulls his hips back, my breath shudders, and a

moan escapes my lips. He catches the sound in his mouth, swallowing it and every one that comes after. Everything is heavenly. His touch, the way he feels inside me, the look on his face.

I've craved having him like this ever since the last time five years ago. Even after having other lovers, nothing compares to his precision and the care he holds for me while he pleasures me. He makes me feel powerful. Like he'll do anything for me if I ask.

"You feel so fucking good," he whispers, breath warm on my ear. "So tight."

A wave of heat rushes through me, and my stomach starts tying in knots. Wrapping my legs around his waist, I dig my heels into his lower back to spur him forward. I want more. I *need* more.

Cole is perceptive, I don't even need to tell him *what* I need. He obliges happily. Reaching between us, he rubs circles against me. They're slow with just the right amount of pressure to send me flying over the edge. The bubble bursts. Butterflies swarm as I come undone around him, leaving me a moaning mess and crying out his name like a mantra.

When I scratch down his arms mid-euphoria, he stills, spilling inside me with a moan. I love him like this. Eyebrows furrowed, lips parted, and eyes clenched shut. Pure pleasure written on his face.

Neither of us moves. We wouldn't dare break this connection right now, not when it feels so good to be together like this. He presses kisses to the base of my neck, hand rubbing up and down my leg.

"This may be a little late," he says, chuckling. "You still have that IUD, right?"

"Got a new one last year," I reply, smiling and patting his shoulder.

"That's good." He gives me a lazy smile as he rocks his hips. "You gotta move your legs. I wanna take care of you."

As absolutely spent as I am, the last thing I want is for him to move. But being taken care of by Cole sounds enticing, so I remove my legs from his waist. He kisses the corner of my lips. After one more gentle thrust, he pulls out slowly. I whine at the loss and slump into the mattress. The sweat shines on his skin as he makes his way over to the closet, disappearing inside until he comes out with a towel.

"Old habits die hard, I see." Cole smiles.

Cole cleans me up the best he can. The bed dips as he crawls in beside me, one of his fingers trailing down my body. I sigh in content, shuffling as close to him as I can get.

"I've missed you so much," he whispers, kissing my forehead. "I don't ever want us to be apart."

"I think we can arrange that. I've missed you, too." I rest my head on his chest, smiling when I hear how fast his heart is racing.

"I'm not fucking this up again." Cole pulls the blanket over us. "And I'm going to make sure you know how much I love you. Every day."

I shift so I can kiss him. He needs to know I appreciate what he's saying to me and that I believe him. His hand is still warm when it finds the small of my back. Our lips work together softly. Slowly. Beautifully.

Regardless of the world crashing down around us, I'm absolutely certain this is how it was always supposed to be.

Finally, we are no longer water and sky. Sadness and fear. Forever close but never truly touching.

Now, we are earth and water. Happiness and peace. Forever imbued deep within each other while still being our own.

Cole

Chapter Twenty-Five

W hen I wake without Sadie, my first instinct is to find her. I sigh in relief when I see no sign of daylight. Knowing I haven't been asleep long, I sit up and rub my eyes before sliding out of bed to grab my clothes.

I put my boxers and shirt on. A slight breeze drifts through one of the windows, and I figure out where Sadie's at. I should've known. A lot of New Orleans homes have galleries attached, this one included. Back when they were all built, property taxes were determined by the amount of doors in and out of the house—so, to avoid paying more in taxes, a lot of these structures were built with window exits to their respective galleries.

As soon as I'm in front of it, I see her.

Sadie.

And God, does it feel so nice to see her like this.

She leans on the iron lace railings, a silky, patterned green robe covering almost every inch of her skin. I've always loved seeing her in this color. It matches her eyes, making them that much brighter every time I look at them. Her head is angled to the sky. A deep breath wracks her chest, and all I can do is wonder what she's thinking about.

She could regret what happened.

Maybe she wants me to leave and never come back, and I can't honestly say I'd blame her for that.

But seeing her illuminated by the faint, yellow light attached to the gallery quells any sort of anxiety I have over this situation. How can I be worried when she's standing right in front of me?

I haven't had Sadie Dupont like this in years, yet somehow, I know everything about this feels better than it did back then. We've been through a lot. Together, and apart. After five years, we reconvene, letting go of every last worry.

I'm not the same Cole I was. Escaping my parents and their grasp on me was exactly what I needed. Even back then, I knew Sadie was the one. I wanted to marry her, love her in the way she deserves, and have kids with her, but I was scared.

And I let that fear overpower me so much, I walked away without so much as an argument. My pride wouldn't let me beg her to stay.

Swallowing the nerves threatening to overtake me, I step out onto the gallery and approach her. I snake my arms around her waist, pleasantly surprised by the way she hums and leans on me when I rest my head on top of hers.

"What could possibly be going on in that beautiful brain of yours?" I ask her.

"Wouldn't you love to know?" She turns toward me, a teasing glint in her eye as she rests her hands on my chest.

I nod, smiling. "More than anything."

After spending all this time away from her, I figured things would feel different. As in, my feelings. Holding her in my arms. Even the sex, I guess.

And while everything feels better, it's all the same somehow.

What hurts the most is knowing I could've had this the whole time if I hadn't let her walk away. I'll never forgive myself for that.

Sadie's lips part as she opens her mouth to speak. A short laugh escapes instead, she shakes her head.

"You don't have to be nervous telling me anything," I tell her, moving to massage her shoulders. "I won't make fun of you."

"Oh, yeah, that's what I'm worried about." She rolls her eyes.

I pause. "I want this. I want you. Things ended between us because I didn't know how to express that to you properly, but I'm not the same person."

"I know," she says.

With nothing left to say, I kiss her instead. She takes everything I give her, not afraid of sending it right back to me. For a moment, I feel guilty. My stomach twists at the thought of having her this way when she said so many times that she wanted to respect her father.

I think that's who she was communicating with out here.

Asking him for forgiveness, since her heart works on its own accord.

"I love you, Sadie. I'm never going to stop telling you that, okay?"

"I hope not," she replies. "You have some pretty big shoes to fill."

She's right. I do. "I'm going to give you everything you deserve and more." I brush her hair behind her ear.

"Cole?"

"Yes?"

"I love you, too."

She said it earlier, too, but it feels so much more real this time. I kiss her again, turning her around and walking her back toward her house until her back is pressed to the wall between two windows. My heart thuds against my ribcage. She reaches between us, keeping her eyes on mine as she pulls the tie of her robe.

I swear she's moving in slow motion. All of it is way too slow for my liking, but too fast at the same time. If I could unwrap her every day for the rest of my life, I'd be the happiest man to ever exist.

Much to my distaste, it still covers the parts of her I crave to see.

Thank God her house is surrounded by trees. No one can see us as I dip my hand between her thighs. Ghosting along her skin, I smile at how eager she is for me, how she seems to be enjoying the choice she made last night.

She gulps and drops her head back. The expanse of her

neck is far too smooth and kissable to ignore, so I run my tongue along it. Her hips shift forward. When my fingers finally find where she wants me, her whole body jolts, as if my touch is a lightning bolt.

An unyielding fire burns within me when I feel how soft she is. Warm, with a beautiful wetness that makes me want to take her now. Her skin glows. Every inch of her is illuminated under the light, allowing me to explore parts I haven't had in so long.

"Cole," she whines, attempting to grind down.

I swallow hard. "I was impatient earlier. Not this time."

With my lips on her neck, I slide a finger inside her, my eyes fluttering shut at the feeling of her wrapped around me. We sigh together. She cups my cheeks, her gaze dark with arousal as she brings my mouth to hers. One isn't enough for her, and I know it. She wants more. A shuddering breath escapes her when I give her the second.

I keep a steady pace, fighting every urge I have.

Sadie's noises are so beautiful.

How she calls out my name.

Her moans.

She starts clenching, her eyes rolling as her head thuds onto the house behind her. Her nails dig into my arms through my shirt, lips parting and eyebrows furrowing. She's mine. All mine.

Slow and precise, I remove my fingers from her. Chest heaving, she tightens her grip as she regains her breath.

"Maybe we should go inside." I'm panting, too, hoping more than anything that she wants to continue.

Sadie bites her bottom lip, shaking her head. "Right here, Cole. I want it here."

Another thing I missed about her. Spontaneity. I'm practically shaking from how much I need her at this point.

Apparently, I'm in shock for too long. She shrugs the robe from her shoulders, allowing it to bunch at her elbows. Putting my hand on the back of her neck, I pull her to me and kiss her hard. She palms me over my boxers until she pushes them down.

Suddenly, I can't move fast enough. I hoist her upward before I line up with her. When I look at her one more time for confirmation, she gives a quick nod. I'm buried inside her with one thrust. She cries out, clawing at my shoulders.

Pinned between me and the wall, Sadie doesn't have much room to squirm. Not as much as she wants. I pull my shirt off, craving the feeling of her bare skin on mine. And then, I lose myself.

I fuck Sadie outside on her gallery, not caring in the slightest about how loud she is. Or how often she hits the wall. Five years without feeling her should be a crime. Her mouth is frantic on mine, each thrust pulling a new sound from her.

"Cole, I'm–" she cuts herself off, head falling backward as she tightens around me. The end hits us both like a grenade. Her first, like she's plucking the pin with a beautiful, pleasured sound falling from her swollen lips.

I'm not far behind. Shuddering, I push as deep as I can

before I spill inside her. I roll my hips to help us both come down.

"Fuck," Sadie says, patting my chest.

I laugh, heart thrashing. "You're something else, Sadie. Truly."

"Says the man who fucked me on a gallery."

"Says the woman who asked for it that way." I smile at her, leaning in and kissing her. "Ask and you shall receive."

She opens her mouth to say something else, but that's when I pull out of her and help her back to the ground. Her breath catches as I put her on her feet.

Sadie lets out a short chuckle, her soft, pretty face tinted pink. "I can't remember the last time I felt like that."

I bring her back inside, helping her clean up before climbing into bed with her. "I remember the last time. For me, at least." When she's this close, I can't help but take in the details of her. The wide, green doe-eyes, the graceful arch of her nose, full lips parted into a smile.

"Oh, yeah?" She playfully narrows her eyes at me. "When?"

"January. Five-ish years ago. This girl took me to the bayou. Gave me the time of my life in my car." I bite the inside of my cheek to stop my grin.

"In the car, huh?" Sadie clicks her tongue. "She sounds too wild for your taste."

"You'd think, wouldn't you?" I pull her closer, tracing shapes on the soft skin of her hip.

"Cole..." she trails off, intertwining her fingers with mine as her head rests on my chest.

"Sadie."

"Do you think we can do it this time?" Her voice is so quiet, it barely reaches my ears.

I pause. She has every reason to be nervous. A lot of what happened to us was because of who I was, but I'm not that man anymore. I need her to know that.

"I do. When I tell you there isn't one other place that I'd rather be, I mean it. It's always been you, Sadie. I knew it five years ago. I knew it when I let you walk away. And I sure as hell know it now."

She smiles at me, bracing herself on my chest as she sits up. "It's always been you, too."

"You've got that look in your eyes," I point out, narrowing mine and resting my head on my palm. "What's going on up there?"

"I wanna show you something. Come with me?"

"Of course," I say without hesitation.

Sadie gets out of bed, grabbing her robe from the desk chair. She ties it, blocking her body from my view. With or without fabric on her skin, she's the most beautiful woman I've ever seen.

I stare at her for a moment, truly appreciating how we're here again. How we fell apart, only to come back together.

She turns around and catches me watching her.
Smiling, she tilts her head.
Her hair falls from her shoulder.
This is it.
For me, for her, for us.
We're it.

"You're staring," she says, holding out her hand.
I take it.

Quickly.

Easily.

Happily.

Sadie helps me out of bed, even though I don't need it. I put my clothes back on. She leads me down the stairs, and they creak beneath our feet. We tread carefully, regardless of if no one else is here.

Everything is better. *I'm* better.

For me.

For her.

For *us*.

I'm not exactly sure what I expect. Her fingers are inter-twined with mine, leading me through a house she has memorized like the back of her hand. She's an angel, even in the dark. The curtains are closed, but slivers of starlight shine through the cracks.

A pale blue glow accentuates how the fabric clings to her skin. How electric we are when we're together.

She looks back at me as we enter the music room—a room I've only been in once. Her father's instruments still reside here. Bronze metal shines differently in the moonlight.

She sits on the piano bench, scooting over and patting the spot next to her. My mind whirls. She's going to play for me.

After years of yearning to hear her play, I'm going to.

"You said you would give anything to hear me sing again." Sadie nudges my shoulder. "What if all I want is you?"

"You have me." I brush her hair behind her ear before placing my hand on her thigh. "Forever this time."

Her eyes glisten with tears as she smiles at me. "This will be the second time I play after he died."

A dull ache overtakes my chest. When I found out Sadie's dad died, my heart broke. It hasn't quite yet healed, so I can only imagine what hers has gone through. Sadie is commit-ting to significant *seconds* tonight.

Being with me for the second time.

Playing for the second time since her dad's death.

"He loves you, Sadie," I remind her, wrapping my arm around her silk-covered waist. "And wherever he's at...all he wants is for you to be happy."

She pauses for a brief moment, her sparkling gaze meeting mine. "I know."

An overwhelming surge of pride flutters through me. Sadie has always been strong. Confident. Forever unwavering in her resolve. Some things never change, and I'm so glad Sadie kept the best parts of herself over the last five years.

"*I* love you." I smile at her.

A pink tint rises on her cheeks—one so deep, I see it even in the dark.

"I love you, too."

As she puts her fingers on the keys, I realize she's giving me a part of her I've never had before. I make sure I give her enough room, watching as she straightens her back and traces along the piano to find her placement. Studying the smile on her face, I recognize the notes she's playing as soon as she starts.

Sadie looks at me, grinning while she shows me the beginning of *Can't Help Falling in Love*. I swallow hard as eagerness swarms me, waiting to hear her. She opens her mouth to sing, and every piece of me crumbles. Her voice is angelic. Like someone drifted down from the high heavens and wove magic into her vocal chords.

And then the chorus.

Every coherent thought leaves my brain except for one.

I

   can't

      help

         falling

           in

              love

                with

                  you

                    either.

I'm falling in love right now.

Can you fall in love twice? Concurrently? I'm already *in love*, but I feel as though I've unlocked a new piece of it. Like I'm falling for her twice all at once.

When the song is over, her fingers pause on the keys. She's waiting for me to say something. Anything. My voice is caught in my throat, so the only thing I can do is tilt her chin upward and kiss her.

She sighs into it, her hand moving to grip my shirt. I touch the small of her back, and it looks like a spark shoots through her, making her arch into me. Without another thought, I pull her onto my lap.

"I love you, Sadie," I whisper, my lips still brushing hers.

"I love you, too." Her words are just like her—confident, beautiful.

She pulls away from me, the smallest of smiles gracing her face. For some reason, I'm almost positive this is a dream. I'm not really here. I'm certain there is absolutely no way

Sadie Dupont has opened her heart to me for the second time.

"Forever?" She traces along my jawline.

"Forever."

Sadie connects our lips. She leans backward, the abrupt sound from the piano making her spring apart from me. We both laugh, even as I grip her waist tightly and rest my head on her shoulder.

I feel her pulse against my cheek, rapid and erratic.

The light flickers on, making us flinch from the sudden change. I wrap my arms around her tightly, holding her to my chest before we look over to see who's ruining our moment.

Kat stands in the entryway, leaning on the arch. "Off-limits. The music room is off-limits to sexy-time shenanigans."

"We—Katherine, we weren't planning on it." Sadie narrows her eyes at her sister. "Did you find Mason?"

"Yeah, he's okay." Kat shrugs. "Does this mean you two are together?"

Sadie looks at me instead, irises of pine gleaming under the new light.

"I'd say so," she says, smiling.

A current of relief floods through me, and I squeeze her. Happiness like this is a once in a lifetime thing, yet somehow, I've captured it twice.

"I have words." Kat clicks her tongue.

"Oh, no," Sadie mutters under her breath.

"Cole Anderson, if you hurt my sister again, I'm kicking

your ass. I should've kicked it five years ago, but I'm telling you now. Watch your back." She turns her glare to me.

I try so hard not to laugh, but given the circumstances, I really can't help it. "Yes, ma'am."

"Don't laugh at me." She pouts, crossing her arms over her chest. "Sadie, tell him how easy it is to make me cry."

"She's...very hormonal." Sadie chuckles, shifting off my lap to stand. She brushes off her robe and tightens it. Afterward, she turns her attention back to Kat. "Why are you back so late?"

"Mason and I had a heart-to-heart." Kat scratches the top of her head.

"A...heart-to-heart?" Sadie raises her eyebrows.

In the light, I'm noticing how tangled her hair is. The patterned green silk clings to her skin, and all I want to do is take it off her. I reach out, fingertips skimming the fabric on her thigh.

"Yep. Told him it was never going to happen. And that I can't force my feelings, so maybe he should find someone else." Kat nods.

"Right...and then what?" Sadie shifts closer to me.

"Okay, hear me out. Being pregnant sucks. My belly is starting to get in the way of things, and I don't have that glow...you know, the one where it makes your skin all shiny? And you look really good?" Kat sighs, running her fingers through her hair. "Anyway, so I told him that, and he did the thing. The Mason thing."

Sadie frowns. "The Mason thing?"

"Oh, come on, you've never seen the Mason thing?" Kat scoffs.

Sadie looks at me. "Definitely not."

"Okay, *fine*, I'll spell it out for you. I slept with him again. But you can't even be mad at me for sleeping with him more than once, because the last time you slept with Cole was five years ago, and here you are—"

"Who said I slept with Cole?"

"Look at you," Kat says, snorting. "Seriously?"

Sadie runs her tongue over her teeth, seemingly conceding. "Okay, well...We're gonna go to bed. And in case you didn't know, sleeping with Mason isn't going to help how he feels about you."

"You don't think I know that? Honestly, this baby is making me want to be a little more...active, and Mason's hot, and he's good at—"

"Okay, Kat, goodnight." Sadie grabs my hand and pulls me away from the piano bench. "Wallow in your own sins. We've got enough of our own."

I give Kat a quick nod before I follow Sadie upstairs. She pushes her bedroom door open, waiting until I close it behind us to throw her arms around me and squeeze me. I don't hesitate to reciprocate.

"Are you tired?" I ask her, rubbing her back.

"Exhausted," she replies, moving away slightly so she can meet my eyes. Her fingers work with delicate precision on the buttons of my shirt. "Come get comfy with me?"

I smile. "Absolutely."

She steps back, allowing me to undress before I pull her

closer to me. Finally, I can do what I refrained from earlier. Reaching toward her, I find the tie holding her robe together and tug.

Sadie gives me a tired grin as she shrugs it from her shoulders. It crumbles to the ground, like every last one of my defenses around her. I never thought I'd be here. In this house. With Sadie. Regardless, nothing has ever felt so right.

We climb into bed together, skin pressed to skin, and relax in each other's embrace.

"I'm happy you're here," she says, kissing my jaw.

"Me too." I cradle her closer to me. "You have no idea."

She shifts once more, a soft sigh escaping her lips as she wraps her arms around me. Her skin is so soft, silky like the robe she wore a few moments ago. I can't get this smile off my face. No matter what I do, or how hard I try, she has permanently made me the happiest man alive.

I have Sadie.

Sadie has me, and we have each other.

Finally, everything is right in this chaotic, evil world.

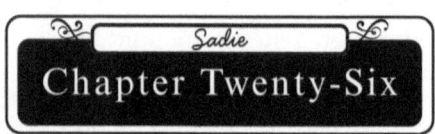

I heard two four-word sentences today that surprised me.

Sadie, the baby's coming!

But, before that: *We should get married.*

Yeah, safe to say my mind is whirling at the moment. And it's my birthday, so today is a bit overwhelming to say the least. This is the first one without Dad, and I spent the entire first half of the day crying. Cole tried to make me feel better. I'm not entirely sure he meant for those words to come out of his mouth, but they did. We're both internally freaking out about both the impromptu proposal and the fact that Kat's in labor.

We'd been standing in the kitchen when he asked. Mason ran in not two seconds later, screaming the words of the first sentence I mentioned.

Kat's baby was due in the second week of January, so she's

a week late. Mason drives to the hospital, and I call Mom on the way there. Everything is happening so damn quickly, I'm not even sure which hospital we're going to.

"This shit hurts," Kat groans, letting her head fall back. "Can't you drive any faster?"

"I'm already going ten over." Mason rolls his eyes, reaching over to pat her leg. "It'll be okay."

Cole and I exchange a look, knowing that won't go over well.

"Mason, it'll be okay for *you*. You're not about to push a watermelon out of your vagina. If she has your big ass head, I'm gonna be pissed." Kat glares daggers at him.

I can't help but laugh. Kat isn't the nicest, and adding a baby into the mix isn't making her any nicer. Cole's arm snakes around my waist. I want to talk to him about everything, but we'll have to wait.

My niece is about to be born.

When we arrive at the hospital, they don't waste any time taking her into a room. They'll only allow two people, so Mason and Mom go with her. Gabe shows up a little late, he ends up sitting with Cole and I out in the hallway.

Hospitals make me nervous. I haven't been in one since Dad died. Sure, this is a completely different circumstance, but worry sinks into my heart regardless.

Cole intertwines his fingers with mine. "You okay?"

"What? Yeah, of course." I nod. "I...don't really think I like hospitals all that much."

"She'll be okay." He leans back in his chair. "We'll be out of here in no time."

No time was a bit of an exaggeration. Kat's actively in labor for twelve hours. Gabe, Cole, and I spend the time trying our best to engage in small-talk, but Gabe still hasn't completely come around to the idea of Cole being back. Kat's exhausted by the time we're allowed in the room, rightfully so. Mason's holding the baby when we walk in, his eyes glistening as he stares at her.

"Guys, we have a little girl." Mason rocks her steadily.

I look over at Kat. She wipes her tears as she stares at him.

"I never knew it would be possible to love someone so much," Mason says, more to his daughter than anyone else. "But here you are. So tiny."

"What name did you decide on?" Cole asks.

"Victoria." Kat smiles.

Mason walks over to me. "Did you want to hold her?"

"Of course, I do." I take her from him, my heart swelling at the feeling of her in my arms.

Victoria is tiny, despite being a week overdue. Luckily for Kat, it doesn't seem like she inherited Mason's big head. Kat tells me she's seven pounds. I catch Cole's gaze. The smallest smile graces his face as he looks between Victoria and me. He wraps his arm around my waist and kisses the top of my head.

For a second, the only thing I see is him. Everything else fades away, and not a damn thing matters except Cole. I snap out of it quickly, but moments like these never cease to amaze me.

"Uh oh." Kat narrows her eyes at us. "I think he wants one."

My face blazes. "What?"

"All in due time." Cole laughs, shaking his head.

I smile down at Victoria as her little fingers wrap around one of mine. Even as I hand her back to Mason, I can't take my eyes off her. She doesn't have any hair quite yet, but she looks just like Kat did as a baby.

Mason brings her over to Gabe, who smiles down at his kind-of-niece. I never thought he'd be one for children, considering he'd never talked about having a family of his own, but maybe Victoria is changing more minds than just his. Eventually, and almost unwillingly, he gives her back to Kat.

"Can you guys give us a minute?" Kat asks quietly.

"Yeah, of course." I grab Cole's hand, leading him back into the hallway after Gabe.

The white walls are almost too bright to look at, and it doesn't help that the floors are the same. We sit in a couple plastic chairs, and I sigh as I lean my head back. Cole intertwines our fingers.

"It's been a long day," he says.

"Probably longer for Kat." I laugh.

An awkward silence falls around us. He chews the inside of his cheek, and his foot taps on laminate flooring. I scratch the top of my head.

"I'm gonna head out, if you guys need a ride," Gabe offers.

"Oh, Mom already said she would," I tell him. "Thank you though."

Gabe offers a nod in Cole's direction before he shoves his hands in his pockets and walks away. I ponder on if he'll ever trust Cole again.

"Kat was right, you know." Cole turns his head to look at me.

"About what? Mason having a big head?"

He snorts. "Yeah, he does have a big head, but no, that's not what I mean."

"Do tell."

"I want one."

It shouldn't come as such a big shock, considering I've always wanted children of my own, too. Given Cole's background, I figured he may be a bit hesitant. He doesn't show an ounce of that.

"Right now?" I raise my eyebrows.

"Not now." He grins, looking down at his hands in his lap. "Soon, though. And only if it's with you."

My heart melts for the second time today. Cole and I have been dating for a little over six months. We've passed our previous timeline, and things between us have never been better. I kiss his cheek.

"I don't know if I want a lot," I tell him. "Maybe two."

Cole hums to himself, nodding slowly. "Compromise on three?"

"I guess we'll have to wait and see where life takes us, huh?" I scrunch my nose, meeting his eyes.

When I first walked into this hospital, I was uneasy. The white walls and floors, endless amounts of doctors and nurses bustling around, all of it made reminded me of when my father died. He's been gone for eight months, and a day has yet to come where I don't think of him.

But here I am: waiting with Cole to go back in to see my niece. Cole brings warmth. Comfort. And even in a setting like this, he relaxes me.

"I was serious earlier, Sadie," he says quietly. "About getting married. I know that was a terrible way to ask, but I feel like...we've lost all this time. We'll never get it back, and I really don't see the point of waiting any longer. I've known for six years that you're the one I want. To the day, oddly enough."

I nudge his arm. "You sure you won't change your mind?"

"Look, I don't know what the future holds. Not a single clue, but the one thing I do know, is that I want you with me. No matter where we're at or what we're doing." He pauses, reaching up to play with a few strands of my hair. "You. Always you."

For a moment, I forget we're sitting in a hospital. I lean over and kiss him, sighing when he cups my cheek. Mom exits Kat's room, her hands in the back pockets of her jeans as she approaches us. She smiles.

"You two want a ride home? Kat's asleep."

"Yeah, let me say bye to Mase real quick." I pat Cole's leg before standing and walking back down the hall.

Mason sits in a chair next to Kat's bed, Victoria cradled to his chest. He doesn't notice me. Pressing his lips to Victoria's head, he rocks her back and forth.

"Daddy loves you, Tori," he whispers to her. "You look like

your mommy. And that's a good thing, because she's the pret-tiest woman in the world."

My heart twists.

Mason boops her little nose. "You're so loved already. You've got Mommy and Daddy, your Aunt Sadie. She's mean. She'll beat people up for you."

He has a point there.

"I'm gonna be better for you. Promise. Maybe if I'd been better in the first place, I could give you a real family. I hope you don't get mad at me for that in the future."

I step back, deciding not to interrupt his chat with Victo-ria. Part of me feels terrible for Mason. He's clearly still encumbered by his feelings for Kat, especially now that Victoria's here.

Mason has changed a lot since he found out Kat was preg-nant. I think back to him six years ago. That Mason would've dropped dead on the spot at a single mention of children, let alone having feelings for someone as long as he's had them for Kat.

I'm rooting for a happy ending for them. Maybe Kat will realize she has feelings for him or maybe they'll find other people who can love them each the way they should be loved.

I make it back to Cole and Mom, letting them know I'm ready to head home. The ride isn't that long, and Mom leaves Cole and I alone. As soon as she drives off, we head to my bedroom, and he sits on the edge of my bed while I look for something to change into.

"Sadie."

"Yeah?" I ask, shuffling around in my drawer.

"Sadie," he repeats. "Come here."

The firmness of his voice takes me off guard. I give up on my search for a moment and make my way over to him. Sitting down, I meet his eyes through the darkness of the room around us.

"If there's a reason you don't want this, tell me." His eyebrows crease, tongue darting to wet his lips. "I want you. And everything that entails. No matter what."

He reaches over to my desk chair where his jacket hangs.

"I've thought about this." He hands me a small black box. "It wasn't something random I brought up. I bought that last month."

With wide eyes, I look between him and the box. An incessant flutter overtakes my heart.

"I've been through a lot of shit, Sadie. A lot. I've seen marriages fall apart, and I've even seen some that should fall apart, but never do. Whatever's holding you back...I need you to know that I'm not joking around." He grabs my other hand.

My chest deflates. "Cole...you've done this before."

"Yeah, I have." He nods. "But I dated Miranda for three years. She was someone my parents wanted me to be with, so if I ever loved her, it's nothing like the way I love you. You challenge me. You make me want to be a better person. I can do that as long as you're by my side."

"What will your parents think of this?" I ask, looping my pinky with his. "My parents' opinions are so important to me, it feels wrong for you to go against yours."

"They don't really care about me," Cole replies. "This isn't about them. It's about me and you, and the future we could have together."

"I don't want to be the reason you lose them."

"You're not. It's not that much of a loss for me, honestly. If they wanted to be in my life, they'd treat me better. And whoever the hell it is I choose to love."

He opens the box and pulls the ring out.

"Marry me, Sadie. Have kids with me. I know we'll be happy for the rest of our lives if you say yes."

"Yes," I whisper, watching a smile spread across his face. "I want all of those things, too."

He's beautiful like this, even when he's exhausted from being up for God knows how long. Grabbing my hand, he slides the ring on my finger. I shift toward him. He puts his hand on the back of my neck and pulls me toward him, his lips meeting mine ever-so-softly.

"I'll prove myself to you every day," Cole promises. "You'll never wonder. Never doubt. I won't hurt you again. Ever."

I kiss him, throwing my leg over his lap to straddle him. Without a second thought, he reciprocates. He flips us over, and he finds his spot between my legs with ease.

Cole pulls away and swallows hard. "Forever with you feels good, Sadie Dupont."

"I look forward to it, Cole Anderson." Pulling him back to me, I grin. "I can't wait."

"Where's the wedding binder?" He quirks an eyebrow at me.

"Wedding binder?" I narrow my eyes.

He bites back a smile. "Kat told me a few days ago that

you may or may not have a wedding binder. And since we're getting married, I think that means I'm granted access to it."

"Oh, no." My head falls onto the mattress, and I laugh. "I was ten when I made that. Access denied."

He fakes a gasp. "How are we supposed to build a foundation of trust if you don't trust me with your plans?"

"All in due time." I cup his cheeks. "Maybe one day."

"It's okay. I'll have Kat find it. Surprisingly, she's become very supportive of us. I thought she hated me." He pops the button on my jeans. "You can change now. I'll go make you something to eat."

I pull him down to me and kiss him. "Thank you."

"Anything for you." He grabs my left hand and presses his lips to my palm. "Always."

Cole lifts himself off me and leaves my room. Smiling to myself, I stare at the ceiling. I realize, for the first time since Dad died, I'm watching the fan turn with excitement rather than dread.

I count how many times it whirls—not to lull me to sleep, but to see how long it takes for Cole to return to me.

The more I think of him, the warmer I become. I can't keep this smile off my face. After everything we've been through, we're finally getting the ending we deserve.

Each other.

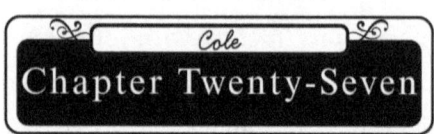

Chapter Twenty-Seven

Cole

I married Sadie Dupont today.

We started in a church, vowing our lives to each other in front of friends and family.

She looks so beautiful in white.

So many thoughts ran through my head when she smiled up at me.

And then, we paraded in the French Quarter.

Up and down the streets until we made it to our final destination.

The corner of Decatur and Frenchmen.

The place where we started, ended, and began all over again.

With all these faces on Frenchmen Street,

and all the mistakes I made, I still cannot believe she chose me.

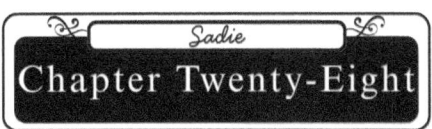

Sadie

Chapter Twenty-Eight

EIGHT YEARS LATER...

"Tori, stop it!" Kat sighs, nudging her daughter with her hip. "I'm trying to have a conversation with Aunt Sadie and Nana."

"Will says I can't play the piano," Tori whines, tugging on Kat's sleeve.

Victoria is eight years old, and she's the spitting image of Kat. The only real difference between them is Tori has Mason's curly blond hair.

"Okay, well you tell Will that I said you could." Kat gives Tori a pointed look.

I shake my head and chuckle. Kat won't win. Like everything else, Tori also inherited her sass. My niece groans, throws her head back, and stomps out of the room. Mom sits in one of the stools by the island, while I rinse off a celery stalk in the sink.

"She reminds me of you." Mom laughs, giving Kat a teasing look.

"Mason and I are both so hardheaded. Who let us have a damn kid?" Kat runs her fingers through her hair.

"She's trouble, that's for sure." Mason enters the kitchen, heading right to the fridge and grabbing a juicebox.

My phone vibrates on the counter, and I don't even have to check it to see what it says. Cole always texts me when he pulls up to the house. I quickly dry my hands before heading into the foyer while Mom, Kat, and Mason talk amongst themselves. Leaning on the archway of the music room, I watch as Cole walks in.

It's Friday—meaning he comes bearing gifts. Three dozen red roses, like my father used to do for Mom, Kat, and me.

His face lights up when he sees me, like this isn't our routine. I always wait for him in this very spot when he gets home. He barely has time to kiss my cheek. The kids are like blurs, I've come to realize, meaning they're fast, and they don't really care if Dad is trying to love Mom.

Cole chuckles, kneeling down to hug our children.

One, two...

Wait, *two*?

Delilah waddles in after William and Cara, her short legs only carrying her so fast. William is the oldest at six. He's exactly like his father. I'm not sure there's one thing he got from me. Cara, who just turned four, has Cole's black hair, but her eyes, nose, and mouth come from me. Delilah, our two-year-old, is the opposite of Cara—my hair with Cole's facial features.

I grab the flowers from Cole and set them on the table next to the door. As he stands, he grabs Delilah and puts her on his hip. Now, he has plenty of time to kiss me.

"How was work?" I ask him, tilting my head.

"Same old stuff." He shrugs. "Gabe said he's working late. He probably won't make it tonight." Cara clings to his leg, so he ruffles her hair. Will has since disappeared, probably back to gatekeeping the piano.

Delilah holds her hands out to me. "Mama, you."

I chuckle, taking her from Cole and leading him into the kitchen. Cara finally lets him go. We've made a new rule for the family. Every Friday, no matter what, we have dinner together.

It can range anywhere from home cooked meals to pizza to takeout, but we always eat together. Though this typically includes Gabe, he's been increasingly busy lately. He was at dinner last week, but he's had a hard time showing up to every single one. Thankfully, he's long since forgiven Cole for the past, and I'd even say they're friends again. Miracles *do* exist.

The table isn't large enough for everyone, so we bought a second one for the kids. I smile at them as they sit. Theirs is small, perfectly sized for the four of them. We'll have to buy a new one soon.

Cole sits at the head of the table. I sit to his right, and Mason to his left. Mom is next to me, Kat's next to Mason, and the other end is saved as an honorary spot for my dad.

He would've loved this—getting the family together and seeing his grandkids.

Dad was the first person I told when I found out I was pregnant with William.

Cole squeezes my hand, sending a smile my way. I look over at the kids, watching them in adoration as they eat together.

After everyone is done, Cole and Mason do the dishes. Kat and Mom drink wine, but I opt for water. Both of them give me knowing looks, it's not like I'm trying to hide it, but I want to tell Cole first.

Eventually, everyone filters out. Mom is the last to leave, as always. She hugs Cole and then me, patting my back.

"I'll see you next week?" she asks.

"Always." I nod in response, grinning at her as she walks out the door.

Cole and I both sigh in relief. We love these nights, but they're terribly long, and the day isn't quite over yet. As if they know exactly what time it is, the kids swarm Cole as he grabs the roses from the table. He scoops Delilah up in his other arm and kisses her cheek.

"You guys know the rules," he says, clicking his tongue. "Mom first."

Typically, Cole will bring William in and have him help, but today seems to be different. He leaves the kids in the living room and turns the television on before he leads me to our room. The canopy is still gray. We switched to the master bedroom, so the walls match the canopy. All of my furniture is the same—solid oak dressers and a desk.

The dark ice of his gaze sends shivers down my body as I undress. I raise my eyebrows at him and grab my robe, tying it around my waist.

The bathroom is through a dark wood door. Tile chills my bare feet. Cole walks over to the edge of the white porcelain tub and starts the water, concentrating on the temperature. Once he's satisfied, he grabs the roses and starts plucking the petals off. I take in the granite countertops. The double sinks. A small chandelier hangs from the ceiling, illuminating everything in a delicate yellow glow.

The tub fills slowly, so he stands when he's finished.

I shuffle over to him. "Thanks for this."

"We've gone over this every Friday for years, Sades. You deserve this and more." He smiles, rubbing my arms. After he grabs a hair tie from the counter, he pulls my hair up for me and secures it on top of my head. "And you know this is my favorite part of the evening." Winking at me, he slowly pulls on the tie of my robe.

"Care to join me today?" I shrug the fabric from my shoulders, letting it crumple to the floor.

"Of course," Cole replies, his eyes trailing over newly exposed skin. "Hopefully the water's still warm by the time I get the kids to bed."

"You'd better get started, then."

"I'll bring some candles." He kisses my cheek. "Really set the mood." My jaw. "Because I could not stop thinking about you today." The tip of my nose. "I love you." Finally, my lips.

"And I love you." I grin, still unable to fight the blush he brings to my cheeks. "You'd better go before I don't let you leave."

"Damn kids." He laughs, shaking his head.

I make my way over to the edge of the tub, dipping my toes in. Cole somehow always gets it to the perfect temperature. He watches me, taking note of every movement with his bottom lip between his teeth. I've had three kids. My body looks different, but he's never once stopped looking at me like that. Like I'm the most beautiful thing he's ever seen. I settle in the water, whirling the rose petals around with my fingers and letting myself relax.

"Alright, I'll be back." Cole leans down to kiss my forehead.

I hum in response and close my eyes, resting my head back on the porcelain. Mindless, I wait for him to come back. I'm not sure how long he takes, but when he returns, he's already unbuttoning his shirt. When he slides it off his shoulders, he reaches beneath the sink to grab candles. He arranges them around the tub and on the counters. Soon enough the room is filled with firelight, and he turns the chandelier off.

"Water's cooled off a little," I tell him, sitting up while I watch him finish undressing the same way he watched me.

"That's okay."

I scoot forward so he can settle in behind me. He pulls me to his chest and clasps his hands together by my stomach. He sighs, content. Every Friday, without fail, he brings home flowers for the girls. Mom or Kat must've told him about it, because I don't ever recall telling him to do it. He doesn't join me every time. Usually, when he does, it means he's a bit more stressed out than normal.

"I have some news," I say, closing my eyes.

His chest rumbles as he laughs. "You don't sound very excited."

"Oh, I am. I'm just...relaxed." I shrug.

"I'm on the edge of my seat."

"Remember when we said we'd probably stop at three kids?" I ask, scrunching my face. Leaning forward a bit so I can turn to see him, I meet his gaze.

His eyes widen, an excited gleam reflecting in the candlelight around us.

"Most likely not gonna happen." I chuckle, waiting for his reaction.

Cole pulls me to him until I straddle his lap. Running his hands up and down my sides, he grins at me before pressing his lips to mine. He leans back onto the tub, looking at every part of me he can see.

"God, Sadie, you're fucking amazing." Cole stares at me, and for a moment, I swear he's in awe. "When did you find out?"

"This morning," I tell him. "I took the kids to get beignets, and you know how much I love those. When I opened the bag, I started gagging. So pissed."

He laughs, squeezing my hips. "Another girl, you think? You only had aversions with Cara and Delilah."

"I think William could use a brother." I shrug. "He's gonna have a lot of work cut out for him with three sisters."

"Did you ever think we'd be here?" Cole whispers,

eyebrows furrowing. "I mean, after everything we've been through...Did you ever see it working out for us like this? In love, happy, four kids."

"I think so." I nod. "Maybe not the four kids part, but I've always known I could love you for the rest of my life."

"For the longest time, I never thought it was possible. I mean, after seeing my parents and how miserable my family was, I assumed that's how it was supposed to be. And I really hope I'm doing better for our family."

Sometimes, Cole gets anxious. His eyes shine with insecurity. It only comes out when he's thinking of how he's doing for the kids. He doesn't want to be his parents. I don't think he has anything to worry about.

"Cole." I cup his cheeks, rubbing them with my thumbs. "Everything is so perfect. I couldn't ask for anything more from you."

"Thank you, Sadie." He gives me another squeeze. "For this. For giving me the chance to make everything right. You're the best mom. The best wife. I wouldn't trade this for anything."

I kiss him, relishing in the softness of his lips and how every part of me responds to him. "Water's cold. Take me to bed?"

Cole hums quietly, nodding. We grab towels and step out of the tub. He plucks flower petals from my skin, fingertips brushing all over me as he drops them back into the water one by one. When I take a moment to look at him, to truly appreciate him like this, I can't help but grin. Cole is exactly the same as he was eight years ago.

His eyes crinkle when he smiles. He's starting to age, but to me, he has never been more perfect.

"I don't know how you do it," he says. "You get more and more beautiful every day."

"Well, unlike Kat, I do get the pregnancy glow."

Cole snorts, rolling his eyes as he tugs me toward him. His hands find my lower back, forehead resting on mine.

"I love you, and it's the most powerful thing I've ever felt in my life."

"You're so sentimental today." I giggle, placing my hands on his chest.

"Some days hit me harder than others," he admits. "Some days force me to remember that we're here because you forgave me. You and William and Cara and Delilah...All of you are perfect."

"Trust me, we'd be nothing without you. You are to them what my father was to me, and that's everything."

He lets out a sigh of relief, pressing his lips to mine. I smile, taken aback by his urgency. Water still clings to my skin, but Cole pulls the towel away from me. A cold chill sends a shiver through me, but Cole's quick to engulf me with his warmth, walking me backward until the back of my knees hit our bed.

"Time to celebrate baby number four?" Cole quirks an eyebrow at me.

"I think celebrating is what led to baby number four." I laugh, ultimately pulling his mouth back to mine.

He hums, his tongue dancing with mine as he carefully lowers me onto the mattress. Climbing over me, he starts kissing down my neck. Before he continues downward, he nips my collarbone. He pauses at my stomach, eyes flicking up to me before he presses his lips to my skin.

"I love you, Sadie, and everything you've given me."

My heart flutters, a smile fighting its way to my face. Even after all this time, he manages to give me butterflies.

"I love you, too." Lifting myself on my elbows, I watch him closely as his head dips between my thighs.

My body reacts to him the same way. Simple touch is never enough, not when I can have all of him. Cole Anderson is perfect. He knows how to make me tick, how to love me. If someone had asked me when I first met him if I thought this would be possible, I'd laugh. He's nothing short of everything I've ever needed.

Here I am, being loved in a way I've never been loved before, living in a house where so many good things have happened.

I play music here.

Brought my kids home from the hospital.

Loved and lost so deeply that the cuts still bleed to this day.

But grief, while seemingly complicated, is much simpler than people let on. Losing someone you love—metaphorically or literally—is never easy. Nor does it get any easier as time goes on. You mourn every single day, but it's not the pain that fades eventually. It doesn't change.

You change. Your heart changes, and the ways you honor those you've lost change.

I honor my father by giving my own children his love of music.

By teaching my kids the importance of family.

By loving deeply and unafraid.

By remembering him.

William, Cara, Delilah, and baby number four will never know their grandfather except through pieces of him that are instilled in me—pieces of him that will never go away. When they're old enough, I'll tell them stories.

Of my dad.

Of their dad.

Of how things can happen when you least expect them to.

Because eight years ago, while I was falling apart, Cole Anderson came back.

He came back, and instead of falling apart, we fell together.

ACKNOWLEDGMENTS

Sitting down to write my acknowledgements is both a surreal and terrifying experience. Little seven-year-old me dreamed of this day, but she truly never thought it'd come true. The fact that I'm here is some dream I'm still waiting to wake up from—let's just hope that never happens...

The first and biggest thank you I'd like to give is to Brittany Weisrock and the Lake Country Press team. Britt, you have no idea how much you've impacted my life, and not just because you're publishing my book. I hold so much love and respect for you, and I am so proud to not only call you my publisher, but my friend. There are not enough thanks in the world I could give to accurately portray how I truly feel.

Isabelle Martinsen, my best friend and the person I can trust to call me out on my bullshit (and unnecessary anxiety), I never knew true, lasting friendship until I met you. I hate to break this to you, but you are stuck with me for the rest of our lives. We have been through our writing journeys together, and I am more and more proud of you every day for your tenacity and determination. I wouldn't be who I am today without you. Faces on Frenchmen Street would simply not exist without you. Thank you for everything you've done for me—and, of course, Sadie and Cole (and Mason and Kat and Gabe and everyone else) thank you for that, too.

True Sloan, we're going through this publishing process together. I'm so glad we both signed with LCP, and even happier that we met each other and became so close as a result. I went into this with a book and a dream, and I never thought such good people would pop into my life as a result. We are forever book buddies, publishing siblings, whatever you want to call it—thank you for stepping in to read and evaluate FOFS. This portion of my life (and all future parts, duh) just wouldn't be the same without you. Through thick and thin, we're in this together...you aren't allowed to escape me. I'm not sorry.

Alex Lake, I cannot even fathom where I'd be without meeting you guys. I started writing again because of you. My biggest hope is that one day, we'll give Olivia that copy I made at Barnes & Noble Press (you know, the one that'll be really old and *definitely* outdated by the time she's old enough to be allowed to read it...maybe I should just get her a real copy of the book.......?). Life is full of uncertainties, but if there is one thing I absolutely know, it's that I couldn't have done or accomplished any of this without you. Your endless support means everything to me, and I hope you know I will always adore you and your family.

McKensie Carr and Lara Aikman, you two...where do I begin? Talk about never ending support. Not even just with my writing, but in my real life 9 to 5! I have grown so much both personally and professionally, and you guys are easily some of my favorite people in the whole world...even if you say I can't quit just because I got a book deal...rude. Whatever, I like you guys, and I like my job too much to quit anyway—regardless, two things here were great. 1, that you thought my book was good enough to make enough money to quit my day job, and 2, that you like me so much that you had to tell me I'm not allowed to quit. I like it.

Now, I don't want to make this section too long, but I do have to say I am more than lucky to have people who support me. I never imagined I'd be here, let alone that I'd have so many people who love me and want my success. While I can't go on too much longer, I also want to thank the entire LCP family, my beta readers, my friends, the Call family, and everyone who has supported Faces on Frenchmen Street. This book is very near and dear to my heart, and I'm so happy to share it with you all.

Haley Warrington is an Arizona-based author where she lives with her two cats, Sweet Potato and Sugar Cookie. Ever since she was young, writing took her life by storm. She crafts stories of love and overcoming hardships in the face of it. She will forever be a hopeless romantic.

www.ingramcontent.com/pod-product-compliance
Lightning Source LLC
Chambersburg PA
CBHW050009120726
47903CB00006B/1693